When Rola... ......, an un...
Government, is sent to the University of Northwell
in North Yorkshire, under the guise of being a
management consultant, he ends up investigating a
little more than he bargained for. Challis thought
his only task was to find out the secret work of a
certain Professor Fletcher. He soon becomes
involved in the private world of the professor, and
his secret loves, especially the mysterious and
beautiful Norma. But then he finds himself in the
midst of a brutal murder . . .

ᵖTHE MERRY MONTH OF MAY

Elvi Rhodes

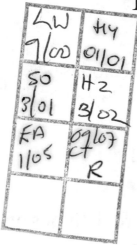

CHIVERS PRESS
BATH

First published 1997
by
Severn House Publishers
This Large Print edition published by
Chivers Press
by arrangement with
Severn House Publishers Ltd
1998

ISBN: 0 7540 2034 7

All situations in this publication are fictitious and
any resemblance
to living persons is purely coincidental.

British Library Cataloguing in Publication Data available

THE MERRY MONTH OF MAY

CHAPTER ONE

'What's happening?' Roland Challis asked. 'When are we to be let out?'

He was standing in the queue of people all waiting to surrender their tickets. There was no one on duty to take them and the exit from the station was firmly locked, presumably to prevent passengers escaping.

He stood with two students with whom he'd shared a compartment all the way from King's Cross. They'd got into conversation around Peterborough and kept it up, on and off, all the way to Northwell. Mike, he'd learnt, was a postgraduate chemist, working for a Ph.D., and Fiona, who was not Mike's girlfriend but had simply met him on the platform, was a second-year student in sociology.

'Anyway, why are *you* going to the university?' Fiona had asked Roland. 'You can't be a student.' She meant that he was too old, and at thirty-three he probably was.

Mike had disagreed. 'Everyone knows Northwell has a reputation for taking on mature students,' he'd said kindly. 'And if they're eccentric so much the better. Not,' he added quickly, 'that you seem eccentric. But a trendy octogenarian is their ultimate goal.'

Roland told them what everyone else would be told—well almost everyone else. 'I'm a Management Consultant, going to take a look at Communications in the University.' It was true, if not entirely. His student days were well behind him. On leaving Oxford with an upper second in history

1

he had had enough of the academic world. Management Consultancy had seemed a good bet at the time, and so it had proved. There'd been plenty of work for a reasonable return, though it wasn't a job he'd like to do forever. He hoped to give the university value for money. He had little doubt that he'd find the job needed to be done, and it was as good a cover as any for digging out the facts for his lords and masters—the government. But as usual they'd given him very little to go on.

There was still no sign of a ticket collector.

'What *is* happening?' he repeated.

'He must be doing the signals,' Fiona said. 'Maurice usually does the signals and sells the tickets. Reg collects the tickets and does the odd jobs. Maurice must be off sick.'

'The signal box is on the down platform,' Mike explained. 'There's a communicating door from the ticket office to the signal box. You think this bit of a wait is a nuisance—and so it is—but it's much worse when you're trying to catch the up train and waiting for your ticket. They abandon the customers at the ticket window to give the green light to the up train, and by the time they get back and sell you your ticket, and you've sprinted along the platform and over the footbridge, you've missed the train. Just. People are always *just* missing trains here.'

'They've never really got themselves organised, poor darlings,' Fiona said sympathetically. 'Apparently this was a dead quiet, teeny little station with about three passengers a day. Due for closure, in fact, until the university came. Now they just can't cope. Not only a lot more trains and passengers, but foreigners who can't understand a word of English and will persist in asking for

2

directions. But not to worry, he'll let us through in a minute.'

'Anyway,' Mike said, 'people aren't usually in that much of a hurry to get into the university.'

'It's not that I'm in a hurry,' Roland said. 'I just don't like hold-ups.' But he had waited around in worse places than this, he thought.

'It's an attractive station,' he said, observing the way in which the name 'Otwood Junction' was picked out in pebbles in a bed bordered with forget-me-nots and wallflowers. 'I like those.' He pointed to the shiny-leaved bay trees, growing in tubs at intervals along the platform.

'You won't when you've had more experience of them,' Mike said. 'They're strategically placed in the best possible positions for falling over them when you're running for a train. Maurice has had to take a first-aid course because of those tubs.'

'And Reg has had to treble the station's stock of sticking plasters of a size suitable for bleeding shins,' Fiona said.

In the end they were let out, Reg carefully scrutinising every ticket.

'It's because we're students,' Fiona said. 'They simply don't trust us. Think we use the same ticket all the time.'

Set free, they shot away like stones from a catapult.

*   *   *

The road, narrow, not made for traffic, ran steeply uphill from the station to the university. Sloping grass banks beyond a ditch on each side were topped by dry limestone walls, bleached to whiteness in the strong light. In the grass cowslips,

3

and a small purple flower of which Roland didn't know the name, moved in the slight breeze. Overhead, wisps of cloud trailed a sky deeply blue and more suited to a Mediterranean summer than to May in North Yorkshire. He had not wanted to come here. The request, order, whatever one chose to call it, had come at the wrong time. But it might turn out better than he had hoped. He recognised his optimism as no more than the result of a sunny day.

London was his scene. He was settled in his flat in Ridgmount Gardens, furnished with Heal's best or with painted orange boxes, according to the moods and financial circumstances of the last few years. In London everything was to hand and there was always something happening. It was ridiculous—the thought occurred to him not for the first time—that he had a job which so often took him away from it. Perhaps he should think seriously about packing it in, though for what he wasn't sure. And Marcia had been none too pleased by his present assignment.

'But you can come up at weekends,' he'd suggested. 'That car of yours will eat up the M1.'

'If you think I'm flogging two hundred and fifty miles with nothing but North Yorkshire at the end of it, you're mistaken, sweetheart. Why do you always expect your women to follow you? I've got better things to do.' She'd been adamant. Loving, on that last occasion, but adamant.

She'd be all right, he knew that. Marcia was always in demand. He was going to miss her, but perhaps not too much. It was as well they hadn't married, although a year ago they'd come near to it.

The university, built in a wide, saucer-shaped dip

4

in the surrounding hills, only came into view as one reached the top of the road from the station. Good job it's hidden, he thought, seeing it now for the first time, otherwise it would just about ruin the landscape. Its buildings, grouped in no discernible pattern, were uniform rectangles of brick, cement and glass, with flat roofs from which ventilation shafts protruded without any attempt at disguise. In fact it was very little different from the light industrial estate which he had passed on the train on the southern outskirts of Northwell, which was not surprising since the same architect had designed both.

Around its perimeter more building was taking place. Cranes, mechanical diggers, bulldozers and dumper trucks were hard at it. A pile driver beat time with loud, rhythmic thuds which echoed back from the hills. A far cry from Oxford, which he'd appreciated only after he'd left it. Yet perhaps, in one way, not so far a cry, since this monument to ugliness attracted, as most people knew, some of the country's top brains.

Indeed, in its short existence many of the world's best intellects had found it worth a visit. Some of them had stayed. It was a fashionable place to be, for both students and academics; from which it inevitably seemed to follow that it had more than its fair share of militants of both kinds. The whole set-up was a godsend to the media, and especially to television to whom it supplied, as well as wit and wisdom for its chat shows, a regular flow of incidents, most of them reprehensible, for its news bulletins.

The University of Northwell provided a scapegoat; satisfied a deep need. Respectable citizens everywhere could, from the comfort of their armchairs in front of the box, blame the state of the country's morals, the economic situation, failures in test cricket, the World Cup and the Olympics, on the students at Northwell. Locally they also had doubts about the weather. There were those who said that the climate in those parts had never been the same since the university had started whatever it was up to in those laboratories.

In the long summer vacation, what with the regular serials going off the air and students dispersing to various dubious parts of the world, life for thousands of viewers became quite dull. Roland's own mother was one such. She wouldn't be at all pleased when she heard where he was. She was always on at him to settle down, by which she meant marry, and buy a nice little house within a dozen miles of Bexhill, where she lived.

Well, he thought, turning his back on the campus, however awful that was, the surrounding countryside made up for it. Bright green hillsides, short cropped, presumably by the sheep though they were now in the lower fields with their half-grown lambs. Clean-looking cattle. A huddle or two of grey stone cottages. Not at all what he'd expected.

Before turning into the university he scrambled to the highest point of the bank, uncapped his binoculars, and looked in detail at the view. He swung leisurely from side to side, surveying the broad countryside. It appeared to be without blemish.

Then he turned right around to face the campus again. Through the binoculars this also was sharpened, brought to life, detailed. Its scars and

6

pockmarks were more clearly visible: damp patches on the cement, heaps of building materials, mean prefabricated huts clustered on the eastern side. But there were a few redeeming features. Lots of birds—his father had taught him to be interested in birds. Chaffinches, gulls, two lapwings, a dunnock quietly scratching around under a shrub. A narrow stream, fed by a small but exuberant waterfall which dropped from the hill on the far side of the campus, ran through the middle of the land. On its banks there were one or two nubile females.

Reluctantly, he turned his head fractionally to the right, seeking a fresh viewpoint. And then suddenly he held the glasses still; froze; concentrated his gaze. Something was happening down there all right.

On a gravel path, bordered on one side by a small plantation of shrubs and on the other by a windowless brick wall, he had picked out two men. Not students. The one whose face he could so clearly see was not much under forty; a tall, big-boned man with bright red hair standing out from his head like copper wire. He wore a light brown tweed jacket. The man with his back to Roland was considerably smaller, not only shorter, but thin, narrow-shouldered. His clothes hung on him. Wisps of dark hair failed to conceal the circular, thinning patch on the back of his head. But it was not these details of appearance which interested Roland. He was not conscious of noting them. Later, they were to come back to him clearly.

Through the binoculars the big man's face was sharply visible, brought so near by the powerful lenses that every line around the pale blue eyes, every fold of skin circling the heavy neck, was plain

7

to be seen. And there was no mistaking his expression of undiluted hatred. Skin flushed; a swollen purple vein running down his temple; eyes bulging; teeth bared. Like a wild animal, Roland thought. His large hands—there were fine red hairs on the backs of the finger joints—held the small man by the throat. He was shaking him violently. Shaking, shaking, shaking—and the small man offered no resistance. It was as if he had neither bone nor muscle; was a rag doll or a puppet unable to move of his own accord, his arms remaining limply by his sides. Then suddenly, with a gesture which seemed almost contemptuous, the big man dropped his victim to the ground, turned swiftly and walked away, disappearing from view between the buildings.

It was not possible to see where he went; the angles of the buildings hid him. The urgency, now, was to get help to the man lying on the grass. But even before Roland lowered the binoculars the man was already rising to his feet. He shook himself, like a terrier after a fight; straightened his clothes, ran a hand across the back of his head. Then he looked around, and walked off in the opposite direction from his aggressor. Strange, Roland thought, how there'd not been a soul in sight during the encounter. Now people began to appear and everything looked normal again. He felt as if he'd dreamed the whole episode.

He fitted the lens caps to the binoculars, put them back in their case, wondered what he should do. Probably nothing. It wouldn't suit his book to be conspicuous, and anyway it wasn't his affair. Except that the man could have been killed, and next time might be. He knew hatred when he saw it, and there

8

had been murder in the big man's eyes. He could mention it to Washington when he saw him. 'By the way, Bursar, does attempted murder fall into your department?' More than likely it was some silly academic squabble which everyone on campus already knew about. Was Bacon, Shakespeare, and how old are the pyramids? Universities were full of them. He picked up his case and walked towards the entrance.

*   *   *

'University of Northwell,' the board said. 'Visitors report here.' By the architect's orders the notice had been carried out in cream lettering on a red-brown background which merged into the brick, and placed inconspicuously near the bottom of the wall. 'Things must *blend in*,' the architect had instructed. 'Not *intrude*. Nothing blatant. All things understated.' 'Function' was a word which made him shudder. Even so, a few sharp-eyed people spotted the notice, and Roland was one of them. He wondered whether he need report since Washington had sent him a map and he was confident of finding his way. But better stick to the rules. Perhaps there were security precautions. He went through the swing doors.

'I have an appointment with the Bursar,' he said to a security guard. 'Roland Challis. I can find my way. I have a campus map.'

The man sitting at the table was quite splendidly uniformed, in navy, with touches of scarlet and ample gold braid. His gleaming medals were the brightest lights in an otherwise dark entrance hall. The gloves tucked into his belt were a new-true-white.

9

He stared at his visitor as a Company Sergeant Major might look at a new recruit who had spoken out of turn on his first day in the army. Not without reason, since Sergeant George Robey Smith—his mother had been a devotee of the music hall and had hoped, had the sex been right, to have named her first-born Vesta Tilley: a name which she gave to his sister instead—had returned after twenty-five years as a Sergeant Major in the Yorkshire Rifles just in time to take up his present post. He had been almost the first person on the scene when the university started and everyone knew that he practically ran it. 'Me and the Vice-Chancellor,' were words frequently on his lips. Their order was not accidental.

'More people,' he boomed, rising to his feet and topping Roland's six feet by a good seven inches. 'More people have been lost from following them maps than I should care to mention.' His tone of voice implied that some of them might still be wandering around, old and hungry, searching in vain for the Arts Centre or Applied Sciences. He stretched out his hand, palm upwards. Since it seemed to be expected of him Roland surrendered the map.

'Thank you sir,' Sergeant Smith said. He dropped it into a large plastic rubbish sack which was clipped to the wall.

'And now . . . First Left . . .' he barked.

Caught unawares by the volume of sound, transported back to his school's Officer Training Corps, Roland sprang as nearly to attention as his suitcase, briefcase and binoculars would allow.

'. . . First left, second right by the boilerhouse, through the car-park, up the steps, under the bridge, turn left at the refectory, third right after the Medical Centre and the Administration's in front of you. Can't miss it,' he threatened.

Who would dare, Roland thought, setting forth. In the end: (though the architect's design seemed to have been, if keeping them out of the university proved impossible, to lose and confuse all visitors) he found himself in the entrance to the Administration building. A man in uniform rather less splendid than Sergeant Smith's, and devoid of medals, was sorting post into wall racks. He broke off to attend to Roland. He spoke briefly into a telephone and a minute or two later a young woman arrived in the lobby.

'I'll take you to the Bursar's office,' she said. 'I'm afraid it's three flights up and there's no lift. Can I carry something for you?'

'Thank you very much,' Roland said, 'but I can manage.'

'Brave words,' she said. 'Don't hesitate to change your mind.'

'I won't. How many times a day do you walk up and down?'

She sighed. 'Thousands. Fifty-eight steps, in case you're not counting. Still, it does mean I can eat what I like.'

'Eat what you like?'

'Yes. No need to diet with all this exercise. It isn't just visitors, you see. Everything the office needs is on the ground floor. Photocopier, post room, filing storage, stationery, coffee machine. It's all down there. We're all as thin as laths on the third floor.'

'I see,' Roland said. 'Or rather, I don't. Why don't the offices move to the ground floor?' He changed his heavy suitcase over to the other hand.

11

'You're getting breathless,' the girl observed. 'Don't worry, nearly there! We couldn't do that. The third floor is purpose built for the Bigwigs. Vice-Chancellor, Bursar, Senate House. It has the best views, you see.'

'Are you the Bursar's secretary?'

'No. I'm Sue Perkins. I help the Vice-Chancellor's Personal Assistant, Marion Richmond. I share an office with Norma. She's the Bursar's secretary. She's out at the moment.'

At the top of the stairs they turned right along a thickly-carpeted corridor, at the far end of which the girl knocked on a door, opened it, and announced him.

'Mr Challis for you, Mr Washington.'

'Ah! Come in my dear fellow! Glad to meet you!'

'I'm sorry I'm a bit late,' Roland said.

Washington laughed. 'Lost your way across the campus I dare say. People usually do because old George Robey Smith won't let them use the maps. Undermines his authority you see. Well never mind. You're here now. Come and sit down. You'll find this chair comfortable, I think.'

He was a large man. Genial, warm. A smile of greeting lit his face. How different he looks now, Roland thought. But it was the same man. There could be no mistake. The pink, smiling face was the one which Roland had seen a short time ago contorted with hatred. The large hands which had gripped his own in a welcoming handshake were the ones which Roland had seen around the little man's neck. From the strength of Washington's handshake Roland thought how nearly the little man must have been throttled. He tried not to stare at the short red hairs on the backs of Washington's fingers.

CHAPTER TWO

Sue Perkins placed the tray of tea on the table in front of the Bursar's desk.

'Any sign of Norma yet?' Washington asked her.

'Not yet. But she shouldn't be long.'

'Well tell her to let me know the minute she comes in.'

'I will. Is there anything else?'

'What? Oh, no thank you.'

He handed a cup of tea to Roland and held out the basin of wrapped sugar lumps. 'Sugar?'

'I'm sorry?'

'Do you have sugar?' Washington repeated.

'Yes. Yes please. One lump.' Roland plopped it into his tea, stirred, tried to sort out his thoughts. Could it be true? Not this kindly-looking man? He must be mistaken. Yet he knew he wasn't; and in any case, when had a man's appearance been a reliable guide to his character?

'Well,' Washington was saying, 'you won't want to start work this afternoon, I'm sure. Here, have a bicky! Try these nutty wafers. They're not bad.' He took one himself and popped it whole into his mouth.

'I thought if you went to see the Accommodations people here you could talk to them about lodgings or a flat. Whatever you fancy. You're not fixed up are you?' he asked hopefully.

'No. I gathered you were going to put me up in the university for tonight.'

'That's right. We've seen to that. Not very luxurious I'm afraid, but comfortable enough. But I'm sure the Accommodations people will find you something more permanent. Very difficult of course. Great shortage of rooms. The place is full of students,' the Bursar complained.

He was no longer smiling now. He walked over to the larger corner window and stared out across the campus. 'Where's that girl got to?' he said.

Washington was uncommonly concerned about the girl, Roland thought. His cheerfulness seemed to have given way to anxiety, perhaps even a little annoyance. Was he a man quick to anger? About relatively small matters? Perhaps, Roland thought, he should put the scene he had witnessed earlier right out of his mind: except that he was not in the habit of ignoring conundrums, preferring to find the solution. There had to be one somewhere. This was a civilised community. The pelting of right-wing political visitors with suet dumplings was one thing—the high spirits of the young, a monotony-breaking demo—but that which he'd seen through his binoculars was something else altogether. But perhaps, he reasoned, drinking his tea while Washington continued to look out of the window, it was no more than a single incident in a moment of red-headed temper. In any case it was nothing to do with him. He had no wish to hamper his own work by getting on the wrong side of Washington.

The Bursar turned round, walked back towards the table. 'Another cup?' He managed a fleeting smile.

'No thank you.'

'Well then, if you're sure you're finished . . .'

I'm being dismissed, Roland thought. Politely, pleasantly, but unmistakably. He picked up his cue. 'Perhaps I should go to the Accommodation Office fairly soon. And I mustn't take up your time. I'm sure you're busy.'

14

'Always busy, old man, as you'll find out for yourself. Always something to be done.'

It was a phrase Roland recognised. They all talked like that about their jobs, defending themselves before they'd been accused.

'But don't let me rush you,' the Bursar said. He walked back to the window as if drawn there by a magnet. For a second or two he remained still, looking out on to the campus, then when he turned back to Roland a relieved smile had replaced the anxiety on his face.

'Here she comes!' he said.

He returned to his seat behind the big desk and sat there, straightening out a wire paperclip in his strong fingers, staring at a console-type piece of equipment which took up a third of the desk surface. It seemed as though he had forgotten his visitor and was simply waiting for time to pass, to bring him to a particular moment. Roland studied the painting on the opposite wall: a Cezanne print of the lake at Annecy, framed in light-coloured wood. Was it Washington's choice or standard university issue?

Then suddenly activated, the Bursar began to flick switches and press buzzers. No words were spoken, but as if it were a magic lamp which he'd rubbed, a beautiful girl appeared in the room. Roland had not heard the door open and her feet made no sound on the thick carpet, but there she was, standing before them both. Roland sprang to his feet, slopping the remains of his tea into his saucer, dropping his biscuit on the floor. Now she really was something!

'*There* you are Norma,' Washington said. 'I was beginning to wonder what had happened to you.'

15

She was quite astoundingly beautiful. Superlative. Palest blonde hair hung like a heavy silk curtain to her tiny waist. Hips curved towards long, long legs under a white skirt of some clinging material. Without seeming to take ordinary mortal steps she was immediately beside Roland. Simultaneously they bent down to pick up the broken biscuit, so close together that he almost nose-dived into her delightfully generous bosom.

Reluctantly, he raised his head as she handed him half a nutty wafer. She smiled at him, her rosy lips—owing everything to health and nothing to artifice—curving to show white, even teeth. So near was her face to his as she handed him the biscuit that her breath, like a bowl of delicate pot-pourri, assailed his nostrils, mingling with the scent of her perfume. She looked directly into his eyes, though he thought without meaning to, and in those sky-blue orbs he saw anxiety and fear, in total contradiction to the smile on her lips. His first thought, even before his head cleared, was to hope that he might be the one to help her.

She stood up, smoothing down her skirt with elegant hands, and turned to Washington.

'I'm sorry I was out when you wanted me. I'd just gone to the campus shop to get something for my dad's supper.'

'Yes, well . . . that's all right then. But try to go in your lunch hour in future.'

That little admonition was for my benefit, Roland thought. He's besotted with her; can't bear her out of his sight, and who can blame him? She could twist him around her little finger. Only somehow he didn't think she would. Nor did he think that the anxiety in her eyes was anything to do

16

with her boss. There had been a remoteness there that had taken her right outside the present situation.

'Well I did actually, Mr Washington,' she said. 'They didn't have it in. Fish in shrimp sauce he fancied, and I saw the delivery van arrive about an hour ago.'

'Yes, well never mind,' Washington said.

Roland found Norma's voice a slight disappointment. It was not so much the north-country vowels, which he liked, as that it had a thinness which was not attractive. When she was discovered by some film magnate, as she must surely be, he would immediately arrange expensive elocution lessons for her.

There was a brief knock at the door and a woman came into the room, hesitating at the sight of Roland. 'I'm sorry Bruce,' she said. 'I didn't know you had a visitor. I'll come back.'

'No, don't go Marion. This is Roland Challis. Meet Marion Richmond, the Vice-Chancellor's Personal Assistant. Challis, as you and I know, Marion, has come to sort us all out, tell us what we ought to be doing! Isn't that what Management Consultants do, eh?' He tried to sound jovial and failed.

'Something like that,' Roland said. So the Bursar didn't want me here, he thought. I wonder who did? Who did the request come from? From what little he had heard of the Vice-Chancellor he wouldn't be the one to call in Management Consultants. Didn't like being disturbed, they said. It seemed likely, then, that it was his own people who'd insisted on a visit. He wished they'd given him a better briefing. 'Find out about Professor Fletcher,' was all he'd

17

been told. How many of these people knew exactly why he was here? That was something he'd have to find out, and until he did he'd assume nothing.

Marion Richmond held out her hand. 'You're welcome,' she said. Her hand was cool; so, in spite of her words, was her voice. 'The Vice-Chancellor isn't in this afternoon but I've made a note in his diary to see you tomorrow at eleven o'clock. I hope that suits you?'

Politely put, but he was sure there was no question of his convenience. What the Vice-Chancellor wanted, or more likely what his secretary decided he wanted, he got. Well, fair enough. He was the number one man around here.

'Perfectly,' he said. 'I'll be here.'

'Isn't Mr Challis going to the Vice-Chancellor's shindig, then?' Norma broke in.

Marion frowned, and then smiled. 'Why of course,' she said courteously. 'I'd almost forgotten. It's not so much of a shindig in fact,'—her smile to Norma took the reproof out of her words—'just a number of people for sherry. The Vice-Chancellor likes to meet people. Eight o'clock in the refectory. I hope you'll be able to come.'

'Delighted. Thank you.'

'Mr Challis was just leaving,' Washington said. 'He's going across to the Accommodation Office. Got to get fixed up with somewhere to live.'

'Do you want me to take him?' Norma asked.

The Bursar frowned. 'I've got a lot of dictation—' he began.

'Don't trouble yourself,' Roland said—and then cursed himself for being a fool. He had just thrown away the chance of having this lovely creature all to himself for several minutes. 'I expect I can find my

18

own way.'

Miss Richmond looked at him, the beginnings of a smile twitching at her mouth. She's nobody's fool, Roland thought.

'I'll walk across with you,' she said demurely. 'It isn't the easiest place to find. And I'll show you where you're staying tonight so that you can drop your cases before we go on to Accommodation.'

*   *   *

The room to which Miss Richmond took him, in one of the university's residential blocks, was pleasant enough, if unremarkable. Oatmeal tweed curtains and matching bedspread, an orange and brown wool rug on the floor. It cried out for the books, clothes and general clutter which would have made it belong to someone. She waited for him while he put his cases down and washed his hands.

'I'd be happy to stay right here all the time,' he said.

'I know. It's a pity you can't. But we have so few spare rooms and so many visitors. And there are no hotels nearer than Northwell.'

'Do most of the university staff come from Northwell?' Roland asked.

'Yes. It's difficult to get them because the train service is so awful and the bus service is worse. They come, but they don't stay.'

'I thought the railway station was quite a busy little place,' he said. 'Though with methods of its own.'

'It is. It's changed a lot since the university came here. Two new waiting rooms, a chocolate machine, even a ladies' loo so they tell me.'

'You don't come in by train?'

'No. I have a car.'

'Do you live in Northwell?'

'Yes.'

'Have you been in the university long?'

'Yes,' Marion said. 'And I'm buying a house on a mortgage, my mother lives with me, and I'm not married. I have a degree in English and I've worked here since I came down from university seven years ago. Are you ready?'

'I'm sorry,' Roland said. 'I didn't mean to be nosy. I'm always interested in what people do.' He wondered why she wasn't married, or living with some man. She was quite attractive in a slim, dark sort of way. Passionate, he wouldn't wonder. Her eyes, dark green and thickly lashed, were particularly beautiful.

'I suppose it goes with your job,' she said.

Now which job did she mean? Did *she* know why he was here? As PA to the Vice-Chancellor she must know most of what went on, confidential or otherwise. Would she be able to tell him about Professor Fletcher? But of course unless her boss gave her the go ahead she wouldn't talk. Good secretaries never did, except for generalities, and he felt sure she was a good secretary whatever else.

'I'm ready,' he said. 'Sorry to have kept you. Have the other people in your office been here long?'

'The Bursar about four years. Norma only six weeks. Sue Perkins has been here more than a year now. I think she's settled. I'm less sure about Norma.'

They walked across to the Accommodation Office, a prefabricated hut on the edge of the

20

campus.

'It's more than a bit out of the way,' Roland said. 'You'd think they didn't want anyone to find it. I'd have expected it to be in the administration complex.'

'So it should be,' Marion said. 'But the Accommodation Officer didn't like that idea and he managed to hold out against it. He says if they were more central they'd have every Tom, Dick and Harry popping in for unfurnished flats. He works on the theory that anyone who is desperate enough will find him in the end. Actually, once you do get a foot in they're usually quite helpful. But I'm sorry, I must fly. We'll see you this evening, then? About eight o'clock.'

'I look forward to it,' Roland said.

The clerk in the Accommodation Office was as helpful as Marion Richmond had promised, but the supply of flats and lodgings was woefully small and they were lukewarm in their recommendations of hotels in Northwell as places in which to spend more than a night or two. Roland took the sheets of addresses he was given and promised to follow up the telephone enquiries they'd made for him.

'I'd do it right away if I were you,' the clerk said. 'All the best places are here today and gone tomorrow.'

'I'll go now,' he promised.

*   *   *

Passing Sergeant George Robey Smith's domain on his way out of the campus, Roland decided to stop and ask him about train and bus times. If he was going to be here for several weeks it might be sensible to buy a cheap car. He didn't possess one, not having found it worthwhile in London. Or how about a bicycle, he thought, in a sudden rush of enthusiasm for all things rural. If the hills weren't too steep.

Sergeant Smith, as he'd expected, had bus and train times. 'Though they're not worth the paper they're written on,' he said. 'They run how and when they like.'

He glanced at the lists Roland was holding. 'I see you've been to the Accommodation Office,' he said. 'Well you'll find nothing in that lot. You don't want to bother with them. As like as not you'll end up in some student ghetto. Guitars everywhere and goodness knows what sort of goings on. Not for the likes of you. What *they* all need is a dose of National Service. Two years in the army. Be the making of some of 'em!'

Roland thought he might enjoy some of the goings on, but perhaps student-type lodgings, if that was what they were and he had no proof of that, might be inconvenient. He might not even be welcome.

'Do you know anywhere else then?' he asked Sergeant Smith. 'I just want somewhere homely for a week or two, where I'll get a reasonable room and some decent food.'

'Oh, I know what you want,' Sergeant Smith assured him. 'I know that all right. What's more, I know where you'll find it!' Triumph shone in his small, black eyes. 'Runswick Avenue's your place. Same road as my brother-in-law. Only a few doors away, in fact. Mrs Thompson. A widow woman. Clean, respectable. She'll do you nicely. Number forty-seven. Tell her I sent you and you'll be all right.'

Runswick Avenue was a long street of tall, late Victorian houses running steeply uphill from the main road where Roland had got off the bus. He wondered why every road he seemed destined to tread ran uphill, never down. Ash trees had been planted at intervals on both sides of the road, which was presumably why it called itself an avenue. Number forty-seven was two-thirds of the way up on the left-hand side. Its fresh white paint, brass letter box and red-polished doorstep marked it out in contrast to its dingy neighbours.

Mrs Thompson, when she opened the door to him, was equally clean and shining in a brightly-flowered print dress and pink cardigan. Her grey hair was backcombed and lacquered in a style so bouffant that it dwarfed the rest of her small frame. Her only informality was the fluffy purple mules she wore on her tiny feet. Roland introduced himself and mentioned Sergeant Smith's name.

'Come in love,' she invited. 'Step into the front room. I've got the colour telly, as you can see, and the gas fire's on a coin meter, not that you need it in this weather. I'm not sure whether I can oblige you or not, but I'd like to. I like university gentlemen. Always have. Not students, you understand, but university gentlemen are always welcome if I have the room. I have one staying with me right now. Would you be wanting full board, do you suppose?'

'Not lunches,' Roland said. 'And I'm not sure yet about meals at weekends.'

'Only I have my own pursuits,' she said, 'and I don't like to be tied down to lunches. Not that I wouldn't make you a sandwich or an omelette if the need arose.'

'I wouldn't want lunches,' Roland assured her. He wondered what her pursuits were.

'He has the first floor back, my present gentleman. He's a foreigner. I like foreigners providing they don't want special food. Indians are difficult because of the curry which hangs in the curtains. But they're very polite. Oh, most polite! You're not a foreigner are you?' she enquired hopefully.

'No. I'm English. Half Irish actually.'

'Ah, the Irish!' She smiled reminiscently. 'Well, yes, come to look at you I can see it. Terry Wogan, that's who you remind me of. I dare say you'll have kissed the Blarney Stone then! Of course I like the Japanese best. Lovely people the Japanese. Small, but lovely. I've had a lot of them since the university came. I could let you have the second floor back if it suits you,' she said suddenly. 'Looks out over the garden and quite secluded. It's the room over my other university gentleman but I'm sure you won't disturb each other. He's very quiet and respectable.'

The room, when she finally showed it to him, was clean and cheerful, looking out on to a pretty but rather overgrown garden at the back of the house. A gate at the bottom of the garden led to a lane which obviously ran between Runswick Avenue and the next road. The gate was almost covered by a rampant clematis in full bloom and had the appearance of seldom being used. He thought the room would do very well, once he had acquired some transport or got used to walking up the hill.

'Well then love,' Mrs Thompson said when he'd accepted it, 'I'm sure that's very satisfactory. A

24

month's rent in advance if you don't mind. Breakfast is at eight and I'm afraid I've had to put the telephone on a call box arrangement, what with the cost of calls going up all the time.' He supposed he would get used to Mrs Thompson's trains of thought.

'A pity my other gentleman is out,' she said. 'But you'll meet him tomorrow I dare say. Dr Maxton, his name is. Here's your keys, love. Front door and back, just in case.'

'Is he Japanese?' Roland asked.

Mrs Thompson shrieked with laughter.

'Dr Maxton! Japanese? That's a good one! Oh no love. Come to think of it, I don't know what he is. Russian, German, South American. I don't rightly know. He's a real gentleman of course.'

'Good! Well I'll move in some time tomorrow, Mrs Thompson. Thank you very much.'

She watched him from the doorway as he walked back down the hill.

CHAPTER THREE

It was not quite true that the Vice-Chancellor liked to meet people. He was reasonably well disposed towards mankind but, given a chance, he would rather be left alone. He preferred plants, small wild animals, and birds, to even the most erudite academics. And in particular he liked such specimens as could be found in the remote parts of the Yorkshire Dales, where he had his cottage.

He was never quite sure how he'd come to be Vice-Chancellor of the University of Northwell. He suspected that it was something his wife had

25

arranged at a party, behind his back. Lavinia, though a regular partygoer, did not attend or give such functions for pleasure, or even as a social obligation. When she was present at a party it was because she had a Cause. This did not in any way cut down the amount or variety of her social life since she was a woman of many causes. There was little doubt, William Spencer thought bitterly, scanning his long thin face in the bathroom mirror as he shaved for the evening's 'do', that at some gathering or other the offer of a Vice-Chancellorship for him had been Lavinia's reason for being there. And as usual she'd achieved her purpose. He'd never stood a chance.

'Damn!'

He had nicked his chin with the new blade. Blood flowed freely, splashing down his neck and spotting the front of his collar. Why were there never any tissues in this bloody bathroom? The lather already drying and itching on the rest of his face, he went into the bedroom.

'Lavinia, I'm bleeding. Give me a tissue.'

She was sitting at the dressing-table, her hair a nest of pink and blue plastic rollers, which meant she didn't rate this evening's party as important enough for a visit to the hairdresser. A bad sign. She handed him a single tissue.

'You should use the electric shaver the children sent you for your birthday,' she reprimanded. 'Now you'll have to change your shirt.'

Sticking a piece of tissue carefully over the cut to staunch the flow of blood, he returned to the bathroom and continued with the rest of his face. Up at his cottage he sometimes went for days without shaving, but in the university it was tricky.

26

He felt constantly obliged to compromise between students and faculty, and appearance came into it. An unshaven appearance, even a beard, could be taken as an attitude of mind, a leaning to the left which he couldn't quite afford. Of course some of his academics were indistinguishable from their students, but such freedom was not for him. In his position, neutrality was all.

Now Lavinia should be Vice-Chancellor, he thought. She'd do it much better than he did. For a start, she came from a long line of Vice-Chancellors, Chancellors, Presidents of the Council. But it was all too late. Had been, in fact, since he was a junior lecturer and she a postgraduate student in biology. She had marked him down then as a man who would rise to the heights she set for him. It wasn't that he had tremendous gifts—more that he was presentable, had no tiresome family to hold him back, and was malleable. Lavinia had always known she could manage the rest.

He went back into the bedroom to change his shirt. He seemed to have stopped bleeding, but better keep the tissue on for a while, just in case.

'Foster's due in ten minutes,' his wife said. 'We don't want to be late.' It was not eagerness to be there. She thought that if she could arrive near the beginning she could set the tone before things got out of hand.

'And I've told him to pick us up at ten sharp. That will be quite long enough.'

There were degrees of importance in the Vice-Chancellor's entertaining, ranging from intimate dinners with never more than eight (influential) people, which took place in his own period dining n off the Wedgwood, to the student start-of-year bangers and beer in the Junior Common ▪m. Tonight's affair came about three from the om and would take place in a curtained-off bit ١e refectory with chairs and tables moved out of ٢ usual rigid lines to give an air of informality.

Vho's going to be there?' he asked.

don't know,' Lavinia said. That meant no one of importance. 'Hasn't your Miss Richmond given you the list?'

Who dealt with the list was also a measure of the importance of the event. Miss Richmond never got her capable secretarial hands on the big events and Mrs Spencer never touched the bottom two. Those in between were a matter for negotiation. The choice of food and drink, however, to the intense annoyance of the university's catering manager, was kept firmly in Mrs Spencer's hands. And she was not one to waste expensive stuff on those, she reckoned, who had not been brought up to appreciate it.

'Well if she has I don't know what I've done with it,' William said.

'She'll have a copy with her. She's nothing if not efficient, your Miss Richmond. I must remember to enquire about her mother,' Lavinia said.

She had taken out the rollers and was brushing her greying hair into a halo effect. The last thing she needs is a bloody halo, her husband thought, turning away from the image of her square, sallow face in the glass.

Mrs Spencer's prime Cause at the party was, though unknown to her husband as were most of her schemes, to inspect Bruce Washington's new secretary. Several faculty wives, she had heard (she

28

made it her business to be well informed) were already apprehensive about the girl's attractive presence on the campus. Sylvia Washington was rumoured to be quite worried, and if the descriptions of the girl were anything to go by then she probably had good reason. Lavinia Spencer was loyal to her sex, especially if they were faculty wives. Washington, of course, could not quite be called faculty. Technically, yes, but a Bursar was not the same as a Professor.

Still, Sylvia Washington was a useful woman, always willing to be treasurer on committees, and good treasurers were hard to come by. She must do what she could. It was a small matter, but she believed in nipping things in the bud. She was thankful that William, whatever his faults, did not have a roving eye. There was a ring at the door.

'There's Foster,' she said. She applied a flurry of pinkish powder to her aristocratic nose. 'Are you ready, William?'

*　　　*　　　*

Marion Richmond stood in the lobby of the refectory, list in hand and an anxious expression on her face. She greeted the Vice-Chancellor and his wife as they came in.

'They're having trouble with the stereo,' she said. 'I've got Guller from Mechanical Engineering to have a look at it. It'll be ghastly if there's no music.'

'Good girl,' the Vice-Chancellor said. 'Have you got a guest list? I seem to have lost mine.'

They stood side by side, reading through the list which Marion produced. Lavinia Spencer waited, tapping her foot impatiently. Marion was aware of

29

the tapping foot and rejoiced. In whatever small ways she could, and short of being overtly rude, she was happy to annoy Mrs Vice-Chancellor in return for the seven years of slights and disparagements, many of them public, which she had suffered at that lady's hands. When she had first come to work for the Vice-Chancellor, an enthusiastic, eager-to-please twenty-one-year-old, she had thought that she and her boss's wife might be friendly, working for the common good of one man, but this had proved impossible. She was not to know that the Vice-Chancellor, in one of his rare moments of perversity, had insisted on engaging the young, pretty, and relatively inexperienced secretary instead of the eminently suitable middle-aged lady his wife had found for him.

The Vice-Chancellor read through to the bottom of the list. 'Do I know everyone, Marion?' he asked.

'Just about. There'll be one or two students you haven't met. In particular there's Mike Carshalton. He's Lord Carshalton's son and you're lunching with him soon in Leeds, so he's bound to ask how Mike is getting on.'

'Mike,' the Vice-Chancellor said. 'Mike. I didn't know Carshalton had a son. Did you know that, Lavinia?'

'No dear.' She made a mental note to ask the young man to tea. One never knew when a Peer of the Realm might be useful.

'And since you've been abroad recently you haven't met the Bursar's new secretary. She'll be here this evening.'

'I don't think you need bother with secretaries, William,' Mrs Spencer said to her husband. 'I'll take that little chore from you.'

'I'm sure you'll enjoy meeting Norma Wishbone, Mrs Spencer,' Marion said politely. And how, she thought!

'Oh, and there's a Mr Roland Challis,' she said to the Vice-Chancellor. 'The Management Consultant. Arrived this afternoon so I invited him here. I hope you approve.'

'Of course. Management Consultant, did you say?'

'Yes. Looking into Communications. Apparently you know all about him.'

'Oh yes! Yes! Challis, was that the name?'

'Roland Challis. I think you must have arranged something on the telephone just before you went to Japan. There was simply a note in your out-tray after you'd left, telling me he was coming and asking me to book a room.'

She would have taken issue with him on this point if his wife had not been present. He had told her nothing about Roland Challis and it was the cardinal sin to withhold information from her. But she had no intention of exposing a flaw in their relationship in front of Mrs Spencer. Marion also prided herself on being fully informed, and usually was, so that whether the Vice-Chancellor was there or not she could keep everything in motion, make everybody happy. Other people said, though loyalty made her disclaim it, that affairs often ran more smoothly in the Vice-Chancellor's absence than when he was there. Sergeant George Robey Smith, someone had once said, might think he could run the university, but Marion Richmond *did*.

'Come along then, William,' Mrs Spencer said.

31

'Duty calls!' They moved off into the main dining room where the party was taking place. Strains of South Pacific showed that Guller had been successful with the tape recorder.

There were quite a number of people there, William thought. He hoped he would remember who they were. He was aware of having seen many of them around over the years, but fitting names to faces was his trouble. It was rumoured (he had heard it himself but never quite believed it) that he'd once, at a party, asked to be introduced to a man who'd been his house guest for three days.

He reckoned that this evening's affair was one of the most useful of all his functions. A good cross-section of people. Lavinia said it served no useful purpose, but he didn't agree. As well as making him out as a democratic man—which he was—it advertised that he existed, which some people doubted, and was actually to be found in his university. Last term someone had chalked on a wall 'Spencer lives', and he knew it was said that there were members of faculty who had been on campus three or four years without ever setting eyes on him. Well, he was here tonight, and once having made contact with all these people, as he had every intention of doing, he could slip away tomorrow to the cottage. People would say 'The Vice-Chancellor? Why yes! I was at his party only the other day!'

'I'll leave you now,' his wife said. 'Make sure Miss Richmond introduces you to the Carshalton boy. We don't want his father to think he's not being looked after, do we? I know how anxious a parent's heart can be when the fledglings have left the nest!'

Well, their own fledglings had taken wing all right. At the first opportunity they'd flown to Canada on one-way tickets. He missed his son and daughter and would have liked to have seen his three grandchildren more often. Lavinia had been an attentive mother to their children, but all she could do now was send them parcels of what she referred to as English tea, knitted garments for the children, and letters of sound advice which they ignored.

'I won't forget,' he promised. But where *was* Marion? She had deserted him, and he liked her to be handy so that she could supply him with information as he needed it. He must remember to tell her that he'd decided to leave in the morning; get her to cancel his appointments.

He'd have to return for the Summer Ball, he supposed. He hoped nothing untoward would happen during the rest of this term. Things were inclined to go off pop in the summer, especially if the weather turned thundery. Student sit-ins, faculty uprisings. And newspaper and television reporters expected him to make pertinent comments on all these things. However, he had devised an all-purpose reply which Marion put out for him when she could. 'The Vice-Chancellor, who is unavoidably absent from the university, is aware of the difficulties on both sides. He is deeply concerned about the outcome as, he is sure, are all those involved, but he would remind you of his policy of non-interference.'

But they were persistent fellows, these reporters. He often thought that they actually enjoyed such mild outbursts of violence as his university offered and would have been even happier to have reported actual bloodshed.

His wife passed him on her purposeful way to somewhere or other. She tapped him lightly on the shoulder with her evening purse.

'Circulate, William! Circulate!'

She looked awful in that droopy black thing. It was typical of her to make the minimum effort for tonight's affair. Circulate indeed! Resentment welled up in him, but habit was stronger and he began to move, his thin face creasing in a benign smile. He was thankful, at least, that Lavinia did not like the country and could seldom be persuaded to accompany him to the cottage.

'Though why you can't have the telephone installed I can't imagine,' she said forcefully from time to time, when she'd been prevented from nagging him.

'I can my dear, but I won't.'

The cottage was several miles from the nearest village and the last mile had to be made on foot, over a rough fellside track. No one called. He had arranged with the village post office that only telemessages need be delivered and he would collect the rest of his post, if any, when it suited him.

In the cottage he was master. His wife had long ago abandoned the attempt to cope with what she called disgusting fungi on every chair and hedgehogs in the bedroom. Also, there was no one of the slightest importance in the dale. Socially, she meant. Ah well! By this time tomorrow he'd be up there. And he had no worries about how things would go in the university in his absence. The faculty and staff were splendid chaps if left to themselves. He didn't believe in poking his nose in.

And there was always Marion. But where was she now?

She was coming towards him with a tall, dark, goodlooking fellow whom he didn't recognise. She looked quite pretty herself in that green get-up, and more lively than she sometimes did. At times she reminded him of a pet hamster the children had once had. A bright-eyed, charming little thing; intelligent but not pushing. She didn't seem to have many men friends—he couldn't think why. All the same, whatever would he do if she should marry? The thought chilled him.

'Vice-Chancellor, may I introduce Roland Challis,' Marion said.

Challis? Now where had he heard that name before? Ah yes! He remembered. They shook hands

'Have some sherry,' the Vice-Chancellor said.

He halted Sergeant George Robey Smith who, with a tray of glasses, was doubling as a waiter (though in his own mind he was not so much a waiter as a sort of host).

'I won't just now,' Marion said. 'I have to go and check on something.'

She moved away. The Vice-Chancellor handed a glass of sherry to Roland Challis and took one for himself.

'Well, cheers!' he said.

'Cheers!'

The Vice-Chancellor sipped, and choked. My God, that cheap muck again! Why did Lavinia economise when there was no need to?

'Well, glad to have you here, Challis,' he said. 'I hope you'll go easy though. Don't upset people. Especially the clerical staff. Clerical staff are the very devil to get hold of. But I'm sure you won't.'

'I hope not,' Roland said. It was an odd conversation, but there was no doubt more to the Vice-Chancellor than met the eye. There had to be.

'All the same,' Roland said, 'I hope you'll give me the freedom to do the job. I'd like to have a word with you about it. And I'd like to make sure that everyone knows that it's OK for me to make enquiries.'

'Oh certainly, my dear fellow! I'll see to all that. Not this evening of course.'

'Naturally.'

There was something of a stir over by the doorway; a sort of wave of movement, mostly by men, though they were followed closely by their attendant women. Had someone fainted? From where Roland was standing with the Vice-Chancellor it didn't seem to be that sort of commotion.

'Something's going on,' the Vice-Chancellor said. 'Let's take a look, Challis.'

The cause of the disturbance was Norma. Her well-timed, late entrance was not planned: she was usually late. She wore a white crepe dress, cut on the cross so that it clung to every line of her body. Above the waist it consisted of two strips of material which crossed low down over her breasts and fastened in a halter at the nape of her neck, so that those who were deprived of the view of her delectable bosom had the consolation of her flawless back, bare to the waist. The thigh-hugging skirt, slit to the knee, was just long enough to reveal her silver-sandalled feet. Her toe-nails were silvered to match. She wore the whole outfit nonchalantly as if, freshly bathed and anointed with

36

sensuous body oils, she had donned something to attend the Northwell Methodists' Summer Bazaar. The result was inflammatory.

'My word!' the Vice-Chancellor said huskily. 'My word! I don't think I know the little lady!' Looking around cautiously for his wife, not seeing her, he strode forward. Washington, Roland noticed, was already by Norma's side; attentive, proprietorial. 'She is mine,' his attitude proclaimed.

The Vice-Chancellor, accustomed to the entry which his status normally gave him, cut through the cluster of eager men and wary females. Roland mingled with the watchers and waiters.

'Ah, Washington!' the Vice-Chancellor said genially. 'I think your wife was looking for you.' He stood there smiling, waiting to be introduced.

'My secretary, Vice-Chancellor. Miss Norma Wishbone.' The Bursar's introduction was reluctant.

'But you haven't got a drink, Miss Wishbone,' the Vice-Chancellor said. 'You're being neglected. No, Bursar! I'll look after your secretary. You'd better see what your wife wants. Bound to be something important. Now my dear, what would you like?' A stupid question, he thought, since there was only that bloody awful sherry.

Norma smiled. 'Anything really. Port and lemon, a snowball, sherry . . .'

'And a sherry you shall have, my dear,' the Vice-Chancellor said.

George Robey Smith with his tray of drinks was nowhere to be seen. The Vice-Chancellor tucked his hand under Norma's elbow and began to lead her towards the bar. Cosier, anyway. They could sit down and have a nice long chat. That, after all, was

37

what he was here for. To get to know people. He moved his guiding hand to the back of her waist. Her perfume swept over him in waves, sweet and musky. What a charming creature she was! He wondered if she was interested in field mice.

But it was not to be. Warned by the danger signals invisibly relayed from one end of the room to the other by members of her own sex, Lavinia Spencer arrived to claim her mate.

'So sorry, William, to drag you away. Miss Richmond has an urgent message for you.'

She bore him off, leaving Norma stranded, which was what every man in sight had been waiting for. Mainly because he was alone and had no excuses to make to anyone, Roland reached her first.

'Hello,' he said. 'I hoped I'd see you this evening. I gather you're almost as new here as I am.'

'I've been here six weeks,' Norma said.

'Do you like it?'

'Oh yes. Quite.'

'You don't sound too sure. Look, you still haven't got a drink. Let's go and find one.'

Before they could move away—they were still not far from the door since the Vice-Chancellor's progress had been slow—a man came through the swing doors and walked straight towards them. Roland saw Norma's eyes widen and the look of fear which he had seen in them earlier in the day returned, only this time a hundred-fold. She put a hand on Roland's arm, as if for protection. The man ignored Roland, seemed not to see him.

'Norma, I meant to be here earlier.' By his speech he was foreign, but Roland couldn't place his nationality. He was small, swarthy, and flamboyant in a cream linen suit.

38

'I've only just arrived,' Norma said. 'Mr Challis is taking me for a drink.' Her voice was sullen.

'I'm sorry,' the man said. 'Not now. I must speak with you alone. It's important, as you very well know. Please excuse us Mr Challis.' Roland started to move away but Norma put her hand through his arm and drew him back.

'Can't it wait?' she pleaded. 'I want to enjoy the party for a bit.'

'No. I'm sorry.'

'Please introduce me,' Roland said. She was so clearly reluctant to go with the man, looked so frightened. Perhaps by small talk he could delay it, find out what was happening.

'This is Dr Maxton,' Norma said. 'Mr Roland Challis.'

'I am sure you will excuse us,' Maxton said. 'We have something we must discuss. After that we are free to enjoy the party.' He gripped Norma by her other arm, so that she was held between the two of them.

'I'd better go,' Norma said to Roland.

He saw Maxton's short stubby fingers press into the girl's flesh as he propelled her towards the far end of the room. Then they disappeared from sight through the velvet curtains which acted as a room divider.

So that's my fellow lodger, Roland thought, walking in the direction they'd taken. Not quite such a gentleman as Mrs Thompson thinks. Also, he knew where he had seen the man before. From behind he recognised the shape of the head and the wispy hair thinning on the crown. Dr Maxton was the man he had seen picking himself up from the ground after Washington's attack.

39

CHAPTER FOUR

He would give her ten minutes, no more, and then go after her. The room was crowded now, and noisy, everyone talking. Even the music had livened up to a South American samba beat. He stood near a pillar towards the far end of the room and looked at his watch. It wasn't his business, but he hadn't liked the look of fear in Norma's eyes.

Washington was on him almost immediately. 'What have you done with my secretary?' he asked. The tone was jokey, but the edge was there. He's demented with jealousy, Roland thought. And surely he hasn't a chance with her. Can't have. There was a slackness about the man, a too-soft mouth, a paunchiness over the stomach, which was slightly disagreeable. But women, Roland had discovered, sometimes had strange preferences. The fact that Washington was also twenty years older than Norma didn't mean a thing. On the other hand, in the short time that he'd known her—if that wasn't too strong a word—she hadn't struck him as a girl who would mess up a marriage. Probably her boss was just another complication to her, and she seemed to have enough of those already.

He smiled, keeping the level light. 'I'm not hiding her.'

'I thought I saw her coming in this direction,' Washington said.

'Well I don't know where she is,' Roland said truthfully. He hoped Washington hadn't actually seen her with Maxton. Certainly he had no intention of setting him on their trail. There'd be murder done; spoil the Vice-Chancellor's party.

40

The best thing would be to keep the Bursar talking for a while.

'I've been meaning to ask you,' he said. 'Do you know a man here name of Fletcher? A pal asked me to keep a look-out for him. They were at Durham together, way back. I said if I came across him I'd pay my respects.'

'Professor Leon Fletcher?' Washington said. 'You'll have to go a long way then. He's in the States, on sabbatical leave.'

'Oh really? Well it's not important I dare say. Do you know him well?'

'Not well. He's a research scientist. They're not the easiest people to know. You have to speak their language for a start.'

'I suppose so. What sort of scientist? My friend didn't tell me much.'

'Chemist. Done a lot of work on precious metals. Very well thought of, I believe. I wonder where she is?'

He's truly obsessed, Roland thought. He can't think of anything except Norma. In spite of himself he felt a sort of pity for Washington. Well at least Fletcher existed here. Or had. Would he now be sent haring off to America after him? He wouldn't mind the trip. It was more than a year since he'd set foot in the States and the place had always had attractions for him.

A woman joined them. She stood beside Washington, put a hand on his arm.

'Introduce me, darling,' she said.

Boston, Roland guessed. He hadn't pictured Washington with an American wife.

'Yes of course,' the Bursar said. 'Roland Challis. My wife, Sylvia.' He explained Roland's function,

41

inaccurately, in the facetious way Roland was used to having his job described.

Sylvia Washington was a tall woman. Her eyes—she looked at him directly as they shook hands—were on a level with his own. Allowing for high heels she must be all of five-foot-ten. Unhappy eyes, she had. It was interesting, not to say saddening, how much anxiety he'd met with in the few hours he'd been in the university, though none of it openly expressed. They all tried to cover it. They were that sort of people. He'd reckon the Vice-Chancellor as being, in spite of his responsibilities, the only person free from real worry. (He knew nothing so far of the Vice-Chancellor's frustrations.) And Sergeant George Robey Smith, of course. He seemed to be the right man in the right job. A kingdom of his own and all the power he could handle.

'I expect you're used to having your job made fun of,' Sylvia Washington said. 'It's never been the same since that Peter Sellers' film—you remember the one, with the man hiding behind the packing cases with the stop watch? Did you see it? It's years ago.'

'I did. I thought it was marvellous. But that's not my line. I've nothing to do with Work Study or Organisation and Methods.'

'I see. Well I hope I do! Perhaps sometime you'd explain. Only not now because I have to drag Bruce away to meet someone who wants to talk about buildings.'

'I'm not here to talk about buildings,' Washington protested. 'It's a party.'

'It won't take many minutes,' his wife promised. She took his hand and led him away.

42

She'd put up a fight, Roland reckoned. She wouldn't let go without a struggle. He wondered why Washington should inspire devotion in such an attractive woman. Perhaps it wasn't so much devotion as a conservation of property. Well at any rate the Bursar had been prevented from going after Norma. But a few minutes more and he would definitely go and look for her himself.

'Are you all right?' Marion Richmond said, appearing by his side. 'I'm sorry to neglect you. Are you meeting people?'

'I've just met Mrs Washington. She seems a nice woman—but nervy.'

'She's probably a worried woman, and I suppose with some cause.'

'Is the Bursar usually one for the girls?'

Marion hesitated. 'I suppose it *is* obvious. Yes he is. But so far it hasn't seemed serious. He can never keep a secretary long, but that's no threat to his marriage. Sometimes the reverse.'

'He looks like a man with a temper,' Roland said. 'All that red hair.'

'Oh he is. It's frightful when he does let go, but mercifully it isn't often. There was the famous occasion when he and Sergeant Smith had an up-and-downer. They're well matched though. Honours were even, though Sergeant Smith likes to think he won.'

'And now Washington's after Norma.'

'Norma's a nice girl,' Marion said firmly. 'She wouldn't hurt a fly. Might kill a wasp but wouldn't hurt a fly. The trouble is, she's completely unaware of the strength of her own attraction. That's what's so nice about her.'

And you, Roland thought. Generous-minded.

43

'But it can lead to complications,' Marion said.

'Hasn't she got a boyfriend of her own?' Roland asked. 'I should have thought that would have been the best solution.'

Marion grinned. 'Why, are you thinking of offering? Naturally, she's got a dozen on a string. Mike Carshalton's the one she sees most, I think.'

'The son of the noble Lord?'

'A Life Peer, actually. Chairman of Chemical Supplies Limited, as you no doubt know. And there's little that *that* doesn't cover amongst its subsidiaries.' Colour suddenly suffused her face. She looked at Roland in confusion. 'I'm sorry! I'm gossiping like mad. What have you done to me? Have I simply been falling for some sort of professional quizzing?'

Roland touched her hand. 'Not really gossip,' he said. 'I'm sure everything you said is public knowledge anyway. And I'd already guessed a lot of it. So no harm done.'

'All the same,' Marion said, 'I shall guard my tongue in future when I talk to you. You seem to have a talent for extracting information.'

'My job,' he said. 'Communications.'

'One-way. I haven't learned a thing about you.'

'Not much to know,' he said. 'But look, I'm a bit worried. Norma was dragged off somewhere by a Dr Maxton almost a quarter of an hour ago. She was definitely not happy about it, and he was a bit rough, I thought. They disappeared through the curtains there. Do you know where it leads to?'

'Naturally. It's nothing sinister. Simply an extension of this room, with a window leading on to a balcony. They use the curtains as dividers to make the room a bit cosier for functions like this. I think

44

we should have drawn them back this evening and opened the window on to the balcony. Why don't we do that now? It's terribly stuffy in here.'

'I really think, if you'll excuse me, I'll go and look for Norma,' Roland said.

'Very well. Though I'm sure she'll be all right. I won't come with you because I have to find Mike Carshalton. He seems to have vanished and the Vice-Chancellor wants to meet him.'

When Marion had left him Roland put down his glass on a nearby table and walked towards the curtains. If Maxton and Norma were on the balcony he could hardly go and join them, but he could perhaps satisfy himself that she was all right. As he reached the curtains they parted, and the student he had met on the train came through.

'Hello Mike,' Roland said.

'Hello there!'

'I've got a feeling you must be Carshalton.'

'That's right.'

'Well Miss Richmond's looking for you. The Vice-Chancellor's secretary. I think she went in the direction of the bar.'

'Thanks. I'll go and find her. What's she like?'

'Medium height. Dark, slim, wearing a long green dress. Very attractive.'

As far as Roland could see there was no one in the curtained-off part of the room. The door to the balcony was open and he could see from where he stood—the sky was not quite dark—that the balcony was also empty. Obviously there was another way out. In fact there were doors in both the left-hand and right-hand walls and it was simply a question of which they had taken. Why, he wondered in passing, had Mike Carshalton come

45

this way?

He went through the doorway on the right and found himself in a short corridor, deserted and almost dark, with cloakrooms on the left. He went into the men's cloakroom. There was no one there, though the lights were full on. Back again in the corridor he walked forward, took a right turn, and eventually found himself at the entrance to the party room again. Norma and Maxton could quite well be back in here, could have been here for some time while he'd been watching the curtained exit. He saw too much drama in straightforward situations, he thought; though perhaps because he'd so often found himself in the middle of it. In this case there was probably a simple explanation.

And as if to prove the point he saw Norma at the far side of the room with Carshalton. Her white dress and pale hair shone like a beacon, and the sight was no less welcome to him. Roland moved towards them, passing the Vice-Chancellor in conversation with a small fat man; observing Mrs Washington sitting on her own; noticing Marion Richmond also moving towards Norma and Mike from the opposite corner. He had not seen Washington, but by the time he reached Norma the Bursar was already with her. Marion was a few seconds behind and in her wake, miraculously considering how recently Roland had seen her sitting half-way down the room, was Sylvia Washington.

'I think you must be Mike Carshalton,' Marion said. 'I'm Marion Richmond. I work for the Vice-Chancellor. I've been looking all over for you because he wants to meet you. Now I've lost him, of course!'

46

No one spoke. Norma looked terrible; as white as her dress, and as if she had hardly the strength to stand. Mike was obviously troubled about Norma; the Bursar angry. Mrs Washington gave nothing away; simply stood beside her husband, clutching his arm.

Marion broke the silence. 'Why don't we all have a drink?' She turned to Roland. 'If you could find Sergeant George Robey Smith with the sherry, I could perhaps track down the Vice-Chancellor and bring him here.' She was not sure what was wrong, but perhaps the V-C would jolly them all up.

'No need to find me, my dear. I'm right behind you,' the Vice-Chancellor said. In the middle of his conversation with a visiting professor in South American Studies he had seen Roland Challis go by, and some instinct had made him look where he was heading for. One sight of Norma had caused him to interrupt a conversation on the small tropical animals of Brazil and fly to her side. It had been an interesting conversation and he hoped he would be able to resume it at a more convenient time.

'And I'm right behind you, William,' Lavinia Spencer said in what passed for a playful manner. Roland sighted Sergeant Smith and signalled him to bring some drinks.

'Well now,' Mrs Spencer said. 'Are we all having one last drink?' Thus, hopefully, she might achieve her twin purpose of winding up the evening and saving what was left of the sherry for another time.

Sergeant Smith handed round the sherry. Norma twisted the stem of her glass around in her fingers, not drinking. Mike tipped back his head and swallowed the sherry in one go. The only way, the Vice-Chancellor thought, watching him. Toss it

47

back. Death where is thy sting? he silently asked himself as, shuddering, he drank. Out loud he said, 'Well it's been a pleasant evening. I hope you've all enjoyed yourselves as much as I have.' No one replied.

'It's terribly stuffy in here,' Marion said. 'Why don't we open the curtains and move out on to the balcony?' She stepped forward and drew the curtains aside. The others, drinks in hand, followed her out of the party area. Norma shivered.

'You should wear warmer clothes,' Mrs Spencer said, looking with distaste at Norma's delicate flesh. 'You young girls! So foolish!' It was not a point at which to say more, since she was outnumbered. Lavinia Spencer only entered battles when she was certain of victory. Besides, she did not wish to make a bad impression on Lord Carshalton's son and heir, who was obviously friendly with the girl. She saw herself being a second mother to the young man, earning the undying gratitude of his father (whom she trusted was a widower). 'What can I do for you, Lavinia?' Lord Carshalton would ask. 'You have only to say . . .' 'I seek nothing for myself. Only for my dear husband.' After that the picture clouded.

She had not had a particularly successful evening with regard to Miss Wishbone. There seemed to be, at the moment, no action she could take. Perhaps Lord Carshalton would object to his son's friendship with the girl. Something might be worked out there. Really, all this was for Sylvia Washington's sake. She wondered if people realised how diligent she was on their behalf?

Marion was the first to go through the French window on to the balcony. It was dusk now, with hardly enough light to see by, so that she almost fell

48

over the body of Dr Maxton, lying face down on the concrete. Roland, immediately behind her, saw that the round bald patch on the back of Maxton's head, which was by now the part of the man's anatomy most familiar to him, was a pulpy, bloody mess. Blood had splashed on to the collar of the cream linen suit. Roland knelt down and felt for a pulse in Maxton's neck. There was none.

A commotion at the foot of the balcony steps cut through the frozen silence which was the group's first reaction to the sight of the dead man. Up the stone stairs marched a dozen students, carrying banners. 'We demand better housing'; 'Homes not Hovels'; 'Cut the Rents'; and one which inexplicably said 'Keating for President'. Even in that terrible moment, with Maxton dead on the ground, Roland noted that Fiona was amongst them. And that she wore a green headband of which tasselled bits hung down and mingled with her own hair, giving her an interesting brown-and-green striped fringe. How the mind clutched at small things, he thought, when larger, unpleasant ones demanded attention.

The student leader was a large, muscular youth, luxuriantly covered in black hair. His banner said 'Dampness kills'.

'We demand to see the Vice-Chancellor,' he shouted. 'We know he's in there at his bloody party! Let him come out and face us!'

His followers cheered, and echoed him. 'Let him come out and face us!'

'Homes not Hovels!' Fiona shrilled.

'I'm right here,' the Vice-Chancellor said politely. 'Of course I'll see you, dear boy—all of you. But not just now. You've arrived at a rather

49

inconvenient moment.' He gave a slight wave of the hand towards Maxton's body, which was almost hidden by the number of people on the balcony.

'Oh my Gawd!' the student said.

'You see?' the Vice-Chancellor said. Outwardly calm, he was thinking that it couldn't have happened worse. He could see the headlines now. 'Student Demo leads to Murder!'

Sylvia Washington laughed suddenly; a high-pitched noise which turned to a continuous shriek. Her husband patted her face, then chafed her hands, trying to calm her. Then Norma closed silver-blue eyelids over her lovely eyes and fainted. Mike failed to catch her as she fell forward and came to rest against the dead man's legs.

There was a further period, infinitesimally short, during which no one moved—as if someone had stopped the film—and the only sound was Sylvia Washington's subsiding hysteria. Then Sergeant Smith pushed his way through towards Norma. Everyone stood aside to let him pass as if, because he was in uniform, he was some sort of St John Ambulance man. He knelt down on the ground, lifted the girl away from Maxton's body and raised her to a more comfortable position, her head resting in the crook of his arm.

'Norma! Norma, love!' His voice was gentle; infinitely concerned. She opened her eyes and saw him and seemed reassured by his presence.

'Uncle George!' she murmured.

Then she closed her eyes again, her thick dark lashes curling against the whiteness of her cheeks.

In a curious way, Norma's words had a more startling impact than Maxton's death. It seemed that, there being nothing more to be done for him on this earth, he lay there almost forgotten: as if shock and disbelief had caused the onlookers to act as though there was no dead body lying at their feet. Marion was the first to recover.

'I must ring for the police,' she said, and went off to do so.

'And a doctor,' the Vice-Chancellor called after her. 'Though I'm sure the poor fellow's quite dead.' He turned to Norma. 'Did you say Uncle George my dear?' He smiled in a kindly fashion.

'Extraordinary!' his wife said.

'My late sister's girl. Vesta Tilley Smith that was,' Sergeant Smith explained briefly. 'Are you feeling better, Norma love?'

'Yes thank you Uncle George.'

'Well then, as you're her uncle,' Mrs Spencer said, 'perhaps you should get her home.'

'We can't go home until the police have been,' Sylvia Washington said. She was in control of herself once more, though her voice was still tearful.

'But we have nothing to do with it,' Mrs Spencer said sharply. 'It's quite obvious that someone came up the stairs from the campus and attacked the poor man.' She looked keenly at the student leader, who had turned pale green and was leaning against the balcony.

'Nothing to do with us,' he said with an effort. 'We saw nothing, none of us. I reckon we'll go now.' He tried to pull himself together.

'I think not,' Washington said. 'As my wife says, we must all wait until the police arrive.'

'What about the party?' Mike Carshalton asked. It was the first time he had spoken. His voice was edgy. 'It doesn't seem right . . .'

51

'It's going on without us,' Roland said. 'Better to do nothing more until the police come.'

Sirens wailed across the campus, the noise drowning every other sound as the vehicle neared the refectory building. Then the sound ran down, like a bagpipe running out of wind, and stopped. Within seconds Marion Richmond came in with two men, not entering from the party room, but from the direction of the back corridor. The first man walked purposefully forward, taking long strides but not hurrying. This, together with his greying hair, well-trimmed moustache and black-rimmed spectacles somehow gave him an air of dependability. The other man, keeping a deferential two paces behind, was shorter, younger, fresh-faced.

The first man went immediately to the Vice-Chancellor, whom he recognised partly from his frequent photographs in the local press, partly because it was his job to recognise local Bigwigs.

'Inspector Murgatroyd,' he introduced himself. 'Northwell CID. And this is Detective-Sergeant Naylor.'

'Well,' the Vice-Chancellor's wife said. 'Now that you are here, Inspector, I'm sure you'll agree that my husband and I should leave. The Vice-Chancellor has to travel tomorrow and he has had a busy day. The Bursar will be here to answer any questions—though I hope you won't keep anyone too long,' she added graciously.

Christ! Inspector Murgatroyd managed not to say it out loud. A busy day! Haven't we all? There would undoubtedly be trouble from his wife when he arrived home, God knew how many hours late. His supper would be dried up in the oven. He'd get indigestion again. He'd have a sleepless night, and

52

tomorrow it would start all over again. A busy day indeed! He'd give that one hell.

'I shan't keep you a moment longer than necessary, madam,' he said pleasantly. 'But I'm afraid you can't leave just yet. Where is the deceased, then?'

By now most of them had come in from the balcony and stood around, not knowing what to do.

'I could make a cup of coffee,' Sergeant Smith volunteered. Norma had recovered and was sitting at a table, Mike close beside her. 'There's a tin of instant, and some milk in the kitchen.'

Mrs Spencer frowned. 'We don't want to turn it into a social occasion, Sergeant Smith.'

'I think it's a very good idea,' Marion said. 'I'm sure you could do with some coffee, Mrs Washington?'

She was anxious about the Bursar's wife who, now that her hysterical outburst was over, lay back in a chair, her eyes closed. Her heavy blue eyeshadow had run into streaks; her mascara was smudged. 'I just want to go home,' she murmured, not opening her eyes.

Inspector Murgatroyd came in from the balcony and beckoned to the photographers who had arrived soon after him. 'He's all yours, chaps.' He turned to the Vice-Chancellor. 'I suppose someone has telephoned the deceased's next-of-kin? He had a wife perhaps?'

'I really don't know,' the Vice-Chancellor said. 'Had he a wife, Lavinia? Have we met her?'

'Dr Maxton wasn't married,' Marion said.

Inspector Murgatroyd eyed her hopefully. She would be the one he could rely on. She looked capable. A tough cookie. 'You knew him?' he asked.

53

'Hardly at all. Not as a person. I just know he wasn't married. But without looking at his file I don't know who should be informed. He's a foreigner.'

'Right. Now I just want to get everyone's name and address, and then I'll need to see you all again tomorrow—those of you I don't get through tonight.'

'I have to go away tomorrow, I'm afraid,' the Vice-Chancellor apologised. He sincerely hoped that this business wasn't going to interfere with his visit to the cottage. It wasn't as if he could do anything. And Marion could make all the arrangements.

'I'd like you not to leave, sir, until I've had time for a chat with you,' the Inspector said. 'But I shall let you know the moment it's convenient for you to go.' Convenient to me, he said to himself. 'Now if you'll all give your names and so on to Detective-Sergeant Naylor . . .' He turned to Marion. 'I'd like a room here tomorrow if you can manage that. I'll be here at nine sharp.'

Nine sharp. One o'clock at the earliest before he was home. Elaine would be in bed and asleep, but at least it would save a row. He'd skip his supper. Have a cup of tea at the station and a bar of whole nut chocolate with it.

CHAPTER FIVE

For a moment, when he awoke, Roland wondered why the walls which he was used to as a medley of brown and orange stripes, had faded to pale porridge. Then he remembered where he was. He got up and drew back the curtains, opened the

54

window wide. The birds were in full voice. Whether by design or accident the view, from this side of the Hall of Residence, was pleasant, overlooking a wide lawn. The architect, in a rare flash of wisdom (or perhaps defeated by nature) had let the stream take its natural course, simply cleaning up the banks and taking the grass to the water's edge.

In spite of the sun the morning air was cool. He moved away from the window, shaved, dressed. A notice behind the door offered breakfast in the refectory at half-past eight. He wondered if they would have cleared up after last night. It had been late by the time they'd all left. Sergeant Smith, refusing Mike Carshalton's offer, had taken Norma home, the Vice-Chancellor and the Bursar having been prevented from doing so by the claims of their wives. Roland had stayed to the end and helped Marion to lock up before she'd driven off in her car to Northwell.

'Not an auspicious beginning for your visit,' she'd said. 'We're not usually quite as violent as this.'

'Have you any ideas?' he'd asked. 'Like why, for instance?'

'None at all. I can't think that anyone would want to kill Dr Maxton. The thing is that I doubt if anyone really knew him. You don't deliberately kill someone you know nothing about, do you? Oh well,' she'd said, 'I expect Inspector Murgatroyd will sort it all out. He struck me as being a wise old boy.'

*   *   *

'You were late again last night, Geoffrey,' Inspector Murgatroyd's wife said. 'I waited up until midnight. What time did you come in?'

'Not long after that, love,' he said soothingly.

55

God, he was tired this morning.

'You didn't eat your dinner. All dried up in the oven. I don't know why I bother!'

'That's a policeman's life, love. You know that.'

'All I know is, it's worse now than when you were a bobby on the beat. I never know when I'm going to see you.'

'Responsibilities love. Responsibilities.'

'And what about responsibilities to your family?' she demanded. 'The children never see you.'

He'd known it would be like this again. There was nothing he could do about it. He just wished she would shut up.

'I'll try to take a few days leave,' he promised. 'We'll go camping. Take the kids. As soon as I get this case off my hands.'

'And the next. And the next. I'll believe that when I get there.' She banged a plate of toast on to the table, went out of the kitchen, banged the door.

Oh well, he'd have to get going; call in at the station and then straight on to the university. The best time for clues was right at the beginning, before people knew what you were after. The trouble was, you had to be able to recognise them. Curious business. A bunch of intelligent people like that, you'd think they'd be too civilised to kill. But when had intelligence had anything to do with it, he reminded himself. Sex, money, power, jealousy. Those were the reasons why people murdered, and none of them related to intelligence. All *that* might do would be to help them cover their tracks.

He reckoned it would be someone inside the university. People always wanted to blame the outsider. The window cleaner was here, or we had a man in to the central heating. Couldn't face the fact that it might be one of their own.

He called up the stairs to his wife. 'Ta-ta love. I'll try not to be late, but don't wait up.'

'I won't,' she yelled.

*   *   *

Breakfast in the Vice-Chancellor's household was a civilised affair. That is to say, both parties sat at the polished oval table in the breakfast room, laid the evening before by Mrs Carstairs who obliged them daily, drinking coffee and eating toast.

The coffee was abominable and was one of the reasons why their house guests often left earlier than they had planned to. The bread could have been good, since there was still a baker in Otwood who made his own and delivered daily, but Mrs Spencer said he was expensive and that all bread, toasted, was more or less the same. The marmalade varied according to what was on offer in the Northwell supermarkets. This week it was a pale, watery jelly. The Vice-Chancellor had long ago ceased to regard meals in his home as anything other than fodder. For real food he relied upon the Senior Common Room lunches, which were surprisingly good, and on the cakes which Marion Richmond baked and brought to the office once a week.

They read their post in comparative silence, broken only by Lavinia who insisted on reading bits from letters which he intended reading later himself, over the top of something in which he was already engrossed. After she had ruined the post for him she opened *The Times:* not for the news, but to find out who had been awarded what and appointed where.

'More coffee, William?'

'No thank you, my love. One cup is more than enough.' Up in his cottage he made good tea, several times a day, of a strength which his wife would have found common.

'You don't eat or drink enough, William. I can't think why you don't lose weight,' Mrs Spencer said.

She cast the newspaper aside. Nothing of importance in it. She wondered about the Birthday Honours next month. Surely William would have told her . . . ? Sometimes, when she was feeling low, she dreamed that William was offered a life peerage and refused it. He was inclined to have leftish views. She couldn't think why.

'Well I suppose I'd better go,' William said, pushing his cup away. 'The sooner I can see the Inspector, the sooner I can get away.'

His wife looked at him in astonishment. 'Surely, William, he'll come here to see you? No need for you to go chasing after him.'

'I thought perhaps he'd like to see me in the university. And Marion will be there if she's needed.'

Lavinia thought he spoke about Miss Richmond as if she were a nanny.

'But I'd overlooked that he'd want to see you, my dear,' the Vice-Chancellor said. 'Perhaps you'd rather I stayed with you?'

'Want to see me? Why on earth should he want to see me just because one of your faculty has died? Not even your faculty, really. A foreign visitor. It's nothing to do with me.'

'He didn't just *die*, Lavinia,' her husband reminded her. 'Not exactly. He was killed. In a very nasty manner.'

58

Punctually at nine o'clock Inspector Murgatroyd, with Detective-Sergeant Naylor behind him, stood before Sergeant George Robey Smith. Sergeant Smith looked distinctly worried, and so far was he from being himself that he offered the services of an under-porter to conduct the policemen to Miss Richmond's office.

'I suppose that's as good a place as any to start,' the Inspector said to his Sergeant. 'The Miss Richmonds of this world usually know what goes on.'

Her office was exactly as he expected it to be. Beige carpet, shelves full of reference books, a formidable array of telephones on the large, L-shaped desk. On the walls two Redouté rose prints in narrow gilt frames. All very predictable. It was also the kind of professional set-up which could completely hide a personality. The real Miss Richmond, where are *you*? He looked around for something which might betray her. The only divergence from bland good taste was a cartoon—sharp, bitter, slightly vulgar, very funny—which had been cut from a newspaper and pinned on the wall by her desk. Not much to go on, but something. She had human flesh, which would bleed if pricked.

'I'm sorry to trouble you so early, Miss Richmond,' he said.

'Not at all Inspector. I'm always in by a quarter to nine. What can I do for you?'

'Who knows? Anything. What time does the Vice-Chancellor get in?'

'He hadn't intended coming in today. He has to go away. Now I expect he'll come in to see you. He shouldn't be long.'

'Much obliged, I'm sure. How well did *you* know Dr Maxton?'

She moved round to the back of the desk and sat down. The seat of authority, he thought. She feels secure there.

'As I said last night, hardly at all. I met him of course, when he first came here.'

'When was that?'

'I think about six months ago. He was certainly here last Christmas because I remember seeing him at the Christmas party in the Admin block. We always invite overseas visitors.'

'Personal details then? Age? Family? Where did he come from? What's his background?'

She hesitated. 'It's probably in the files. But I don't like giving personal details. There can be a lot of trouble about files.'

The Inspector sighed. These kind of people seemed to think they were outside the law.

'I don't doubt it,' he said. 'But we're not talking about student pranks now. This is a police matter. The man's dead. Murdered. Coshed on the head with a heavy object.' Which I've yet to find, he reminded himself. There'd been nothing lying around, obligingly covered in blood and hairs.

'I don't want to lose any time,' he continued. 'Besides there must be someone we should inform.'

'Very well,' she said. 'I don't have Dr Maxton's file myself. It's held by Professor Fletcher's secretary. She happens to be away, but I can get hold of it. I have the authority.'

I'll bet you do, Inspector Murgatroyd thought. Out loud he said, 'Much obliged. And perhaps I should see Professor Fletcher fairly soon.'

'You can't,' Miss Richmond said. 'He's in the States, on sabbatical. His secretary might have known his exact whereabouts but she's in Switzerland for three weeks.'

A buzzer sounded on her desk. She picked up a telephone; smiled as she listened to the voice at the other end.

'Not yet,' she said. 'He's here now. I'll ask him.' She covered the mouthpiece. 'It's the Vice-Chancellor. It is a bit inconvenient for him to come in. He says if you need to see him could you possibly go along to his house?'

'May I?' Inspector Murgatroyd said, taking the receiver from her.

'Good-morning sir. Yes, I'm afraid it is necessary. And Mrs Spencer. I *could* come out to you.' Make a change, he told himself, otherwise I wouldn't. 'Shall we say about noon then?'

'Pity about Professor Fletcher,' he said, replacing the receiver before Miss Richmond could take it from him. 'Still I dare say we'll trace him if it's necessary. And no doubt we'll find what we're looking for in Dr Maxton's file.'

'I wouldn't bank on that,' Marion said.

'Oh? And why not?'

'These arrangements are often quite informal, very little put on paper. University people—scientists especially—meet each other at conferences all over the place. They hand out and take up invitations right, left and centre. It's the easiest thing in the world to arrange a visit, especially if the visitor's financing himself.'

'Don't they take up references, then?'

'Not at that level. They more or less know each other. If not, they know each other's work and

61

reputation. It could be that Maxton simply met Professor Fletcher at a conference. Or even just wrote to him without having met him. Said he'd always admired his work and would like to spend a few months in his laboratory. Something of that sort.'

'But Professor Fletcher would know him?'

'Probably. Or might think he did. It wouldn't matter a great deal,' Marion said. 'Once they're here a lot of visitors just work away on their own. Sometimes I think they use the university as a base while they travel around Europe.'

'Cushy!'

'It's the way things are,' Marion said coolly.

*   *   *

Washington was already at his desk, reading the morning's post, when Roland arrived. He looked pale, his skin sickly against his red hair. His suit was crumpled, as if he'd not had it off his back all night.

'Come in Challis. Sit down. I won't be a minute.'

'I'm sorry to interrupt . . .'

Washington read to the end of a letter, screwed it into a ball and threw it into the waste paper bin.

'I thought I'd get through my post. Norma's not in.'

'Why not?' Roland asked. 'I thought she seemed quite a bit better by the time Sergeant Smith took her home.'

'I don't know.' Washington's reply was terse. 'She hasn't telephoned.'

So that was it. Was it the whole of it?

'Perhaps she's suffering from shock,' Roland suggested.

'We all are. It's a nasty business.'

62

'Did you know Maxton?'

'A little. Not well.'

But well enough to wish him dead, Roland thought. There was no doubt in his mind, and since last night he had thought about it a great deal, that at the moment he had watched the two men through the binoculars, Washington had murder in his face; had had difficulty, in fact, in holding himself in check. He was certainly in a state of shock now, Roland thought, watching him open an envelope with a long steel paper knife. The hand which held the knife trembled.

'I thought it would be a good idea to take my goods and chattels to my new lodgings,' Roland said, changing the subject. 'I dare say you won't want me around for an hour or two, with the Inspector here and so on. I'll be back long before he needs me.'

'He's with Marion,' Washington said.

So he'd have to wait until later to see her. He'd meant to drop into her office before going to Mrs Thompson's. Find out if she was all right. But he didn't want to meet the Inspector just yet. He wondered how much he should tell him when they did meet. Better play it by ear.

'I'll go then,' Roland said.

'That sounds like a good idea.' Washington wasn't really interested. While they were talking he'd picked up a phone and dialled, and was obviously getting no reply. Roland could hear the ringing tone going on and on. He felt sure Washington was phoning Norma's home. In the end Washington put the receiver down, and then shoved the rest of his post to one side.

'A load of rubbish,' he said. 'Far too much paper

being pushed around. Too much communication if you ask me. Where does it all end? How much of it's necessary?'

'Probably not much,' Roland said. 'See you then.'

*   *   *

In view of his suitcases Roland prevailed upon Sergeant Smith to call a taxi for him. When it drew up outside number forty-seven, Mrs Thompson, her hair piled high under a mauve chiffon headsquare, was just leaving the house, scurrying down the path, high heels clattering.

'Can't stop!' she cried. 'Bus due! You know your way around.'

Presumably she was off on her pursuits. She seemed particularly cheerful. He was sure she couldn't know about Maxton. Who, in the university, knew that Maxton lodged here?

He let himself into the house and went up to his new room. He might as well unpack while he was here, get things into place. He hung his clothes in the wardrobe; put the few books he'd brought with him on the shelves; picked up a small table and moved it over to the window; looked out at the garden. He'd been wrong in thinking the back entrance was never used. Someone had recently come in through the gate which yesterday had looked so undisturbed. Where the clematis had covered the edge of the gate and hidden the latch it was now broken away and the iron latch was visible; and not quite closed. The long green strands of clematis, with their profusion of small white flowers, hung loose.

As he turned away from the window he heard the slight noise of a key being inserted into a lock, followed by a squeak as the front door was opened. It was done quietly, but his bedroom door was ajar and in the still house the sound carried up the stairwell. He was confident it was not Mrs Thompson, returning for something she'd left behind. He doubted if, in spite of her diminutive size, she ever moved quietly. But who else would have a key? He went out on to the landing and looked over the banisters, keeping in the shadow so as not to be seen.

Norma was coming up the stairs. She stopped on the floor below him and without hesitation went into the room he knew must be Maxton's, closing the door behind her.

Should he follow her? Or should he let her get on with whatever she'd come to do? Didn't the little fool know that whatever she was up to in that room she'd be leaving her fingerprints all over it? And it couldn't be long before the police arrived and checked on everything. She wouldn't have the sense to wear gloves; probably she had no idea of the trouble she was letting herself in for. Unless, of course, she had a perfectly legitimate reason for being in the dead man's room, which he thought unlikely.

And why, he asked himself, should he be protecting her from the police? If she'd had anything to do with Maxton's death—and certainly she'd had something to do with him alive—then should he consider shielding her? Was it as basic as sexual attraction, or was it because, instinctively, he agreed with Marion Richmond's remark that Norma wouldn't hurt a fly? But—Marion had also said—she'd kill a wasp.

It took him all of five minutes to make up his

mind, after which he walked down the flight of stairs and knocked on Maxton's door.

'It's me. Roland Challis. I know you're in there, Norma. I watched you come up the stairs. Open up, there's a love!'

There was a long silence and then she opened the door a few inches, holding the doorknob in a gloved hand, barring his way. He was shocked by her appearance. She was as immaculate as ever, but there were mauve blotches under her frightened eyes and the skin was taut over her cheekbones. Her mouth twitched, as if she did not have it quite under control. He had the feeling that she hadn't slept at all.

'Let me come in,' he said. He pushed her gently backwards and went into the room. Drawers lay open, books had been pulled off the shelves, papers were scattered on the floor.

'What are you up to?' Roland asked.

'Are you the police? I didn't think you were the police.' She backed away from him. He could see that she was trembling.

'I'm not the police. But they could be here any minute. As soon as they get Maxton's address they'll be down here like vultures. How are you going to explain all this?' He indicated the mess in the room.

'I didn't do this,' she said. 'Not this mess. It was like this when I came in. I swear it was.'

'You're saying Maxton left it like this? I'll bet Mrs Thompson wouldn't approve.'

Norma shook her head. 'No, he couldn't have.' She spoke in a whisper, as if fright had robbed her of the power of speech. 'He was a very tidy man. Neat and tidy. He wouldn't leave a place like this.'

'So he had another visitor?' Roland said.

'I only know it wasn't me.'

'Did you find what you were looking for?' He looked at her gloved hands.

'No.'

'Was it important?'

'Yes.'

'A matter of life and death?' Roland said.

The trembling turned to shivering, her hands, shoulders, body, shaken by convulsions. As he stepped forward to take hold of her the front doorbell rang. Loud, insistent, not stopping.

'Quick!' Roland said. 'Up to my room. Immediately over this one. I'll answer the door. You stay in my room and don't move.'

The doorbell continued to ring. He ran down the stairs to answer it. Inspector Murgatroyd and Detective-Sergeant Naylor stood on the doorstep.

'Why, hello Mr Challis,' the Inspector said. 'I didn't know you lived here.' He sounded genuinely surprised.

'As of today,' Roland told him. 'I expect you want my landlady, Mrs Thompson. I'm afraid she's out.'

'I was beginning to think everyone was out,' the Inspector said. 'Mind if we come in?'

'I was in the bathroom. Come in by all means. Is there something I can do?'

'I think so. It seems Dr Maxton lodged here. I take it you didn't know that, Mr Challis? Well Detective-Sergeant Naylor and I would like a few particulars, which I don't suppose you can give us, you having arrived after he departed, so to speak. But perhaps you know which his room is, do you?'

'How would I know that?' Roland said. 'Mrs Thompson said she had another lodger. I didn't know it was Maxton.'

'Ah well! A process of elimination then,' the Inspector said.

Not if I can stop you, Roland thought. 'I think she said his room was immediately under mine,' he said. 'That would make it first floor back.'

'Then we'll try that,' the Inspector said agreeably.

'I'm not sure that Mrs Thompson would approve—' Roland began.

'Oh I'm sure she wouldn't mind, now that the poor gentleman's dead. People don't usually obstruct the police, not unless they've got something to hide. Up the stairs here I suppose?'

As Roland stepped to one side in the narrow hall to let them pass—it was obvious that nothing he could do would prevent them—the doorbell rang again. Detective-Sergeant Naylor opened the door. Mike Carshalton stood outside. It was clear from his startled expression that he'd expected to see neither Roland nor the police.

'Looking for rooms, Mr Carshalton?' Inspector Murgatroyd asked pleasantly.

CHAPTER SIX

'I said "Looking for rooms, Mr Carshalton?"' Inspector Murgatroyd repeated.

'I'm sorry, Mike,' Roland broke in quickly. 'I thought when I suggested you should come here that Mrs Thompson would be in. Unfortunately she's not.'

Mike stared at Roland.

'So you *are* looking for rooms, Mr Carshalton?' the Inspector said. His voice was as smooth as silk.

68

'I told Mike I thought Mrs Thompson might have a bedsitter,' Roland extemporised. 'I wasn't sure of course.'

'Of course not. So where do you live now, Mr Carshalton? In the university I believe?'

Mike found his voice. 'Yes.'

'And you're not happy there?' The Inspector was all concern.

'No. No, I'm not,' Mike answered.

'I see. And Mr Challis saw an opportunity of helping you? That's nice. A friend in need.'

'It's very kind of him,' Mike said.

For heaven's sake, Roland willed him, act it out! Look as if you know what you're doing! Anyway, what *was* he doing here?

'Mr Challis is a most obliging man, I can see that,' the Inspector said.

Roland thought it was time to change the conversation.

'Look Mike,' he said, 'I'll be going back to the university as soon as the Inspector's finished with me. Shouldn't be long. Would you like to wait in the sitting room?'

'I'll wait,' Mike said, picking up the cue.

'In here then.' Roland opened the door to Mrs Thompson's front room. He hoped there'd be no more unexpected visitors. He was running out of space. Norma, by this time, must have heard Mike. He hoped she'd have the sense to stay where she was.

'This way, I think,' he said, taking the policemen up the stairs. 'I imagine that's the room there.'

'Well we shall see,' Inspector Murgatroyd said.

He opened the door, stood in the entrance, sniffed, and then walked in, followed by the

69

Detective-Sergeant and Roland.

'Dearie me!' he said. 'An untidy fellow, the deceased! Unless he's had a visitor of course. Do you think he might have had a visitor, Mr Challis?'

'How would I know?' Roland asked. 'I only moved in this morning.'

'So you did. So you did. Then he wouldn't have had anyone in the last hour, say? Not without you knowing?'

'No. I shouldn't think so.'

'I thought you'd say that,' the Inspector said. His eyes gleamed behind the thick glasses. 'You've got good hearing have you, Mr Challis? Now we in the police force have to develop all our senses. Hearing, sight, touch, smell.' His tone was conversational, off-hand. He wandered around the room looking at things, not touching anything. But he was not as casual as he seemed, of that Roland was sure. And over Maxton's room hung the unmistakable scent of Norma's perfume. Sweetish, musky, very feminine.

'Well Detective-Sergeant,' the Inspector said finally, 'perhaps we should just seal up this little lot until we get the boys on to it. Any idea when Mrs Thompson'll be back, Mr Challis?'

'None at all.'

'Pity. Well, perhaps as we're here we'll have a little chat with you. Why don't we go up to your room?'

'I think the sitting room would be better,' Roland said.

'Do you? Now I have this little idiosyncrasy about seeing people in their own settings.'

'It's hardly my setting,' Roland said.

'Nevertheless—'

'Actually it's rather delicate,' Roland said

70

diffidently. He tried for a naïve embarrassment in his face, though doubting its success with the Inspector. 'I have a visitor.' They couldn't compel him to let them into his room. He knew that.

'A visitor?'

'That's right. It's a bit awkward . . .'

'Ah! A lady!' The Inspector winked at him. 'Someone we know, then?'

'No,' Roland assured him. 'A friend from London. But—'

'Well,' the Inspector said admiringly, 'she must be very fond of you to be here so early in the day. I'd say you were a lucky man, Mr Challis.'

'I know,' Roland answered. So, he thought, does Inspector Murgatroyd. At least he knows there's something; but there's nothing he can do about it right now.

'Well in that case I'll see you back in the university,' Inspector Murgatroyd said. 'Come to think of it, I'm a bit short of time. Got to see the Vice-Chancellor. Now *there's* an interesting man.'

'Indeed yes,' Roland agreed. He showed them to the door, closed it behind them, and without stopping to see Mike, ran up the stairs to his own room. There was no certainty that the Inspector wouldn't return almost immediately. That was an old trick. He must let Norma out of the back door and then deal with Mike.

His room was empty. No one there at all. All that remained of Norma's presence was the heady smell of *Jardins des Souvenirs*. He ran down to the sitting room. What did the little idiot think she was doing? But the sitting room was also empty; no sign either of Norma or of Mike Carshalton.

*   *   *

71

Garth House, which a grateful university had put at the disposal of whoever undertook to be its Vice-Chancellor, was about half a mile outside the village of Otwood, which gave Mrs Spencer the opportunity of keeping an eye on the village without its inhabitants being able to pop in on her too easily. Many of the inhabitants of the village were, by now, university faculty and their families, the natives having been only too pleased to sell their inconvenient, dampish cottages, which the university incomers inexplicably raved about, for prices higher than their wildest dreams. With the proceeds they had bought newly-built houses, with all mod cons, on the outskirts of Northwell. And since almost all the villagers had moved to the same estate they were able to keep an eye on each other and go in and out of each other's houses with the local gossip exactly as before. It was a situation which satisfied everyone.

'They used to have cockfights up on the hill behind Garth House,' Detective-Sergeant Naylor observed.

Inspector Murgatroyd looked at his assistant with interest. He was a young man of few words, but when he did speak it was usually interesting. Totally irrelevant, but interesting.

'Before it was put a stop to,' the Detective-Sergeant said.

'Fancy that! Do you know if the Spencers have any domestic staff? Housekeeper? Gardener?'

'Mrs Carstairs goes in every day barring Sundays, and Joe Smith does a bit in the garden. Shall I have a word with them while you see sir and madam?'

'Why not?' Inspector Murgatroyd said.

The Vice-Chancellor himself opened the door to

them and took the Inspector off to his study.

'Well, well!' he said. 'Well, well, well! And how can I help, Inspector? We want this thing cleared up as quickly as possible. You'll have a glass of sherry, I hope.'

'Thank you. I'd just like to ask a few questions; get a picture of how things work, what goes on.'

'What goes on? That's a good one!' The Vice-Chancellor handed the Inspector his sherry and cleared a copy of *Country Life*, a tobacco tin, spectacle case and a large pebble from a chair so that his visitor could sit down.

'Thank you sir.'

It was a gloriously untidy room. Books everywhere, not only on shelves, but piled on tables and chairs and on the floor. Drawings were pinned to the walls. A microscope, binoculars, Wellington boots, pot plants, several copies of *Nature*, an anorak, all fought for the available space. All the same, the Inspector liked it. It was a haven from the fair sex. He'd like to bet that madam was never allowed in here. He had already decided that the Vice-Chancellor could only be pushed around so much, and for that he had to admire him.

'What do you know about Dr Maxton?' he asked.

'Practically nothing, I'm afraid. I don't really remember seeing him around at all, as a matter of fact. Miss Richmond says he's been here a few months. But of course I have to be away a lot.'

'Do you know young Mr Carshalton?' the Inspector asked.

'Carshalton?' The Vice-Chancellor seemed surprised by the question. 'Not at all I'm afraid. I know his father, Lord Carshalton. He's in chemicals—and a lot of other things. Why do you

73

ask?'

'And Miss Wishbone? The Bursar's secretary?'

The Vice-Chancellor's face brightened. 'Now there's a charming girl,' he said. 'I wonder where Washington found her?'

'No doubt he'll tell me,' the Inspector said. 'What about Professor Fletcher?'

'Fletcher?'

'I understand he's the link with Dr Maxton.'

'Oh, is he?'

I can't believe the faithful Miss Richmond hasn't told you that much, Inspector Murgatroyd thought. She must have been on the phone the minute I turned my back.

'Professor Fletcher is in America,' the Vice-Chancellor said.

'I realise that, sir.' They talked as though America was Outer Space, which was odd amongst people who were always globe-trotting. He was beginning to feel that Fletcher was a taboo subject. 'Of course we could get in touch with him, Vice-Chancellor, but I thought perhaps you could tell me something. For instance, what did Professor Fletcher *do* when he was here?'

'He's a chemist. Works on precious metals. A very gifted young man. Highly thought of.'

'Young?'

'Not yet forty. He's come a long way. One of the world's experts in his field.'

'Really? Was he working on something special? Something important?'

'Who knows what's important in scientific research?' the Vice-Chancellor said. 'What's insignificant today can change the world tomorrow.'

And you're not answering my questions, the

Inspector thought. You're really quite clever.

'Well let's say anything *you* would consider important, Vice-Chancellor.'

The Vice-Chancellor smiled, shook his head.

'Have some more sherry, Inspector. Now how would I know what was important to a chemist? I'm a biologist.' The smile left his face. 'Not even that any longer. Simply an administrator. Nobody understands a chemist, Inspector, except another chemist.'

It's like swimming in treacle, the Inspector thought. They gang up. He waved away the sherry decanter which the Vice-Chancellor was holding out to him.

'No thank you sir. Now how about Mr Challis,' the Inspector said suddenly. 'What can you tell me about him?' Sometimes you could catch them on the hop if you changed the subject quickly enough. But the Vice-Chancellor was a wily bird.

'Well,' he said, 'Mr Challis himself can tell you best. I expect you'll be questioning him. A pleasant chap, I thought. Here to do an important job.'

'Oh yes? What job?'

'Management Consultant. Expert on Communications. You ask him.'

Expert on non-communication, the Vice-Chancellor. How could you prove that anyone was obstructing the police?

'And when do you think I might go away, Inspector? I'm rather anxious to make a start,' the Vice-Chancellor said.

'I dare say tomorrow, sir, unless anything crops up. Let me know your whereabouts, of course.'

*   *   *

He'd better return to the university right away, Roland thought. He supposed he should warn Norma and that young fool Carshalton. Warn them of what? Not to get mixed up in the affair? Not to go against the police? But Norma was already mixed up in it; he didn't like to think how deeply. One thing he *should* tell her was to change her perfume, and quickly. He had little doubt that the Inspector had been on to it and would probably recognise it again. He would also go and pump Marion about Fletcher. Quite apart from the job, he found he wanted to see her again.

Marion was on the telephone when he entered her office. While she talked, Roland studied her. Creamy skin, in contrast to her dark hair. Fine, silky eyebrows arched over the lively green eyes which were her chief attraction. The red silk blouse she was wearing showed off her dark beauty. She had capable-looking hands: square palms, long fingers, no rings. She scribbled words on a piece of paper and pushed it across the desk to him.

'Five minutes', she'd written.

'I'll come back', he wrote. 'Will you have lunch with me?' She read it, smiled and nodded. Roland decided to drop in and tell Washington he'd returned.

The Bursar was sitting in the armchair in front of his desk. Norma sat opposite him with a shorthand pad on her knee. Seeing Roland, the Bursar broke off his dictation.

'Just popped in to let you know I'm back,' Roland said. 'I'll be with Miss Richmond. See you after lunch to talk about work, if that suits you.'

Washington waved a hand in acknowledgement. 'OK,' he said. 'I expect a visit from the Inspector sometime this afternoon, but shall we say about two?' He looked happier than he had earlier in the day—no doubt because Norma had turned up—but there was still a look of strain in his face.

From behind Washington's chair Roland looked hard at Norma, willing her to look up at him, but she kept her eyes on the shorthand notebook and refused to acknowledge him.

'That's a nice perfume you're wearing, Norma,' he said. The room reeked of *Jardins des Souvenirs*.

'Thank you,' she said, but not looking at him. Had she taken his meaning? He doubted it. Washington's reaction was immediate. Before Norma had had time to say 'thank you' he turned around in his chair and glared at Roland.

'If you don't mind, Challis,' he said, 'we're rather busy.'

'I'm going.'

The man's insane, Roland thought. He went back to Marion's office.

'I want to find out how to contact Professor Fletcher,' he said to her 'I promised a friend I'd find out where he was. No one seems sure, except that he's in the States, but I thought if I could meet his secretary.'

'Everyone wants to meet Professor Fletcher's secretary,' Marion said. 'She's on holiday in Switzerland.'

Hellfire! How could he push it further without seeming too insistent?

'But there'll be a note of his whereabouts in his file,' he said casually. 'Do you have access to that?'

'I do. Personal files on faculty are in the Vice-Chancellor's care, which means in mine. They're locked up in the filing store on the ground floor.

You do go to a lot of trouble for your friends.'

Roland laughed, shook his head. 'I wouldn't have promised if I'd known. Fletcher seems to be an elusive bloke. Do you know him?' He kept his tone light.

'Yes,' Marion said.

Stalemate. He'd have to get the file.

'I really don't want to drag you down to the ground floor. Could I fetch the file for you?'

She raised her eyebrows. 'Certainly not. The personal files are under lock and key.'

'Of course. Stupid of me. Then perhaps your nice Sue Perkins could get it. I don't want you to go to a lot of trouble.'

She took a bunch of keys from a drawer. 'It's not a lot of trouble,' she said. 'Though I doubt if I can help you. I've no recollection of Professor Fletcher's itinerary being sent to me for filing. However, I go to lunch about now, so if you're going with me we'll call in the filing room on the way.'

On the ground floor they turned right into the corridor, in the opposite direction from the front entrance. Marion picked out a key on her bunch and unlocked a door. Inside the room, Roland looked around. If everyone was going to be uptight about Fletcher he'd somehow have to get hold of the file for himself. Knowing the man's present whereabouts was only the beginning. He needed to know what he was up to, both here and in the States. Probably he was just beavering about with some incomprehensible chemistry which might or might not be of importance. But *they* must think it was.

If he had to get into this room, only the door key would be the difficulty. He noticed that Marion

didn't have to unlock the cabinets before consulting the files. They simply relied on the door being locked. If the door wasn't possible he might have to find another way in. He walked across to the only window. Outside, people were passing with fair frequency. While looking out, he studied the catch. It looked just about foolproof. He turned back to Marion, who stood in front of a filing cabinet, frowning.

'I don't understand it,' she said. 'Professor Fletcher's file isn't here. There's the sling where it ought to be, but the file itself is missing.'

Missing! Hell! Was nothing going to be straightforward? 'Perhaps it's out of place,' Roland suggested. Highly unlikely. Someone had beaten him to it. And for why?

'No,' Marion said. 'No, I don't think so. There are no other empty slings and it's quite obvious that no sling has two files. You can see at a glance with this type of filing. It's definitely gone . . . but how on earth . . . ?'

'Perhaps someone's borrowed it,' Roland said. 'Let's go to lunch.' He'd as soon she didn't start a hue and cry for the file at this point; not until he'd had time to decide what to do next. 'I dare say you'll find the explanation.'

*   *   *

The long bar was crowded: students, staff, workmen. Roland and Marion collected beer and sandwiches and took them to a table.

'Do you usually come here?' Roland asked.

'No. More often than not I lunch in my office. It's not a meal I bother about much.'

'Why not? Why don't you come here?'

'Habit partly. And then I feel conspicuous—although I know perfectly well I'm not—because I'm on my own.'

'You don't have many friends in the university?'

'Not really,' she said. 'Mine isn't a job where one makes friends. One doesn't quite fit in anywhere.'

Under all that efficiency she's lonely, Roland thought. Why does she have no confidence in herself as a person, apart from her job?

'I'm really worried about Professor Fletcher's file,' Marion said. 'Why should it be missing?'

Why indeed, Roland wondered. Either there was something in it so hot that the file had been removed for security reasons, and in that case surely Marion would know, or someone besides himself was curious about Fletcher. He reckoned that was it. Maxton was the obvious one, but how would he get the file? There'd been no signs of break-in on the window-catch. Collusion, perhaps. It needed no more than the borrowing of a key. By whom? Presumably only Marion had the keys.

'Have you seen the file recently?' he asked.

'Not really. But I've used the same filing cabinet and I think I'd have noticed if anything was missing. You develop an eye for these things.'

'Well perhaps it's been borrowed and will be returned,' Roland said.

'By whom? I have the keys.'

'No one else?'

'There's a spare set of everything in the key cupboard, but I also hold the key to that. The Vice-Chancellor has master keys, of course. But he never goes near the files. If he wanted a file he'd simply ask me for it.'

Unless he didn't want you to know, Roland said

to himself. Out loud he asked, 'Why would anyone want Fletcher's file enough to steal it? What would be in it? Results of his work perhaps?'

'Could be,' Marion said. 'Perhaps something for safe-keeping while he was in the States.'

'But you'd know?'

'I'd expect to have filed it.' Then the expression on her face changed, became bland. Her tone of voice levelled. 'But I don't understand it at present, and if I did I wouldn't tell you.'

'I'm sorry. Another beer?'

'No thank you. I can't stay. But don't let me rush you. I expect I'll see you later.'

'I want to send a telemessage,' Roland said. 'Is there a post office on campus?'

'Yes. If you walk in the direction of the library you'll pass it on the way.'

As Marion got up from the table they saw Norma and Mike Carshalton come into the bar. Marion waved to them to come and share the table.

'Are you sure you won't stay?' Roland asked.

Marion shook her head.

'Then will you have some dinner with me this evening? Please! I'm a stranger in a strange land.'

'You needn't appeal to my pity,' she said, smiling. 'I'd like to.'

Marion left the bar and Roland watched Mike drag an unwilling Norma across to share the table.

'I'm sorry about this morning,' Mike said. 'Thanks a lot for what you did. I can't explain anything. Not yet.'

Roland turned to Norma. 'And I suppose the same goes for you?'

'Yes,' she said. 'But it's not what you think.' She was making no attempt to eat the food Mike had

81

pushed in front of her and her drink—a tomato juice—remained untouched. She clenched her hands until the knuckles showed white.

'Well, if you say so,' Roland said. 'But I might be able to help you.'

'Thank you,' Mike broke in. 'But Norma's quite right. We can't say anything at all.'

Roland shrugged. 'Very well then. But please do one thing. Mike, you go into Northwell the minute you've finished that beer, and buy Norma the biggest bottle of Chanel No. 5 you can find. And Norma, you get rid of that *Jardins des Souvenirs*, the quicker the better. Like the minute you get back to the office.'

She stared at him, uncomprehending. It was the first time since Maxton's appearance on the scene last night that he had seen her dragged out of her frightening thoughts.

'Get rid of it? But it's my favourite! And Mike gave it to me!'

'I don't care if Prince Charles gave it to you. Just you smother yourself in Chanel No. 5.'

'I've got it!' Mike said suddenly. 'Thanks for the tip.' Roland left them and went to the post office, from where he despatched a lengthy telemessage to his lords and masters.

CHAPTER SEVEN

'Ah there you are Miss Richmond,' Mrs Spencer said, walking into Marion's office.

'I'm usually to be found here in working hours,' Marion said with civility. 'Did you want me for something?'

'Not at the moment, Miss Richmond, though we might a little later.'

'We?'

'The Summer Ball Ladies' Committee of course. I thought that as my husband has had to leave, we would use his office. So much more convenient for everyone.'

Mrs Spencer never acknowledged, even to herself, that her husband had escaped; deserted her. When he had shot off to his cottage she spoke of his departure as if some reason of scholarship, the need to seek quiet for some *magnum opus*, had taken him reluctantly away from her. She had never before, though, taken over his office. Marion wondered how much authority she had to refuse her entry. But short of standing in the doorway, arms outstretched against the advance, there was little she could do about it.

'I'm not sure that the Vice-Chancellor—' she began.

'The others will be here any minute,' Mrs Spencer said. 'I'm expecting Mrs Washington, Mrs Keswick, the Chaplain's wife—what's the little woman's name?'

'Mrs Prince-Patterson.'

'Mrs Prince-Patterson. Such an unsuitable name. And Miss Hardwick from the catering staff. Just show them in will you? Oh, and it's possible we might need you to take a few notes. I'll ring when I want you.'

'I'm sorry, Mrs Spencer,' Marion said, controlling herself with difficulty. 'That won't be possible. I've got stacks of work for the Vice-Chancellor and that must have priority.'

'Oh! Oh well, we'll have to manage. Or perhaps

the Bursar will spare *his* secretary. Yes, that would be a splendid idea. And we'll all have tea at whatever time you have yours. With a few biscuits or perhaps a little cake or two if someone can slip out for them.' Her face creased momentarily into the beginnings of a stiff smile before she disappeared into her husband's office.

Why doesn't someone murder *you*, Marion thought. I'd volunteer to be an accessory both before and after.

The other members of the committee arrived within the next few minutes.

'Are you feeling better, Mrs Washington?' Marion asked the Bursar's wife. She still looked strained; her eyes wary, her cheek rouge two patches of bright colour on her white face. She was clearly a very anxious lady.

'Yes thank you. I'm sorry I made such a fool of myself last night.'

'You didn't,' Marion assured her. 'It was a nasty shock. One doesn't expect to meet murder.'

'But you always manage to keep so calm,' Mrs Washington said, going into the Vice-Chancellor's office. 'You never flap.'

One of these days, Marion promised herself, I shall run amok, screaming at the top of my voice and throwing things. And it'll be right after some well-meaning person has told me how calm I always am. They made her feel as if she was devoid of the human emotions which activated the rest of them. She spent an angry minute thinking what she would say and do when the day arrived, but she couldn't sustain her annoyance for long. She was in a happy mood this afternoon. In spite of everything, she felt that life was all right. She was looking forward to the evening with Roland Challis. As he didn't know the area, perhaps she would take him to Harrogate, or Ripon. They could get a good meal in either place, and the drive would be beautiful at this time of the year. She attacked the heap of correspondence on her desk with vigour.

After a while Norma came in.

'Inspector Murgatroyd wants to see me.' She bit her lower lip, twisted her fingers nervously. Marion smiled at her.

'Don't worry, Norma. He won't eat you. Just refuse to be afraid of him.'

'But I *am* afraid,' Norma admitted.

'Then don't let him see it.' She wondered why Norma should be so frightened.

*   *   *

Why is she so afraid, Inspector Murgatroyd asked himself, studying Norma. She made a pleasant study, one to which he would willingly have devoted himself for a long period. She was wearing tight black trousers and a silky black jumper which curved with her figure. Her hair was tied back with a multi-coloured silk scarf and gold hoop earrings pierced her neat ears. They were not the sort of earrings the Inspector would have considered suitable for office wear, but on her they were perfect.

'That's a nice perfume you're wearing, Miss Wishbone,' he said pleasantly. 'What is it?'

Norma looked at him in surprise. 'Chanel No. 5.'

'Very nice. A gift, was it?'

'Yes. Mike Carshalton gave it to me.'

'Ah yes! A good friend of yours, is he, Mr Carshalton?' Sometimes if you got them talking

85

about someone else they forgot themselves. Gave themselves away.

'Yes he is.'

'Known him for long?'

'Since I came to work here.'

'And that's . . .' he consulted his notes, '. . . about six weeks?'

'That's right.'

She was giving nothing. Shock tactics, should he try? But it went against the grain to bully such a beautiful creature.

'And was Dr Maxton a friend of yours?' he asked.

'No! No he wasn't!' She spoke quickly, raising her voice from the whisper which was all he'd had from her so far.

'Well now, and I'd got the impression he was. Where did I get that I wonder?'

'He wasn't. If anyone said that they were lying.'

'You sound as though you didn't like him, my dear.' His voice was gentle, sympathetic.

'I hated him!' Too late she realised her mistake; watched the smile spread over the Inspector's broad face.

'Tell me why,' he invited.

'I don't know why.' Her guard was up again.

'No matter,' he lied. 'How did you come to know him?'

'He lodged in Runswick Avenue, where I live. Sometimes he gave me a lift into work, if he saw me standing at the bus stop.'

'And who wouldn't?' Inspector Murgatroyd said. 'So you haven't known him long? Only since you came to work in the university?'

'Before that I used to work at Picketts, the car components factory. I was in the office there. It's on the same bus route as the university. He'd give me a lift.'

'Very considerate. Friend of the family, was he? I mean, living so close.'

'No!' She was emphatic.

'Your Uncle George, did he know him? Sergeant George Robey Smith.'

'I don't know. I shouldn't think so except that Uncle George knows everyone.'

She was perking up a bit, feeling a bit more sure of herself, the Inspector noticed. Her hands were no longer tightly clasped. Any minute now she'll tell me to ask her Uncle George myself, he thought.

'Why don't you ask him?' she said, right on cue.

'Oh I shall, my dear. I shall. So Dr Maxton was just someone who lived down the road and kindly gave you a lift in his car from time to time? That's all, is it?'

'That's all.'

'Then it wasn't very nice of you to hate him, was it?' he chided her. 'Perhaps he made a pass at you? Was that it?'

'I didn't hate him,' Norma said. 'I shouldn't have said that. He just wasn't my sort.'

'I see.' He'd get no more out of her now. 'Well, thank you very much, Miss Wishbone.'

'Can I go now?'

It wasn't flattering, he reckoned, the way they all wanted to get away from him. He studied her from behind as she walked out of the room. When the last delicious curve had disappeared he turned his attention to the list in front of him. Washington, Challis, Smith, Carshalton. Mrs Washington, he supposed; and some of those students who'd been in at the death. Perhaps he'd see Sergeant Smith

87

next. He'd follow on nicely from his beautiful niece.

*　　　*　　　*

'What were you doing then?' he asked Sergeant Smith several minutes later. 'Let's say, just the few minutes before you went on the balcony? What made you go out on to the balcony, by the way?'

Sergeant Smith drew himself to attention as far as was compatible with sitting in the armchair where Inspector Murgatroyd had placed him. He would rather have been standing on his two feet.

'I was beginning to tidy up the room,' he said. 'The sherry was running out—we don't have a very generous allowance to my way of thinking. Now if I had the running of—'

He was ready to expand on that subject, so the Inspector quickly interrupted him. 'You were tidying up,' he prompted.

'That's right. Cleaning glasses. Emptying ashtrays, that sort of thing. Giving people the general idea . . .'

'That the party was over?'

'That's right.'

'So why did you go out on to the balcony?'

'I saw the curtains was drawn back, didn't I? No business to be drawn back. People weren't supposed to go into that part of the room. I don't know who did it.'

'It was Miss Richmond. She told me so. She thought the room was getting stuffy.'

Sergeant Smith thrust out his chin. 'Miss Richmond knew we wasn't to use that part of the room,' he said. They were old adversaries, the Inspector thought, the Sergeant and Miss Richmond. At least they were in the Sergeant's

88

eyes.

'So you went to draw the curtains together again?'

'I went to *investigate*,' the Sergeant corrected. 'It was while I was investigating that I heard Mrs Bursar scream.'

Investigating; snooping; call it what you like. The Inspector reckoned that Sergeant Smith would always be early on the scene.

'Had you seen the students, the ones who were demonstrating?'

'If I had,' the Sergeant said firmly, 'I'd have sent them packing. Discipline, that's what's lacking here. The Vice-Chancellor's a very nice man, and a gentleman, but two years in the army would be the making of some of 'em.'

'Did you know Dr Maxton?' the Inspector asked.

'Not to speak of. I knew him by sight, of course. In my job I make it my business to know everybody.'

'Quite. But you didn't know him well?'

'No.'

'He lived quite near to your niece, I understand.'

'I believe so.'

'A charming young woman, your niece.'

The craggy lines and folds of the Sergeant's face softened. The hardness went out of his voice. 'She's a good girl, our Norma. The spitting image of her mother, my late sister Vesta.'

'You were very fond of your sister?'

'She meant a lot to me,' Sergeant Smith said. 'Having no family of my own. She was a lot younger than me, of course. I took her death very badly. So did Henry.'

'Henry?'

'Her husband. Norma's dad. Norma's been a

89

good girl to her dad. Thinks the world of him.'

'And of you, I shouldn't wonder,' the Inspector said.

Sergeant Smith was not to be drawn any further. If he'd remained on his feet instead of being forced into this sitting position, he thought, he'd have kept his feelings to himself.

'If that's all,' he said, 'I have to get back to my job. God knows who'll be coming and going while I'm wasting time here.'

'That's all for now,' Inspector Murgatroyd said.

Sergeant Smith stood up, did a smart about turn, and marched towards the door.

'Oh, by the way,' the Inspector said casually, thereby interrupting the rhythm. 'Do you know Professor Fletcher?'

The Sergeant, caught off balance, halted clumsily. 'Professor Fletcher? Of course I do. He's in America.'

'Whereabouts in America?'

'How would I know?' the Sergeant said. 'I'm only the Head Porter. Not God Almighty.'

*   *   *

'Well I think that's about all,' Mrs Spencer said to her ladies. 'We'll get my husband's secretary to serve us with tea and then one of the other girls can make notes of what we've decided. I've asked for Miss Wishbone. She can type the necessary memos and get the notices out.'

Mrs Washington looked up sharply. Mrs Spencer looked hard back at her. What she hoped—indeed intended, since for the moment she could think of no satisfactory way of getting Norma permanently out of her job with the Bursar—was to show the

Bursar's wife (and anyone else present, who could then spread it abroad) that Norma was of no account, not to be feared. That she would find a way of accomplishing this Mrs Spencer had little doubt. Then in the fullness of time she could perhaps ease the girl out of her job: if not out of the university altogether, then to some man who was less susceptible than the Bursar. There must be a dedicated scientist or mathematician who would not notice Norma. Better still, perhaps she could get her to work for some woman or other.

Mrs Spencer pressed the buzzer to summon Miss Richmond. Marion heard it but chose to ignore it, so that in the end the Chaplain's wife had to be sent out of the meeting to ask for tea.

'If you're sure it's no trouble,' Mrs Prince-Patterson said apologetically.

'Did Mrs Spencer say that?' Marion asked. 'Anyway, tell her someone will fetch it as soon as possible.'

She rang Sue Perkins and asked her to get the tea.

'The machine stuff will do,' she said. 'Cardboard cups.'

Marion crossed the corridor to the Bursar's office.

'Mrs Spencer is in,' she told him. 'She'd like to have Norma for a little while. If it's not convenient I suggest you say so.'

'Curse the woman! What does she want her for?'

'It's the women's committee for the Summer Ball. Isn't Mrs Washington the treasurer?'

'I'd forgotten. Is Sylvia here?'

'Yes. They're about to have tea.'

'Well tell Mrs Vice-Chancellor she can have
91

Norma for half an hour or so. No longer. Pressure of work, et cetera. Will you tell Norma on your way out?'

'But I'll be petrified,' Norma said when faced with the news. 'She hates me.'

'Just be yourself,' Marion advised her. 'You can't lose.'

Fortified, Norma faced her inquisitor.

'I don't suppose you know much about university balls?' Mrs Spencer said. She would start by putting the girl where she belonged.

'No, not really,' Norma said. 'I usually go to the Northwell Palais. It's very good.' Marion had said not to be afraid and she was determined not to be.

Mrs Spencer looked around her committee, her expression of patient pity with one not born to privilege inviting them to smile with her.

'Well yes,' she said, 'though this is a very different affair, Miss Wishbone. Not so much for *dancing* as for meeting people. The Lord Lieutenant, the Chief Constable, the High Sheriff, the Chancellor . . . But it needn't worry you. I'm sure it's not a function you would wish to attend.'

'Oh but I am,' Norma informed her pleasantly. 'Mike Carshalton's asked me. His dad's coming as well.'

Bother! She had forgotten the Carshalton boy. This was going to be very awkward and really she wondered why Mrs Washington and the other wives couldn't deal with their own problems. They could hardly expect her to make all the sacrifices.

'Well never mind that now,' she said uncertainly. 'To work, to work! If this affair is to be a success we all know where the responsibility will lie!'

For the next thirty minutes Norma, with great

competence, did all that was required of her by the ladies. Then she closed her notebook, gathered her various bits of paper together, and left them.

'Well,' Mrs Spencer said, scooping up her belongings, 'she's an ordinary little thing, really, don't you think? No sophistication. I thought she looked quite drab in that black outfit. Don't you agree?'

The members of the committee, preparing to leave, looked at each other behind the back of their leader with raised eyebrows. Except for Mrs Washington, who opened her handbag and frantically searched for something or other inside it, not looking up to meet anyone's eyes.

*   *   *

In the corridor leading to the stairs Inspector Murgatroyd passed the ladies on their way out, recognising Mrs Spencer, who ignored him, stopping Mrs Washington who followed a little behind the others.

'Good afternoon Mrs Washington,' he said genially. 'I was hoping to see you. I'm wondering if, as you're here, it might be convenient for me to have a word with you.'

The other women disappeared down the staircase. The Bursar's wife was trapped, looking for a way of escape.

'It won't take a minute, madam,' the Inspector said soothingly. 'Miss Richmond has put an office at my disposal just along the corridor here. Save you coming in another time, or me coming to your house.'

'There's nothing I can tell you Inspector,' she said quickly. 'Nothing at all.'

93

'Nevertheless,' the Inspector said, 'if you wouldn't mind . . .' With a touch as light as air on her elbow he propelled her towards the interview room. It was a small room, normally used for interviewing would-be staff. There was the minimum of furniture: a desk, a table, two cheap armchairs.

'Please sit down, Mrs Washington. Now just relax and tell me about last night. Anything you can think of.'

'Have you spoken to my husband?' She was clasping and unclasping the fastening of her handbag in a manner which, although he felt sorry for her, irritated him.

'Yes,' he said. 'I had a word with the Bursar. He was very helpful.' If she thought she was going to get any more out of him she was mistaken. In fact, the Bursar hadn't been helpful. Obviously worried about something; scared, even. Equally obviously obsessed by the fair Norma. But about as helpful as a table top. He'd admitted to knowing Maxton, but not well. Met him in the Senior Common Room sometimes at lunch, he'd said. Pressed, he'd recalled that it was Maxton who'd recommended Norma to him when he said he was looking for another secretary. He could think of no reason, no reason at all, he'd said, why anyone should want to harm Maxton. No one, as far as he knew, was that well acquainted with him.

'Yes,' the Inspector repeated. 'Very helpful.'

Not so Mrs Washington, either. At the end of twenty minutes he couldn't decide whether she really didn't know anything or was hiding something. If she had nothing to hide why was she so scared? He had seen fear often enough to

94

recognise it. She maintained that she'd simply seen her husband and the others going into the other bit of the room, beyond the curtains which Miss Richmond had drawn back. She'd joined them because she was at that time on her own and was, so to speak, one of the party.

'It was awful for everyone,' she said, 'seeing him lying there on the floor like that. I'm afraid I just went to pieces. I haven't been very well recently.' She looked pinched and cold, in spite of the heat in the room.

'Did you know Dr Maxton well, then?'

'Oh no! Hardly at all!' She was quick off the mark with that one.

Everyone else there, except Mr Challis and Miss Wishbone, she'd known for some time. She liked and respected Miss Richmond. And of course the Vice-Chancellor and his wife, she said when pushed.

'Well thank you for answering my questions,' the Inspector said, standing up, seeing her to the door. She'd been right when she'd said she couldn't be much help, he thought. Or wouldn't. And now he wanted a further word with Miss Richmond.

When he entered Marion's office he sniffed the air appreciatively and smiled at her. He looks mighty pleased with himself, Marion thought.

'I must say, you ladies go in for nice perfumes,' the Inspector said. 'What's this one called, then? I might like to buy some for the wife.' Would it do the trick with Elaine he wondered.

'*Jardins des Souvenirs*,' Marion said.

'*Jardins des Souvenirs* is it?' He had no difficulty in remembering where he'd smelt it before.

*   *   *

95

Roland had called in Marion's office briefly while the committee ladies were in session, to make arrangements for the evening. Marion had suggested a small pub she knew, between Harrogate and Knaresborough, where they could eat well, and perhaps walk by the river if the evening stayed fine.

'I'll pick you up at your place,' she said. 'Can we make it seven-ish? People dine early in this part of the world, and we have to drive out there.'

So when, at five minutes past seven, she tooted her car horn outside number forty-seven, Roland ran downstairs and out of the house.

The car was a Triumph convertible and Marion had put the top down. 'I hope you don't mind,' she said. 'It's such a lovely evening and I enjoy the smells of the countryside, which one doesn't get in a closed car.'

'It's great,' Roland said. 'Speaking of smells, that's a nice perfume.'

'Everyone's on about perfume today,' Marion said. 'It was a gift. Oh, by the way, I've brought a telemessage for you. I'm sorry, but I opened it. You couldn't be found and it's routine in those circumstances, in case it's something urgent.'

'I see. And is it?'

'I wouldn't know. Judge for yourself.'

He took the envelope. If it was what he was expecting he'd rather she hadn't seen it. They hardly ever used code with him. He read the message. 'URGENT YOU CONTACT V-C RE FLETCHER STOP POLICE INFORMED.'

'Well!' he said. 'It calls for explanations, is that what you're thinking?'

She didn't answer, let in the clutch and drove

forward. Driving down the hill they passed Norma walking arm-in-arm with a middle-aged man.

'Probably her father,' Marion said. 'She's very fond of her father.'

She turned right into the main road and drove towards the outskirts of Northwell, neither of them speaking as she negotiated the traffic. Leaving the houses behind, Marion spoke first.

'I have to admit, I'm consumed with curiosity. But you don't have to tell me a thing. In my job I'm used to putting confidential matters right out of my head.'

'I intend to explain,' Roland said. 'Can it wait until we get wherever we're going?'

'Surely.'

At the derestriction sign she put her foot down and the little red car leapt forward.

*   *   *

At five minutes to midnight she stopped the car quietly outside Roland's lodgings. The evening was cool now and she had put up the hood.

'Like Cinderella,' she said. 'You can be in before it strikes midnight.'

Roland leaned across and turned off the engine. Then he took her in his arms and fastened her mouth under his. She pushed him away, but gently. In the light from the street lamp her eyes shone.

'No more,' she said quietly. 'Not now. I can't take it.'

'Come up to my room,' he said. 'Come and have a last drink.'

'If I come up to your room it won't be for a drink,' she said. 'And we both know it. Some other time I will. But not now.'

97

'Soon?'

'Soon,' she promised.

They kissed again, gently, her fingers exploring the contours of his face. Then Roland got out of the car and she drove away. He watched until the car was out of sight at the bottom of the deserted avenue, then he let himself into the house quietly, not wanting to disturb Mrs Thompson. As he tiptoed up the stairs the treads creaked, though not, he thought, enough to waken her if she was already asleep. The house was in complete darkness. He opened the door of his room and as he entered, groping for the light switch, a searing pain ran across the back of his head, enveloping him, shooting through his whole body. The stars which he saw just before he lost consciousness illuminated the whole world, and then blinded him.

CHAPTER EIGHT

He was swimming in thick, velvet darkness. In a cave. And in the distance, at the entrance to the cave, he could see a pinpoint of light, and knew that he must reach that light if he was to be saved. All around him, as he tried to swim towards it, was the roar of the sea. He must swim as strongly as he could, using every ounce of strength, lashing out his arms and legs; but his limbs were heavy and uncoordinated, refusing to obey him. He seemed to make no progress and yet, though he himself was not advancing, the mouth of the cave was getting bigger; brighter. Though he was powerless to swim towards it, the light came nearer.

And then he saw that Inspector Murgatroyd was

98

standing in the mouth of the cave, sitting on a throne, surrounded by the light as if by a halo.

Roland opened his eyes.

'Good-morning Mr Challis,' the Inspector said.

'Good-morning Inspector.' His voice echoed somewhere above him. 'I thought you were on a throne, with a halo around you.'

The Inspector chuckled. 'You're not in heaven yet, Mr Challis. I doubt if there was any danger of that, even if Mrs Thompson hadn't found you when she did. On a throne, did you say? With a halo? Was there sweet music then, and beautiful girls?' He seemed gratified by the idea.

The throne had resolved itself into the chair on which the Inspector sat by Roland's bedside. Silly to say 'Where am I?' because it was obvious by all the trappings that he was in a hospital room. Narrow, white-counterpaned bed, stainless steel trolley, gleaming paint, and a nurse standing in the doorway.

'Back with us, Mr Challis?' she chirped. She advanced towards the bed, straightened out a few imaginary wrinkles in the bedspread, felt the pulse in his wrist. 'Not much talking then, Inspector. We mustn't tire the patient.'

'I'll be good, Sister,' the Inspector promised. 'They like bossing the police around,' he said to Roland when she'd left the room.

'Who wouldn't?' Roland said. 'That's real power.' His voice was returning to normal, no longer lost at the end of a tunnel. 'What happened?'

'You tell me,' Inspector Murgatroyd said. 'Only don't tell Sister I let you. Mrs Thompson found you. Got up in the early hours to go to the bathroom. Saw your door open and your feet sticking out on to

99

the landing. Rang the police.'

'How did *you* get in on the act?'

'Oh we've heard about you! Had communications from above, you might say. The Super thought I'd better be the lucky one in case it tied up with Maxton's murder. Anyway, I'm a natural for being dragged out of bed at five in the morning. Who else?'

'I'm sorry I inconvenienced you,' Roland apologised.

'So you should be. But I was scheduled to see you today about whatever it is you're up to in the university, and I don't mean playing at Management Consultants.'

'Oh I don't play at it,' Roland assured him. 'It's just that I do other little jobs from time to time for a persuasive government.' His head was aching. He didn't really feel like talking.

'So I understand,' the Inspector said. He couldn't pretend to be pleased about that. He'd been wanting to see this affair through on his own. He didn't get many murders and it made a pleasant change from petty thieving. He'd been lucky to persuade the Super not to call in the Yard, and now he had this know-all to contend with.

'I'm not the police,' Roland said, reading the Inspector's thoughts. 'As you very well know.'

'How would you describe yourself?' Inspector Murgatroyd asked.

'On the whole, I wouldn't. But for you . . . Well, it's common knowledge that the government has a "think tank": a sort of unofficial group of people with enquiring minds, always prying into this and that for the rest of us.'

'I've heard of it. I thought it had broken up.'

100

'That's probably what they'd like you to think. But it exists.'

'And you're a member?'

'Good God no!' Roland said. 'I suppose you could call me an errand boy. They send me out to— how shall I put it?—to collect information for them. I'm not the only one. They send me where I can get an entry.'

'Spies,' the Inspector said.

Roland laughed. 'Nothing so grand. And Maxton's little lot is all yours unless there's a definite tie-up with Fletcher. He's the one we want to know about, and it's his research we're interested in. Some of these people plodding away in universities don't realise the implications of their research. Or don't want to. He could be on to something this country badly needs.'

'I thought those scientific bods published everything they did. In highbrow journals nobody else understands.'

'They do,' Roland agreed. 'It's a way of life with them. And Fletcher hasn't been publishing anything. That's what's odd.'

'And the chances are that if *we* can use it, the rest can?' the Inspector queried. 'Is that the urgency?'

'That's right.'

'You're talking too much. Sister'll send me away if she catches you at it. How do you feel?'

'I thought you'd never ask,' Roland said. 'Head aches a bit. But I'm all right.'

'Fit enough to describe what happened?'

'Except that I don't know. I'd been out for the evening—'

'Who with?'

Roland raised his eyebrows. 'It's irrelevant,' he

101

said. 'But if my love life interests you, it was Marion Richmond. And while we're at it, she knows why I'm in Northwell.'

'Does she indeed?'

'More or less. Anyway, I let myself in, went upstairs to my room. I'm sure there was no light on or I'd have seen it under the door and been prepared.'

'Using a torch. Probably what he hit you with. Any idea who? Or why?'

'Not the faintest. You're ruling out a perfectly ordinary burglar, disturbed on the job?'

'Oh I think so,' the Inspector said. 'Why pick on your room? It wasn't the handiest. And nothing else in the house was disturbed.'

'Well as far as I know,' Roland said, 'no one here knows me, or knows why I'm here, except the Vice-Chancellor. And now Miss Richmond, but I'd only told her during the evening. Besides she wouldn't . . .'

'Don't give me that,' the Inspector said wearily. 'A man of your experience. Of course she would, given the motive and the opportunity. You should know that.'

He did know. But he trusted his instincts; and Marion was sound, he was sure of that.

'Why did you tell her?' the Inspector asked.

'I wanted to.' Which was only partly true. Would he have told her if she hadn't read the telemessage? He doubted it. And she'd had that at least a couple of hours before she'd handed it to him. She could, in theory, have set up the whole thing; but he wasn't going to tell the Inspector that.

'How long am I going to be here?' he asked.

The Inspector shrugged. 'Up to the Doc. They

102

don't think there's anything more than concussion. You're a lucky man.'

'One way of putting it,' Roland said. 'I can think of others.'

Sister came into the room, ran a smoothing hand over the counterpane again, and spoke firmly to the Inspector. 'I'm sorry, sir. Time's up! Mr Challis must get some sleep now.'

Sleep, the Inspector thought. His eyes lingered on the crisp white sheets, the flawless bedcover, the window shaded with a venetian blind. 'Have you a spare bed, Sister?' he asked.

She allowed herself to smile, then she closed the window blinds completely, rearranged the contents of the locker top in a symmetrical pattern, and ushered the Inspector from the room. Roland called her back as she was about to close the door.

'Sister, may I have another visitor this afternoon?'

'Who?'

'Miss Marion Richmond.'

'Is she a relative?'

'A friend.'

'Well, if you're good,' she promised. 'If you get some rest now.'

'I'll be good,' Roland promised. 'Will you telephone her, please? She's in the university.'

'No need to. She telephoned earlier this morning. She'll be ringing again at lunchtime. Now go to sleep.' She closed the door softly behind her as she left.

He didn't want to go to sleep. He wanted to work things out. Was the plan to cosh him, or had he simply turned up at the wrong time? What would have happened if Marion had come up to the room with him, as he'd more than half expected she would do? But he found he couldn't think clearly. Willingly side-tracked into thoughts of the pleasanter parts of last evening, he fell asleep.

*   *   *

This must be heaven, he thought, wakening later. No moustached policeman sitting in the chair, haloed in light, but a beautiful girl in a white dress, her pale yellow hair falling over her shoulders. The vision resolved itself into Norma.

'Hello,' he said. 'I didn't expect to see you.'

'I know. I think perhaps the nurse thought I was Marion. I didn't actually say I was. Anyway, she let me in—and I had to see you, Mr Challis.'

'I'm glad about that. You sound a little troubled for an angel.'

'Angel?'

'I keep thinking I'm in heaven. I was looking for your harp.' He tried to jolly her, seeing the strain on her face, but she refused to respond.

'Marion told me you were here. I had to see you,' she repeated. 'But I wouldn't want to make you worse.'

'You'd never do that,' he assured her. He felt distinctly better since his sleep. Perhaps they'd let him out later in the day. There was a lot to be done. 'I'm glad you came. What was it about?'

'I wanted you to know it was nothing to do with me. Your . . . accident. I know I was in the house yesterday, but it wasn't me in your room last night. I swear it.'

He hadn't considered Norma. He wondered why she should be defending herself so fiercely. Given that anyone had a reason for being in his room, he supposed she was as physically capable as most people of hitting him on the head. He looked at her hands, lying in her lap. Strong hands, but now nervously uncontrolled.

'Did you find what you were after in Dr Maxton's room?' he asked. She owed him that much.

'No.'

'No use me asking what it was, I suppose?'

'I can't tell you. But I didn't kill him. That was nothing to do with me.'

'Where did you get the key to Mrs Thompson's house?' Roland asked.

Colour ebbed from her face. Beads of sweat gathered on her grey forehead. She raised a clenched fist to cover her mouth and he thought she was going to be sick.

'Here!' he said. 'Take it easy! I'm not the police.'

'Have you told the police I was in the house yesterday?' Her voice was a whisper.

'No. Though you just about did that yourself. It was a lovely scent you left behind you. I notice you've changed it.'

She stared at him. Surely she'd realised what he meant about changing her perfume? Really, she was too innocent to be let out of the house. It was for this reason, he supposed, that he'd ruled her out as his attacker.

'But that's awful!' she said.

'What is?'

'The perfume. The *Jardins des Souvenirs*. When Mike said "Get rid of it" I thought he'd suddenly taken against it. But I couldn't throw it away. It was too lovely.'

'So you gave it to . . . ?'

'Marion. What will happen?'

'Nothing much I shouldn't think. Marion will sort that out with the Inspector. I suppose there are plenty of people who can say she was in her office all yesterday morning. But the Inspector did notice the perfume in Maxton's room. I'm certain of that. Don't underestimate him, Norma.'

And here I am again, he thought, helping her to evade the law. Would he have done it if she'd been plain, plump and fifty? He refused to answer himself.

'So you're not going to tell me what you were looking for, Norma?' He stretched out his hand and took one of hers in it. Hers was icy cold.

'I can't tell you anything,' she said. There was sadness as well as finality in her voice, as if she would have liked to have confided in him. But the subject, he realised, was now closed.

'OK,' he said. 'Forget it. How's Mike?'

'Fine.'

'How's his work going? He's writing his thesis isn't he?'

'That's right.'

'Who's his supervisor?'

'Professor Fletcher.' Was it his imagination, or did she hesitate over Fletcher's name? Careful now.

'It must be quite difficult working on one's thesis with one's supervisor three thousand miles away. Mike must need to get in touch from time to time.' He spoke casually.

'Oh yes,' Norma said. 'He writes to Professor Fletcher whenever he has a problem.'

So simple. Right under their clever noses.

A nurse, one he hadn't seen before, put her head around the door.

'Time's up I'm afraid,' she said. 'If Sister comes

106

back and finds Miss Richmond still here I'll be for the high jump.'

'But I'm not—' Norma began.

Roland interrupted. 'She's just leaving, nurse. You were a bonus,' he whispered to Norma. 'Your visit's done me good. Sister will let Marion in when she arrives.'

He was tired after Norma left. All the same, he hoped they'd let him out by tomorrow at the latest.

*   *   *

Life in hospital, he decided a little later on, if one wasn't actually ill, was a series of pleasant awakenings. This time it was Marion who sat at his bedside. She looked serious and managed only a slight lift of the corners of her mouth in return for his smile of welcome. He held out his hand and she took it in hers.

'Why are you looking so solemn?' he asked.

Her eyes widened. 'Really, Roland, that's a silly question. You go and get yourself half-killed and then you ask me why I look solemn. I'm worried, that's why.'

'I didn't exactly *seek* it,' Roland protested. 'All I did was walk into my own room. A man's entitled to do that, I suppose?'

'Well isn't that just what I mean? If a man's going to get nobbled walking into his own room, what hope has he when he goes looking for trouble?'

'Don't worry,' Roland said. 'I can take care of myself.'

'That's why you're here I suppose?' She gave him a real smile now, the kind which crinkled her eyes and a few years from now would leave fine lines on her skin. She had the kind of looks, he reckoned, which would get better and better.

'I didn't know the game had begun, that's all,' he said. 'I missed the starting pistol.'

'Seriously, Roland, please be careful.'

'I will,' he promised. 'Now tell me what's going on in the university.'

'Today? Inspector Murgatroyd hovers. Mrs Spencer was around again, signing memos for the Summer Ball. Since it all takes place in a few days time all the arrangements must have been made ages ago. She's simply making changes, driving everyone mad. Norma had to type out all the memos again and Bruce Washington was furious.'

'I can imagine,' Roland said. 'Look here, I've found out something which could be useful. Mike Carshalton is Fletcher's student. He's writing up his thesis and, according to Norma, can get in touch with Fletcher whenever he wants to.'

'I didn't know that,' Marion said quickly. There was something in the way the words rushed out, as if the information had taken her unawares. She met Roland's intent look and was clearly ill at ease.

'Should you have?' Roland said. 'I wouldn't have thought you'd have had much contact with students, especially on the science side.'

'No. No of course not. Will it help?'

'Of course it will,' Roland said. 'Apart from knowing Fletcher's whereabouts, he's almost sure to know what his Professor's working on. Research students usually do, wouldn't you say?'

'I suppose so.'

'Will you do something for me, then? Will you get Mike to come and see me? I don't want to waste time.'

She looked doubtful. 'I don't think you should. Couldn't it wait?'

'I don't want to wait. If I don't get what I want from Mike I'll have to talk to the Vice-Chancellor. You saw the telemessage. When will the V-C be back?'

'For the Summer Ball,' Marion said. 'I think not before then.'

'It can't wait,' Roland said firmly. 'Failing Mike I'll have to go and seek out the Vice-Chancellor.'

'He'd flay you alive,' Marion said. 'No one, but *no one* goes up to the cottage.'

'Well here's one who will. Why hasn't he contacted me, or at least made himself available? He must know I need to see him. Anyway, Mike Carshalton first. If I'm going to be let out tomorrow I'll telephone you and perhaps you could arrange for me to see him in the university. If I'm stuck here will you ask him to come in?' It would come as no surprise to Mike, he thought. He owes me an explanation about yesterday.

Marion rose abruptly from the chair by his bedside and walked over to the window; fiddled with the blind; looked out.

'It won't be necessary,' she said.

'What won't?'

'For you to see Mike Carshalton.'

'Not necessary? Why not?'

She turned around and faced him. He watched her draw in a quick breath, square her shoulders before she answered.

'Because I can tell you what you want to know. It's true that I don't know where Leon Fletcher is right now, but I do know something about his work.'

109

'*You* know? Did the Vice-Chancellor tell you?'
'No.'
'Then who . . . ?'
'Professor Fletcher told me himself. He's a friend of mine. I've known all along,' she admitted.

CHAPTER NINE

'You *know* him? You know Leon Fletcher?' Roland said.

Marion raised her head, looked at him defiantly. 'Yes.'

'Well? Do you know him well?'

'Quite well. Should I not?' It was obvious that she resented his question. She turned away and looked out of the window again.

'I'm sorry,' Roland said. 'It's just that it comes as a surprise. You knew I was interested in him. I'd told you that was why I was here. I'd have expected you to have said something before this, instead of stringing me along.'

'How much sooner? I only knew about you last night, and then only what you told me.'

'You mean you don't believe me?' Roland asked. 'Everything I said was true. And will you stop looking out of the bloody window! Look at me!'

She wheeled round and faced him. 'I don't disbelieve you; but I don't know you. Sexual attraction is not a guide to logic. Quite the reverse. I saw no reason to tell you anything about Leon Fletcher. As far as I was concerned he didn't come into yesterday evening. I thought I was there for my own sake, not to be pumped for information.'

'You know damned well you were there for

yourself,' Roland said irritably. 'And for God's sake come away from that window and sit down. The light hurts my eyes.'

'Actually, I think I should go,' Marion said. 'I don't think I'm doing you any good.'

'Oh no you don't!' Roland cried. 'Not even if I have to keep you here by force.'

She smiled in spite of herself. Then she crossed to the chair by the bed and sat down again, perching on the edge of the seat as if poised for flight. Roland sensed that if he said the wrong thing she would walk out, and knew that in spite of his brave words he was in no state to prevent it. His headache was worse, and when he raised himself from the pillow the objects in the room tended to spin around. Hell and damnation that he should be in this stupid state just when action was needed!

'All right,' he said. 'For the moment you win. I can't stop you going, but please don't.'

'I'll stay five minutes,' she promised. 'Make the most of it.'

'*Why* didn't you tell me you knew Fletcher?' Roland persisted.

'I've already answered that question. But if you want a further reason it's because I don't usually choose to talk about other people's affairs. And as I said, I *don't* know you. It's not as if you were Inspector Murgatroyd, even.'

'The power of the police!' Roland said. 'I suppose if I'd turned up with sirens shrieking you'd have told me anything?'

'Not really. Not quite.'

'Well you know me now,' Roland said. 'I've been honest with you. And being hit on the head must surely put me on the side of the angels?'

111

'I know you a little better,' Marion corrected him. 'Instinctively I trust you, but there's no good reason why I should. As I said, sexual attraction is the worst possible guide.'

'Well I'm glad you admit to that much,' Roland said. 'Are you always as cautious as this?'

'If it concerns my job I am.'

'Then why are you suddenly prepared to tell me about Fletcher's work? Or were, a few minutes ago.'

'I shall only tell you what he told me when there were several other people around. He didn't say it was a secret—in fact he rather boasted about it.'

There was a hardness in her voice which was new to him, as if she were reviving a memory she didn't like.

'Was Fletcher a special friend of yours?' Roland asked. 'Or more than a friend, as they say in the gossip columns?'

She didn't answer. He wondered if he'd gone too far.

Sorry,' he said. 'Don't bother to answer that.'

'It was an affair which never worked,' Marion said quietly.

'Affair?'

'You could call it that. I was very fond of him.'

'Fond of? Loved?'

'Yes, I loved him all right.'

'Past tense?'

'Oh yes!' The words were very definite. 'Leon Fletcher was—is—a brilliant scientist. Dedicated. He was heading straight for the top.'

'I gathered that. And . . . ?'

'He'd have got there, and stayed, if he hadn't started to drink.'

'Was that what broke it up?'

'No,' Marion said. 'I'd have coped with that. He's not an alcoholic, you know. Possibly it was his work which made him drink. He worked all hours, until he was too tired to relax. And it seemed that only alcohol could do it. And then of course it affected his work. I don't think it showed—I'm sure it didn't—but *he* knew. And sometimes he would go on a bit in front of other people.'

'Where did you come in?'

She shook her head. 'I didn't for very long. I was no help to him. I wanted to be—tried to be—but women don't rate high in Leon Fletcher's life.'

And that's why you don't rate high in your own eyes, Roland thought.

'I'm sorry,' he said.

'I'm over it,' Marion said quietly.

There was a silence between them, then Roland said, 'Is this why he hasn't published anything recently? It's more than two years now, and that's got my people very puzzled. He was a most prolific man before that. Scientific papers all over the place. They just don't believe that a man of his calibre is doing nothing. *Has* he been doing nothing?'

'I would think that highly unlikely,' Marion said. 'Work was everything to him.'

'If you don't want to tell me about it,' Roland said, 'I don't doubt that I'll get it from Mike Carshalton. Only as I'm stuck in here that will waste time.'

'Very well. As I said. I shall just tell you what he said once, out loud at a party,' Marion said. 'There must be other people who know. It can't be all that secret. He's working on something to do with car exhaust systems.'

'Exhaust systems?' Roland couldn't keep the

astonishment out of his voice.

'You sound surprised,' Marion said.

'I am a bit,' he admitted. 'It's not what I expected.' What had he expected? Something more exciting. Nuclear stuff; revolutionary war weapons? Oil? Car exhausts sounded mundane.

'He considered it very important. Said it would make a difference in every country in the world. Pollution came into it.'

'It would, of course. Tell me, did you believe him?'

'Oh yes.' She sounded positive. 'He wouldn't lie about his work.'

'You don't think he was in any way deluding himself?'

'Not at all. I'm certain that if he said he was on to something of great importance, then that was so.'

'There'd be a lot of money in it,' Roland said thoughtfully.

'No doubt. But not for him.'

'Why not?'

'Scientists aren't the ones who get the money. They do the work and then some government, or manufacturer, comes along, puts up the cash, and makes a fortune out of it. Whoever heard of a rich scientist?' she asked.

'Is that what Fletcher said?'

'Only once. He was rather bitter about it on one occasion. And I don't blame him.' Roland was surprised by her vehemence.

'Would that have turned him, do you think?' he asked.

'Turned him?'

'In the wrong direction. To sell to the highest bidder.'

114

'He was a man of integrity,' Marion said coldly.
'Was?'

'*Is*. Always will be. You're on the wrong tack there.'

She could be right. She was the one who knew Fletcher. But money was a powerful draw, especially when it seemed to be morally yours.

'I think you don't understand the scientific mind,' Marion said.

'What was the process?' Roland asked.

'I don't know. Everyone knows he works on platinum, but I don't know about this one.'

Or you're not telling me, Roland thought, watching the curtain come down over her face. Does she know? In a way, it didn't matter too much as long as she didn't leak it to anyone else. And he thought that was unlikely since she seemed to dislike discussing it.

'Well I *shall* get to know the details,' he said. 'Or rather, my bosses will. It's only a matter of locating Fletcher. But you must see that speed is important? That's implicit in what you've told me. Whoever gets at him first is home and dry.'

'No one's going to get at him,' Marion said.

'Don't misunderstand me,' Roland said slowly. 'Getting at him isn't simply a matter of asking him what it's all about. That's the well-mannered way we play it, but there are others not so gentlemanly. If there's important information which only he holds, which he hasn't troubled to patent, Professor Fletcher could be in danger.'

She looked at him in disbelief. 'You're too used to playing cops and robbers,' she accused him.

'Not at all. I'm quite serious. Whoever gets there first is, as I said, home and dry. Don't you want it to

115

be the right people?'

Marion shook her head. 'It will never be the right people,' she said. 'I would want it to be the scientist. Anyone else who profits isn't entitled.'

'Not even if they pay?'

'It won't be the scientist they pay,' she said passionately. 'Only a bent scientist gets that kind of money. There aren't many of them around.'

But one or two, Roland thought, though not voicing it. He was surprised at the obvious intensity of her feelings. Her cheeks were two burning spots of colour, her eyes too bright.

'What was your father?' he asked gently.

She looked up at him, startled. 'He was one of the very best scientists,' she said defiantly. 'He died poor, while those who use his inventions are still rich. Oh I don't mind for myself, but it's so horribly unfair. And my mother has nothing.'

'Did your father mind?'

'Not as much as I do. There were things he wanted, mostly for my mother, and couldn't have. But he said it was the way things were. Research scientists didn't work for financial gain.'

He reached out and took her hand. He wanted to believe in her integrity; he was surprised that it was important for him to do so. But here was a motivation which could take her in any direction. Would she stand by her father's beliefs, or take her revenge? Did she know more than she'd said? She was in a strong position to do so.

He felt a strong anger against himself. This was what the job did to him. He could trust no one all the way, even when he wanted to. It was no foundation for living and he thought, not for the first time, that he should get out of it. But that

116

wouldn't be easy. They had a habit, if they found you uscful, of not letting you go.

'Can't you tell me any more?' he asked. 'You must know what was in Fletcher's file before it went missing. Since it seems that someone else has it now, your knowledge could be vital.'

She snatched her hand away from his and jumped to her feet. Now she was really angry. 'And if I did know,' she cried, 'do you think I'd tell you? Is that what you think of me?'

'Even if the information wasn't important?' he persisted in spite of her anger.

'I'm not the judge of what's important! As far as I'm concerned, whatever's in a pcrson's file is confidcntial. Unless the Vice-Chancellor himself ordered me to, I wouldn't reveal the contents to anyone.'

'Steady on!' Roland said. 'You make it sound like the confessional!'

'Well as far as I'm concerned, it is.'

'You take yourself very seriously,' Roland said.

'I do *not* take myself seriously,' she protested. 'I take my job seriously. Are you so stupid that you can't see the differencc?'

'All right,' Roland said. 'Calm down! I didn't mean to offend you. I shouldn't have pushed it.'

'Well you have offended me,' she snapped. 'I think it's time I left.'

'Marion, don't go!' he pleaded.

Oh God! Blast this bloody head! He wanted to leap out of bed and take her in his arms; to kiss all the hurt and anger out of her face. He threw back the bedclothes and was half-way out of bed when Sister came into the room. She leapt in his direction.

117

'Mr Challis, what *are* you doing? Really, if you go on like this I don't know what we shall do with you. Forbid all visitors for a start. You're a very naughty man.'

She turned and glared at Marion. 'I'm afraid you've upset my patient, Miss Richmond,' she said icily.

Then she pushed Roland back into bed and tucked the bedclothes in tightly all the way round. By the time she had him once more in a neat parcel, Marion had left.

'Now don't you dare move an inch,' Sister threatened. 'Dr Macfarlane's due any minute now. You've got to look tidy.'

'Why?' Roland demanded.

'Why?' She seemed nonplussed. 'You just have to, that's all. Doctors like all patients to be tidy.'

'When can I go home, Sister?' he asked.

She frowned. 'That's not for me to say, Mr Challis. That's the doctor's decision. But the sooner we learn to behave ourselves, the sooner we'll be out. Perhaps the doctor will let us go to the bathroom today if we're good!'

She gave a final twitch to the top sheet, smiled winningly. 'Try to sleep,' she said.

But it was impossible to sleep. There were too many things to think about. He tried to put thoughts of Marion out of his mind and to concentrate on car exhaust systems. What did he know about them? Precious little except that they were a damned nuisance. Pollution? Rust? Safety? Cost? As far as he knew the problems they presented had never been solved. Somewhere at the back of his mind he thought that there were countries which had special requirements for car

118

exhausts. On the face of it, it seemed a small matter, not one to provoke death, or coshings on the head. But a solution to the problem could have far-reaching results, of course, and the amount of money involved worldwide could be enormous. Whoever got the patent, cornered the market, would end up in the multi-millionaire class. It would be worth the while of any industrialist, perhaps any government.

How near the end was Fletcher? That was the crucial question; and who except the man himself could answer it? He might not be anywhere near a solution—though in that case why would he have gone off for a sabbatical? Would such a dedicated scientist leave an exciting piece of work unfinished? It seemed unlikely. It seemed much more reasonable that he should have found the answer he was looking for, but in that case what and where was it?

Had Maxton been after this information, Roland wondered. Had he perhaps had it before he was killed, in time to pass it on to whoever he was working for? He hated to think where Norma fitted into all this. It was just possible that Maxton's death had nothing to do with the Fletcher business, though he doubted that. There seemed, still, to be a dearth of information about Maxton, unless Inspector Murgatroyd had unearthed any more while *he* was lying here as useless as a dummy in this hospital bed.

He'd got to get out. He simply couldn't stand it much longer. He must see Mike Carshalton as soon as possible, and now that bitch of a Sister probably wouldn't let him have any more visitors. Also, he'd got to get at the Vice-Chancellor. He must be the key. He must have the information which they wanted in London, or why the telemessage? Why did the idiot have to go and hide himself away where no one could find him? It was totally irresponsible. He was sure Marion wouldn't give him her boss's whereabouts. Who else would know them? Mrs Vice-Chancellor, of course, but he wouldn't cut much ice there. Also Inspector Murgatroyd, who might or might not play ball, and he was not yet sure that he wanted a ball game with the Inspector. Sergeant Smith knew everything. He might give. But how the hell could he get at Sergeant Smith, lying here like a rag doll?

It was a relief when the doctor came in and interrupted his thoughts. Comic relief, Roland thought, watching the entry of the faithful band of nursing and medical staff who stood to attention around his bed, respectfully awaiting the words of wisdom which might fall from the lips of their Chief.

'How are we then?' the doctor asked.

A pert reply rose to Roland's lips, and froze there. He wanted out, and if being polite (or being a good boy, as Sister would have put it) made any difference, then he was willing to be polite.

'I'm fine. A bit of a fraud, lying here with all these people waiting on me hand and foot.'

'Mr Challis was wondering whether he might get up to go to the bathroom?' Sister said.

'I don't see why not,' the doctor replied. 'Take it easy though.'

'Thank you,' Roland said. For this relief much thanks. Even to be able to get out of bed he'd feel less like a prisoner. But it wasn't enough. 'When can I go home, do you think?' he asked.

The doctor put out a hand and Sister put the patient's chart into it. Dr Macfarlane studied it intently. Roland couldn't imagine why, since he'd had a good look at it himself and found nothing spectacular there.

'Early next week, I dare say,' the doctor said. 'If all goes well. That was a nasty bump you had. Any idea yet who did it?'

'None whatever,' Roland said truthfully. 'Not before next week, you think? I really feel quite fit.'

'Afraid not. We can't take any chances. Anything special you want?'

'Yes.' Roland made no attempt to keep the bitter disappointment out of his voice. The thought of having to stay in hospital over the weekend was unbearable. 'I'd like a book on car mechanics.'

'Car mechanics? You know something about cars?' the doctor said cheerfully.

'No I don't,' Roland snapped. 'That's why I want the book.'

CHAPTER TEN

When the doctor had finished his round of the ward Sister came back into Roland's room.

'I'd like to make a telephone call, Sister,' Roland said.

'I'm sorry, Mr Challis. You've got to keep quiet. No excitement. Just get up to go to the bathroom, and quickly back into bed again. Doctor's orders. Otherwise we're not going to be let out next week, are we?' The corners of her mouth turned up in a smile which did not reach her eyes.

How a little power goes to the head, Roland

121

thought, watching her. She thinks she's in charge of my life. The truth was, she *was*. Well, the only thing to do was to persuade her to use her power for him instead of against him.

'OK, Sister, you're the boss!' he said. 'Then would *you* telephone for me? Or better still, let one of your nurses do so? I know how busy you are.'

She sighed. 'You're not an easy patient, Mr Challis. All that's required of you is that you lie there quietly and read a nice book. I've asked a porter to get you something on car mechanics from the hospital library, though I shouldn't think it would be very soothing. What about a nice thriller?'

'Please Sister, the telephone call!' Roland persisted. 'It's only to the university.'

'Well I'll see what I can do,' she said reluctantly. 'To whom? And what's the message?'

'To a student, name of Mike Carshalton. He's in Chemistry. I'd like him to come in and see me, Sister. Just for a couple of minutes. It's urgent— and really very important. I wouldn't ask otherwise.'

She shook her head, pursed her lips, not at all moved by his plea. 'Oh no, Mr Challis! We're having no more visitors today. Not at any price!'

'But Sister . . . !'

She raised her hand in a stop sign. 'I'm sorry, Mr Challis. It's just not on. The doctor said you were to take things quietly. And it's my professional duty to see that you and I obey him. So let's have no more fuss, Mr Challis.' She spoke in the bright, clear voice especially reserved for soothing fractious patients. Roland could have hit her.

'And when you want to go to the bathroom,' she said, patting his hand, 'just ring for a nurse and she'll take you.'

She most emphatically will *not*, Roland thought. But there was no point in saying anything. From his position all that argument would get him would be an armed guard outside his door.

He watched her leave, and then lay still, wondering what to do next. There must be a public telephone somewhere, even in this turn-of-the-century place. It was simply a question of finding it. As far as he knew, he was on the fifth floor, but having been brought in unconscious he knew nothing of the geography of the place. From his bed he could sometimes hear the clanging of lift gates, and near to a lift there was usually a staircase. If he couldn't find a telephone on this floor—he was now determined to make the call himself—he would go up or down the stairs until he came across one. He decided to exercise his new measure of freedom and go to the bathroom (as Sister preferred to call it) at once. And unaccompanied.

On his feet he felt weaker than he'd expected to. He took the hospital dressing-gown from the peg behind the door and put it on. The last occupant of this room must have been a giant. A Sergeant Smith of a man. He pouched the spare material over the belt and looked around for slippers. He believed there were some in the bottom of the locker, and so it proved: red and brown checked felt, and about three sizes too big.

Dressed for the expedition, he opened the door a crack and peeped out. It was a stroke of luck that the police had requested a private room for him. In the public ward this would have been impossible. His room, as he had thought, was in an area just outside the main ward. The doors of all the other rooms were obligingly labelled. Sister's room was directly opposite to his, with its door mercifully closed. The rest were marked 'sluice', 'kitchen', 'bathroom' and 'toilet', with the last conveniently close to the swing doors which led to the corridor outside. Through the circular panes of glass in the upper halves of the swing doors he could see into the world of comparative freedom.

He set off towards the toilet and then, there being no one in sight, pushed open the swing doors and went out. A sign on the wall confirmed that this was Floor Five and that he had just left Stanley Ward. There was no sign of a telephone booth anywhere. He hoped it wasn't too far away; he hadn't expected to feel so shaky. As he had hoped, there was a large service lift not far from the entrance to the ward, and close by a polished wood staircase. Should he go up or down? A toss-up.

The thought of a toss-up reminded him that he had no coins. His wallet was in his locker drawer, and he had a fair amount of money in that. But his trousers, with the loose change in the pockets, must have been taken away with the rest of his clothes. God knew where! Well, find the telephone first and then solve the coin problem. Perhaps the university switchboard would let him reverse the charges. Or if the worst came to the worst he could dial the police and ask for Inspector Murgatroyd. He didn't want to do that. This was not a point at which he wished to involve the police, though he had the greatest respect for Inspector Murgatroyd.

It was interesting how little notice anyone took of him, wandering around the hospital in his oversize dressing-gown. And once he had started down the staircase and was out of sight of the ward, he felt more confident. If he was missed then too bad.

Reaching the fourth floor corridor he halted a woman wheeling a trolley of books.

'Could you please tell me where the telephone is?' he asked her.

'Yes. It's along there and round to the right.'

While she was speaking he was feeling in his pockets. An expression of what he hoped was utter dismay came into his face. 'Oh no!' he cried. 'Oh no, I can't have! Oh damn!'

'What's wrong?' the woman asked.

'I've come without my money. I thought I had it in my dressing-gown pocket and now I realise I must have left it on my locker top. Well that's it! I can't do all this again. It's my first day up and it's amazing how wobbly one feels.' Was he overdoing it? Why not ask straight out for the loan of ten pence?

'That's all right,' the woman said pleasantly. 'No problem. Here, you'd better have two ten pence pieces in case the first one goes wrong.' She took two coins from the tin box on the trolley. What a nice woman she was!

'We'll charge it to the Comforts fund,' she said cheerfully.

He thanked her, and set off in the direction she'd indicated. The telephone was in use so he sat on a bench nearby and waited while a man had a long argument with someone who seemed to be his wife. Roland was glad to sit down, but beginning to worry now about the time. Sister must have missed him, and she was not above searching the lavatories. Supposing she sent out a posse and they found him before he'd had time to make the call? And what nonsense it was that he should be making a big production out of this very minor escapade. It was

125

something hospital did to one. God save us, the man was feeding in another coin! Would he never finish? Roland got up from his seat and went and tapped the man on the arm.

'Would you mind?' he said. 'I'm not supposed to be here. Got to get back into bed before I'm found out. Or flake out.'

The man broke off his conversation and looked at Roland. 'My word you do look bad, mate,' he said. 'Anyway, I'll be glad to chop it. I've had enough.'

He spoke briefly into the telephone and slammed down the receiver. 'Women!' he said, walking away. 'If you're thinking of ringing a woman, mate, then my advice is *don't*!'

Roland took over the telephone, dialled the university number, waited for the pips. He would have liked to have telephoned Marion, but now wasn't the time. Why the devil didn't the switchboard answer?

Eventually they did. While he waited to be put through to Mike's laboratory he wondered whether his money would last out. By the time Mike was found and brought to the telephone, Roland was on his second coin. He spoke quickly.

'Look,' he said. 'I've got to get in touch with Fletcher. No time to explain, but if you can get that bloody Ward Sister to let you in here I'll tell you more. Right now, just trust me and tell me where Fletcher is. You owe me a small favour,' he reminded him.

'I would if I could.' Mike's voice crackled over the line as if he was calling from Siberia.

'What do you mean? You know how to get in touch with him. Norma told me so. And speak up.

126

It's difficult to hear you.'

'I *did* know,' Mike said. 'He was at Ithaca last, New York State. I telephoned there last night. They said he'd left for the UK four days ago.'

'What? Are you sure?' The pips started to go, indicating his money was about to run out.

'Absolutely. The guy I spoke to had seen him off at Kennedy airport—'

Then the line went dead. Roland looked around for another possible source for some more change, but there were only nurses now in the corridor and he didn't want to get involved with them. He stood near to the telephone for a minute or two, but Mike didn't ring back. Then he turned and walked back along the corridor and up the steps to the ward. Luck was with him and once through the swing doors he slipped into the lavatory unseen. He was emerging again when Sister spotted him.

'Mr Challis, did I not distinctly tell you that you were to wait for a nurse?' she cried.

'I'm sorry, Sister. You all seemed so busy, and suddenly I couldn't wait.'

She stood in front of him, barring his way. They looked steadily at each other.

'Don't you believe me, Sister?' Roland asked.

'I do not, Mr Challis. Now get back into bed.'

At least, he thought, he hadn't been missed.

*   *   *

Curiously thankful to be lying between the cool sheets, Roland looked at his watch. Five minutes to six, so he must have slept again. Too late now for any more action on his part, even if he could summon the strength. Physically he was almost pleased by his enforced inaction. He felt foul. It

127

must, as the doctor had said, have been some blow on his head. He had formed no opinion as to who had hit him. Had the idea been to eliminate him altogether, or simply to put him out of action for a few days? If it was the latter, round one to them. He was growing careless. Normally he would never have walked into a darkened room, even his own, late at night without taking precautions.

But his concern at the moment was with the news Mike had given him on the telephone. If he couldn't contact Fletcher, and he presumed, though Mike had had no time to say so before they were cut off, that the Professor hadn't returned to his own home—then it was more than ever urgent that he should get to grips with the Vice-Chancellor. The instructions in the telemessage were quite explicit on that point.

Maxton's murder, the theft of Fletcher's file, the attack on himself, and now Fletcher's unscheduled return said to him that things were hotting up. If Fletcher's work was as valuable as Marion (and presumably his own bosses) seemed to think it was, then it could be out of the country, gone for good to whoever was in the market for it, very quickly. By the time Fletcher could repeat the work it would almost certainly be too late.

And how could one be sure that Fletcher would be around to repeat the work? These people were not fussy about men's lives. Also, whose side was Fletcher on? That was a question which had to be answered. What was he up to right now?

The questions spun round in his head. He would never find the answers lying in a hospital bed. Apart from the fact that everything was moving and he somehow had to stop it, he'd go mad with frustration. He wondered if Mike Carshalton would make an effort to get in to see him. But the urgency now was not only to see Mike—though he would like to fill in some details—but to get after the Vice-Chancellor. His bosses were usually right.

The nurse arrived with his supper.

'Shepherd's pie and peas; jelly and custard,' she said cheerfully, trying to make it sound like a gourmet's dream.

He ate without tasting, absorbed in his thoughts. He *had* to get out; tomorrow at the latest. After which he had to get to the Vice-Chancellor's cottage, of which he didn't know the whereabouts. And he was sick in the head, more or less imprisoned, and had no clothes.

This place was like bloody Colditz. He indulged himself for a minute in considering Sister as the Camp Commandant. 'No one has ever escaped from here, Lieutenant Challis.' He supposed that he could actually discharge himself. But then he would have to get his clothes and he was quite sure that, between blank refusals and delaying tactics, Sister and the doctors were capable of holding him up for quite some time. They'd inform Inspector Murgatroyd for a start. No, he had to slip away as quietly as possible. Just leave; no fuss. His preliminary jaunt to the telephone had been fairly easy. It would simply be an extension of that, with clothes. Clothes were the immediate problem. He indulged in the fantasy of kidnapping Sister, locking her in a cupboard and escaping in her uniform. He'd seen it done in a hundred films.

There was a knock at the door and a hospital porter walked in, holding out a book which he gave to Roland.

129

'There you are sir, *Car Mechanics for the Million*. Is that what you was wanting?'

'Thank you,' Roland said. But he didn't look at the book. He was staring at the porter's clothes. Blue overalls, one-piece, a bit like a tracksuit.

'Thank you very much,' he repeated. 'Would you like to earn twenty pounds?'

'Earn twenty pounds? What do you mean, Guv?' The porter looked suspicious.

'Those overalls you're wearing. They're exactly what I want. If you can get hold of a pair for me I'll give you twenty pounds.'

'You mean *steal* 'em?'

'No. Just borrow. I'd send them back to you in a day or two. No one would be any the worse off.'

The man hesitated. 'Well, I don't know . . .'

'Twenty pounds. Cash on delivery. Only I've got to have them first thing tomorrow morning; preferably this evening. Later than that they'd be no good.'

'It's not easy,' the man said.

'That's why I'm offering twenty pounds.'

'They're hospital issue.'

'That's the idea.'

'If it's for anything illegal . . . I have my job to think about.'

'It's straight,' Roland assured him. 'No trouble. Just a practical joke I have in mind. I'll definitely return them to you.'

The man relaxed, spread his hands. 'Well in that case. I'm one for a bit of a joke meself. How would it be if I was to bring 'em in just after the day staff goes off duty and before the night staff gets going? I'm on until nine tonight.'

'Perfect,' Roland said.

The porter grinned. 'You'd be surprised how often stuff goes astray in the laundry for a few days,' he said with a wink.

'I wouldn't,' Roland said. 'And by the way, not a word in Sister's direction.'

'Not me,' the man said firmly. 'I wouldn't give that one the skin off me rice pudding!'

*   *   *

Five minutes after Sister and her day nurses had left, the porter came quietly into Roland's room and handed him the overalls, and Roland gave him the money. Neither of them spoke. It was only as Roland watched the man leaving that he noticed that he was about five-foot-three and as thin as a lath. If they were his own overalls . . . Oh well, it was too late now. He hid the garment under the mattress. It would be safe enough there since all the night staff ever did to his bed was straighten the top sheet and shake up the pillows.

He planned to be away before Sister and her minions were back on the scene in the morning. The night nurses were grossly overworked and the hours between early morning tea and the time when the day staff came on duty were usually chaotic. There would be little time for looking after a patient in a private ward, especially one who was no longer bed bound. He settled down for a night's sleep.

*   *   *

'Wakey, wakey!' the nurse said brightly, when he'd been asleep what seemed like ten minutes. She crossed to the window and opened the blind. The

131

early morning light filtered in.

'A lovely May morning,' she said. 'Can you look after yourself while I get on in the ward?'

'Of course,' Roland said, remembering. 'Don't bother about me, nurse.'

When he had drunk his tea he took the overalls into the bathroom under his dressing-gown. They were newly laundered and as stiff as a board against his skin. Also, as he'd feared they were sized to fit the porter. Fortunately the manufacturer seemed to have decided that only length counted, so that there was room enough around the middle for almost any size of body, but on Roland's six-foot frame the trousers reached only to mid-calf. And he possessed neither socks nor shoes. He looked down with distaste at his lower legs, disappearing into the too-large felt slippers. Then he transferred his wallet and a few personal possessions which had been in his locker drawer to the pockets of the overalls. He left the bath tap running so that the room would sound occupied and, making a final check that there was no one around, he emerged.

Suddenly a nurse came out of the sluice room, carrying a bedpan. She made a half-turn in his direction and he was sure she was going to spot him. He grabbed the rail of a trolley full of dirty crockery and pushed it in front of him through the swing doors into the corridor.

There were people standing by the lift; in fact there were people at various points along the corridor, so that it was impossible to abandon the trolley without attracting attention. He pushed it along the corridor, past the staircase down which he had planned to escape. The trolley gave him an

132

official air, and hid his bare legs, but he wasn't getting out of the place. On the contrary, he was lumbered with it, and now firmly set in the wrong direction.

Then he saw a vaguely familiar figure heading towards him and recognised it as one of the doctors from Macfarlane's gang—by the look of him on his way to Stanley Ward.

'Good-morning,' the doctor said as he passed.

'Good-morning, sir!'

A few yards further along the corridor, Roland looked back. The doctor was standing still, staring in his direction. Roland took a swift right turn and pushed his trolley through a pair of handy swing doors. Various semi-clad women looked up, startled, and a nurse zoomed towards him.

'I'm very sorry,' he apologised. 'I'm new here. I was trying to find the kitchen. Seem to have lost my way.'

She smiled, re-directed him. 'There's a back lift around the next corner,' she said. Then as he turned his trolley she looked down at his slippered feet.

'My feet are killing me, nurse!' he said. 'Not used to being on them all day. Can't bear my shoes on.'

'I know the feeling,' she said sympathetically. 'When you go off duty, soak them in a bowl of hot water with a handful of salt. You'll find it very soothing.'

'I will nurse,' he promised her.

There was no one waiting for the back lift and it was empty when it clanged to a halt in front of him. He pushed the trolley in, followed it, and pressed the button for the ground floor. He was lucky again

133

in that it chugged its way down without stopping, though through the iron grid he saw angry faces as it passed them by.

On the ground floor he got out, left the trolley where it was, and walked out of a nearby door into the May morning. There was a taxi rank not far away and he took a cab to Runswick Avenue. The driver looked at his legs, but said nothing. If my luck holds, Roland thought, I can change into real clothes and be down in time for Mrs Thompson's breakfast. He would decide his next move after he'd had his bacon and eggs, toast and marmalade.

*   *   *

At about the time when Roland was finishing his last piece of toast and enjoying his third cup of tea, the telephone rang in the Vice-Chancellor's elegant hall. Mrs Spencer came through from the breakfast room and picked it up. It really was quite inconsiderate of anyone to call her at this hour.

'Hello!' she snapped.

Then as she listened a smile spread across her face. More than a smile: an expression of rapture.

'Why of *course*, Lord Carshalton! No, certainly it's not too early. So kind of you to ring . . . but I'm afraid dear William is away from home. I don't expect him back until the day of the Summer Ball. So pleased to hear from dear Mike that you're coming to that!'

It had not been dear Mike who had told her, she thought, but that silly little Norma Wishbone. She simply must get to know the Carshalton boy.

'Well, if you say it's important,' she said into the phone, 'I'm quite sure my husband would be delighted to have you contact him. Actually I had

134

planned to go up to the cottage myself, today. Why don't we travel together? You could pick me up on your way there.'

She had not planned any such thing, of course. There was far too much to be done in the way of last-minute preparations for the ball and no one else, she was sure, capable of doing them. But they would just have to manage without her. She had no intention of passing up the present opportunity. A drive in Lord Carshalton's car—she hoped for a chauffeur-driven Rolls—would be the perfect occasion for a little tête-à-tête with his Lordship. On William's behalf, naturally. She wanted nothing for herself. She did not quite trust her husband with Lord Carshalton, not if there was something really important at stake. She had little doubt that whatever Lord Carshalton wanted to see her husband about, it would be to the latter's advantage.

'Ah yes! Business! I understand, Lord Carshalton. A Vice-Chancellor's wife, you know. Well you needn't think that I shall be in the way. I shall take myself off for a nice, long walk. There's so much *nature* around William's cottage.'

*   *   *

Roland decided to go straight to Sergeant George Robey Smith. The Sergeant must know, after all these years, just where the Vice-Chancellor was to be found. Pride wouldn't let him admit that he didn't. And when he'd found out he'd go to Marion and she could choose whether she'd take him at once to her boss, or whether he should hire a car and go it alone. He hoped she would take him, since he doubted if he was up to driving.

135

But in spite of his aching head, he felt singularly hopeful about things in general. So far today, things had worked out for him. It was still early in terms of real time, but a lot had happened since he'd drunk his cup of weak tea in hospital.

CHAPTER ELEVEN

'Know anything about the beautiful Miss Wishbone?' Inspector Murgatroyd asked his assistant. 'Come across her before, have you?'

Detective-Sergeant Naylor grunted. 'I should be so lucky! She's the kind of babe I've been saving myself for. Are you going to turn her over to me, then?'

'I am not. She excites my curiosity.'

'She excites more than my curiosity,' Naylor said. 'And I haven't got a wife to be faithful to.'

Inspector Murgatroyd sighed. 'Finish your tea and let's get going. It could be a long day. Anything on the V-C's set-up? At home, I mean.'

'No. Mrs Carstairs has only been working there six months. On the verge of packing it in, she says, on account of she can't stand madam. One of those women who go around writing 'dust' on the top of the piano, madam is.'

'I can believe that,' the Inspector said. 'Do they quarrel? Mister and Missus?'

'Not really. Apparently madam goes on at him, but he keeps calm, goes his own way. More to him than you'd give him credit for, Mrs Carstairs says.'

'There's got to be,' the Inspector said. 'And what about Washington?'

He got up from the table, walked towards the

canteen exit. At the counter he stopped and surveyed the array of confectionery.

'Hm! Fruit and nut today, I think,' he said.

He was feeling better than usual this morning. A reasonably timed finish yesterday evening. Supper with his wife and the kids. The telly, even if it had been all American cops, and an early night. And for once Elaine hadn't pleaded a headache. He felt almost human. The bar of chocolate which he slipped into his pocket was no more than an insurance against the day to come.

'Nothing on Washington yet,' Naylor said, following his boss out. 'He's been in his present job about four years. Before that he was in some sort of administrative post at the London School of Economics. He met his wife at LSE so they haven't been married all that long. She lectured in Political Economy. Generally thought to be a lot brighter than he is.'

'And right now a very frightened woman. Know why?'

'No,' Naylor answered. 'You're sure you wouldn't like the Washington family in exchange for Norma?'

Inspector Murgatroyd chuckled. 'Rank, my boy! The privilege of rank!'

They crossed to the car-park.

'What about the weapon then?' Naylor asked. 'No further?'

The Inspector tossed the car keys in Naylor's direction. 'You can drive,' he said. 'No further. Possibly never will be.' He buckled himself into the passenger seat. 'The boys say it could have been— probably was—an ashtray of the kind you find all over the university. Heavy glass, and big, so they won't get pinched. But they do, all the time. Some

137

people would nick an elephant. Sergeant Smith was going around emptying them and cleaning them about the time Maxton was killed. And of course obligingly polished off all the fingerprints for what they might have been worth. No, the weapon might or might not turn up. What I'm more interested in is *why* somebody used it. Motive. When we know that we'll get somewhere.'

'To hear them all talk,' Naylor said, 'no one knew or cared a thing about Maxton. Well, one of them cared enough to snuff him. You don't do that because you don't like the colour of a man's tie.'

'True,' the Inspector agreed.

'And what about Mr Challis? Who dislikes him enough to hit him on the bonce?'

'Who knows?' the Inspector said smoothly. 'Though I dare say he's used to it. People in his kind of job come with thick skulls. One of the bright boys, our Mr Challis.'

'Do you think there's a tie-up with Maxton?'

'Who knows that, either? I suppose there has to be one somewhere, because of Fletcher. But it's Fletcher's doings that Challis is interested in, not who killed Maxton. Maxton's death is our baby, and don't you forget it. Once Challis gets the answer to his particular question I suppose he bows out. Depends what it uncovers. Anyway, he's on a cushy number at the moment. Women visiting him, I don't doubt, and all those bosomy nurses fussing around.'

He adjusted the lever under the car seat, leaned back comfortably, clasping his hands over his stomach, closing his eyes. Naylor, glancing at him, recognised the signs and kept quiet. In any case he didn't like chatter when he was at the wheel. It was a beautiful May morning. Not a day for tediously

138

investigating crime. He'd like to be wearing fell boots, striding out across the hills. He envied the Vice-Chancellor of this place, with his cottage up in the Dales. As he turned into the university car-park the air was alive with birdsong.

'I want to know where Maxton met Fletcher,' Inspector Murgatroyd said, coming to life. 'Which conference? Who else was there? In particular, what it was about. Find out.'

'But no one knows,' Naylor remonstrated. 'His secretary's somewhere on top of a mountain. And this lot just seem to come and go as they like; no questions asked.'

'Well, you ask a few more,' the Inspector persisted. 'Spread yourself. Also, follow up on the Bursar and Mrs Washington. Before they came here.'

'While you concentrate on the fair Norma,' Naylor grumbled.

'That sounds very like insubordination, lad,' Inspector Murgatroyd said genially. 'Well if you're good I'll tell you afterwards what went on with Miss Wishbone. As much as is fit for you to hear.'

His assistant despatched, Inspector Murgatroyd seated himself behind the desk in the interview room. Then he got to his feet again and went and stared out of the window. He wasn't used to sitting at a desk; thought better on his feet.

How was he going to crack the fair Norma? He knew there was something there, was quite convinced she'd been in Maxton's lodgings in spite of Mr Clever-pants Challis's cover-up. But why had she been there? Also, how? Well, he wasn't above bullying her for an answer if that would get it out of her; but he wasn't sure that it would. Female

139

psychology—who could understand it? Better find out where she was vulnerable.

Young Carshalton? Washington? What about old Uncle George? He was very fond of her. And on whose advice had she suddenly changed her perfume and given away the first lot, he was fairly sure, to Maid Marion? He left the interview room and walked along the corridor to the secretaries' office, not bothering to knock before he entered. Sue Perkins looked up from her typing. There was no sign of Norma.

'You startled me,' Sue Perkins said pointedly.

'I'm sorry miss. I was looking for Miss Wishbone. Is she around?'

'She's with Mr Washington.'

She would be, he thought. Should he go in and tackle them both together? He decided he would rather, for the time being, concentrate on the girl. He'd see Washington again when Naylor had dug out some more information.

'Will she be long, do you think?'

The girl shrugged. 'Who knows? Would you like me to phone?'

'I would rather,' he said pleasantly. 'Apologise for the intrusion. Tell her Inspector Murgatroyd would like to see her in the interview room. At once,' he added.

It was always a nice point as to whether giving someone time to think made them more nervous or less. Rightly or wrongly, he judged that this time he'd made it urgent.

Norma was wearing her tight black trousers and a yellow cotton blouse. Yellow's not her colour, the Inspector thought. Makes her look washed out. There were dark circles under her eyes, though, which had nothing to do with the reflection from her blouse. She stood in the doorway, looking anxious. He motioned her to a seat.

'I'm very busy,' she said timidly. 'Mr Washington has a lot of dictation, and I haven't even started my filing.'

'Ah yes! Filing!' He came around the desk and took the armchair opposite to her. 'I expect you get a lot of filing? Nasty stuff.'

'I don't mind it,' Norma said.

'And I suppose you all help each other out, eh? You and Miss Perkins and Miss Richmond.'

She looked puzzled. 'I help Miss Richmond if Sue's not there. Sue helps me if I need it.'

'That's what I like to hear,' he said. 'And you're all trusted with the confidential stuff, I suppose.'

'To file it, yes. We don't *read* it. It's mostly quite boring. People always think things are confidential which no one else cares two hoots about.'

'Quite! But Miss Richmond holds the key.'

'Oh yes. In her drawer. We have to ask her for it if we need it.'

'Yes. Well, that wasn't what I really wanted to talk to you about.' It had been useful, though. Quite clearly more than one person could have got at Fletcher's file, which Miss Richmond had told him yesterday afternoon had gone missing.

'I've told you all I know, Inspector,' Norma said.

'Have you really, Miss Wishbone? Have you really?' His voice was benign.

'You know I have, Inspector.' The kindness of his manner, he was happy to note, had given her a little more confidence. With a little more still she might trip herself up. It had been known.

'Do I? Well we'll see. There might be something

141

either of us has thought about.' He looked at her ~~appreciatively~~. 'How's the young Mr Carshalton?' ~~asked~~.

~~She~~ looked surprised. 'Mike Carshalton?'

'A very eligible young man. *And* with a rich father, one hears. All those factories and so on.'

She flushed. 'I'm not interested in his father. I was friends with Mike before I knew about his father.'

It's serious, the Inspector thought.

'You've known him long?' he asked.

'Six weeks. Ever since I came here.'

The Inspector sighed. 'Six weeks! I suppose you feel you've known him forever?'

'You get to know some people quickly,' she said.

'I know. Did Mike Carshalton give you the perfume you were wearing in Dr Maxton's lodgings the other day?' he said suddenly. 'Did he, Miss Wishbone? Or did Dr Maxton give it to you?'

He rapped out the words: bang, bang, bang; leaning forward, his face close to hers. Terror suffused her face. He noted it, was sorry for her, and pressed his advantage.

'I wasn't in . . . It's not true . . . !'

'Come, come, Norma! I *know* you were there. I'm not just guessing,' he lied. 'And you're going to tell me how, but more particularly, why.'

Confusion blended with fright in her eyes. She's wondering if Challis gave her away, he thought. Let her wonder. It was the best possible help to him when people didn't know where they stood.

'I didn't kill Dr Maxton,' she persisted. 'I had nothing to do with it! I swear it!'

'Now who's saying you did? All I want is to get at the truth.' My God, he thought, I sound just like

142

one of those telly cops. 'But you see I *know* you were in Dr Maxton's room.' He was quite certain of it now. She hadn't denied it. 'I just want to know *why*. That's all. What were you looking for? I shall find out in the end, you know.'

And then against all his expectations she seemed suddenly to pull herself together. Apprehension still showed in her eyes, but her mouth, as far as its beautiful curves would allow, was set in an obstinate line.

'Come on,' he coaxed.

She looked down at the floor. 'I've nothing more to say,' she whispered.

'You're wasting my time,' the Inspector chided. '*You* know what you were doing there. *I* shall find out. So come on.'

'I didn't kill Maxton,' Norma said. 'I had nothing to do with it. It's true that I hated him and I'm glad he's dead. But I don't know who did it and I wouldn't tell you if I did. I won't tell you anything. He deserved to die.' Her tone was level, but she still avoided looking at him.

'Why?' the Inspector asked softly.

'Because he was a bully and a cheat and a traitor.'

'A traitor? That's interesting. To whom was he a traitor?'

She remained silent. He rose, walked swiftly over to the window and looked out. People were walking about out there, in the early summer sunshine, looking as though they were enjoying life. Groups of students lay around on the grass, not even pretending to work.

All that he'd gained from this interview was that she'd been searching in Maxton's room, which he'd

143

never doubted anyway. It looked as if it was all he was going to get. That, and the fact that she could have taken Fletcher's file. But there had been no trace of the file, nor any information about Fletcher, when the police had searched the room yesterday. Had she therefore found what she was looking for before they arrived, and taken it away with her?

She was shielding someone. He was absolutely sure of that. He never ceased to be amazed by the obstinate loyalty of women, and usually for the most undeserving of men. It was nearly always for a man. Men had it, if at all, for ideals, politics, their country. Women had it for men. They'd lay their lives on the line for them. In his job, bloody frustrating. He turned away from the window and looked at Norma again.

'Can I go now?' she asked. She was sure of herself again, he thought, knowing that for the moment she'd won.

'One thing before you do,' the Inspector said. 'You realise, I suppose, that I can take you in on suspicion?'

She looked up at him, frightened but defiant, not answering.

'I wouldn't hesitate,' he said quietly. 'Don't think I would. And another thing. If you didn't kill Maxton—in which case somebody else did, because he's very, very dead—then you could be in danger. Think about that. Whoever knows about Maxton well enough to kill him, knows that you're involved. If you've got some information he's after, or he thinks you have, or some clue about him, then you're no safer than Maxton was.' He sighed. 'Perhaps I ought to take you in for your own protection.'

'Can I go now?' Norma repeated.

'Yes. For the moment. But don't think I've finished with you, because I haven't. And for God's sake be careful. Don't go around on your own. You're too beautiful to die!'

In bad taste, that, but it had slipped out. If she hadn't killed—or maybe helped to kill—Maxton, and that he didn't know as yet, then she *was* in danger. There was no doubt about that. But from whom? Don't go around on your own, he'd said, but she'd be safer on her own than with the wrong person. Perhaps he should put someone on to her. They were short of men and it wouldn't be easy.

As she left the room he took the chocolate bar out of his pocket, popped a couple of squares in his mouth and sucked them greedily. She'd got the better of him, but only for the moment. He hadn't finished with her yet, not by any means. Common sense and experience told him that he couldn't assume her innocence. He wasn't usually susceptible to feminine charm, but Norma's brand, by its very lack of self-consciousness, was powerful. He would have to remain at all times aware of its influence. Instinct told him that she wasn't guilty of murder, whatever else, but was instinct anything to go on? Well, on the whole he thought it was. Some people called it flair, which sounded more professional. An open mind, that was what he must keep.

He left the interview room and walked along the corridor to Marion Richmond's office. Her desk was covered with orderly heaps of papers, held down by paperweights. He sat in the armchair, picked up one of the weights—a heavy flint—and

145

examined it.

'Rather nice,' he said. 'You collect these things?'

'I tend to,' Marion said. 'I like lumps of stone. I picked that up on the Sussex Downs when I was there on holiday. Did you want to see me?'

'Nothing special,' he said. 'I'm just a bit puzzled. Thought you might have some bright ideas.' Always try to flatter the intelligent ones by telling them how they could help.

'I doubt it, Inspector,' Marion said. 'I'm not feeling all that bright this morning.'

'Oh? Anything wrong?'

'Nothing at all. Just too much work and not enough time.'

'I suppose you look after all the Vice-Chancellor's affairs when he's away?'

'Yes. And quite a lot when he's here. Unless it's marked "personal". Then I don't touch it.'

'But "confidential"?'

'Oh yes of course.'

'So you're the one who'd know what he was up to?' The Inspector's tone was jocular.

'All he's ever up to, as you put it, is trying to run this university. No easy task, I assure you, Inspector Murgatroyd,' she said severely.

'Of course not,' he soothed. 'What about Miss Wishbone, now?'

'Norma?' She paused in the middle of slitting open an envelope. 'What about her? She doesn't really have anything to do with the Vice-Chancellor. She's the Bursar's secretary. She only gives me a hand if we're short-staffed, or if I'm exceptionally busy and Mr Washington isn't.'

'Of course. Very fond of her boss, is she?'

'I don't know,' Marion replied. 'Why don't you

146

ask her?'

'I will,' the Inspector promised. 'I will. She strikes me as being a loyal, affectionate girl. Wouldn't you say so?'

'I would.'

'I thought so. Do anything for anyone, I imagine. Anyone she was fond of, that is.'

Marion looked at him without speaking, then read through the letter she had just opened and placed it on one of the heaps on her desk.

'Strange thing, loyalty,' the Inspector mused.

'Are you telling me something, or asking me?' Marion said.

The Inspector picked up another paperweight, a heavy glass one with flowers embedded in it, and examined it carefully.

'She could be in danger,' he said softly.

'Norma?'

The telephone rang. Marion picked it up. 'Vice-Chancellor's office.'

While she listened the Inspector watched the expression on her face change from the wariness she had been showing towards him, to incredulity. Then a small dimple at the side of her mouth betrayed amusement at something which, he surmised, was not meant to be funny.

'Well, thank you for telling me,' she said eventually. 'I don't know anything about it, of course. Yes, if I *do* see Mr Challis I'll give him your message. Inspector Murgatroyd? As a matter of fact he's right here. I'll put him on.'

She handed the telephone to the Inspector. 'The hospital,' she said.

He listened, uttered a few monosyllables, and then rang off, smiling broadly.

'Well,' he said. 'So his nibs has escaped? Wouldn't have thought anyone could have got away from that Sister!'

Marion grinned. 'It should be an interesting story,' she said. 'I wonder where he is now?'

Before she had finished the sentence there was a knock on the door and Roland walked in.

'I'll bet you're talking about me,' he said. 'Well here I am, in the somewhat shaky flesh.'

'You look terrible,' Marion told him. 'For goodness' sake sit down. Really you are an idiot. And Sister is hot on your trail.'

'Too late,' he said. 'I'm beyond her power.' He was pleased to see the welcome in Marion's eyes. She was no longer angry. He was less pleased to see Inspector Murgatroyd sitting there. Fair play meant that he must now tell him all he knew about Fletcher, and also that he was going to see the Vice-Chancellor.

'Shall I ask one of the girls to get you some coffee?' Marion asked.

'I'd appreciate that.'

She looked pointedly at Inspector Murgatroyd. If he had any decency he'd go now, but it was obvious that he had no such intention.

'Thank you,' the Inspector said genially. 'White for me. With sugar.' He'd not got his answer from her about Norma, but he'd come back to it.

'I'll be back in a minute,' Marion said. 'I want a word with Sue before she goes off to the dentist.'

'Any developments?' Roland asked the Inspector when Marion had gone out of the room.

Inspector Murgatroyd told him what he had found out about the Washingtons.

'Naylor is working on that one. There might be a

148

political angle. He's also trying to get more on Maxton. And by the way, I *know* Norma was in Maxton's room, so we'll have no more messing about over that. I'm very curious about our Miss Wishbone. However ... what made you leave hospital so suddenly? Couldn't stand the cocoa?'

Roland told him about his telephone call to Mike Carshalton.

'Which means,' the Inspector said slowly, 'that Fletcher was in the UK on the night Maxton was killed. Very interesting, don't you think?'

'I do,' Roland said. 'Also I know more or less what Fletcher's working on. Something to do with car exhausts. I don't know the whys and wherefores as yet. That's something the Vice-Chancellor will have to fill in.'

'Car exhaust systems?' The Inspector sounded interested. 'That begins to make a pattern, wouldn't you say?'

'No,' Roland said. 'It means nothing to me as yet. Of course I can see it's important, and that there's a lot of money in it.'

'Now that's where local knowledge makes all the difference,' the Inspector said smugly. 'You probably don't know that there's a car components factory in Northwell. Picketts. One of the best. Very go ahead, with its own Research and Development department.'

'I didn't know. That does make it interesting.'

'Doesn't it just? And therefore you also didn't know that our Miss Norma Wishbone worked there until just six weeks ago.'

Roland whistled. 'It *does* begin to fit, doesn't it?'

'It does indeed!' The Inspector leaned back in his chair, clasped his hands over his stomach, and smiled like a satisfied cat.

'What we want to know now is, was the university working with or against Picketts, and whose side was Fletcher on,' Roland said.

'Precisely. And how well Maxton knew Norma when she was at Picketts. He got her the job with Washington. Why would he want her to move from Picketts, do you suppose?'

'I haven't the faintest,' Roland said. 'I leave Norma in your hands while I pump the V-C. See what you can find out about collaboration between Picketts and the university, and especially if Fletcher was involved. I suggest we pool all our information from now on. It's one big, beautiful mix-up at the moment, wouldn't you say?'

'I would,' the Inspector agreed.

'I wonder where Fletcher is now,' Roland said. 'Did he or did he not come back to the university when he landed in the UK, I ask myself.'

'Did he even stay in the UK?' the Inspector said. 'There are planes out of Heathrow going all over the place. We still know next to nothing about the man.'

Marion returned, and shortly afterwards Norma stood in the doorway, holding a tray of coffee. Marion was sure the Inspector had seen Norma, but he behaved as if she was invisible.

'So Professor Fletcher's back,' he said. 'Well no doubt he'll have something interesting to tell us. Oh, hello, Miss Wishbone, I hadn't seen you there.'

When Norma put the tray of coffee on the side table it was obvious to all of them that her hands were trembling. She left the room without speaking.

'I still don't see why you had to leave the

hospital,' Marion said after a silence.

'I'm going to see the Vice-Chancellor,' Roland said. 'And before you get on your high horse let me tell you that I know where he's to be found. At least I know the general direction.'

'Who . . . ?'

'Sergeant Smith. Reluctantly, but I was able to persuade him. I'd like you to take me—I have to confess that I'd just as soon not drive—but if you can't, or won't, then Sergeant Smith will hire a car for me.'

'Self-drive or chauffeur-driven?' Marion asked.

'Self-drive, of course,' Roland said.

'Then I'll take you in my car.'

'Great! I want to go almost at once, though.'

'That's impossible,' Marion said. 'There are a few things I must do here. And Sue has just gone off to the dentist. I dare say Bruce Washington will let Norma give me a hand. Even so, I need a couple of hours. But not more, I promise you. And it won't take long to get there. It's not much more than thirty miles.'

'Right,' Roland said. 'I'll come back here for you.'

In the meantime, he thought, he might dig out Mike.

Marion looked at him keenly. 'If you've any sense,' she said, 'which I doubt, you'll forget whatever you're scheming for the next two hours and go back home and rest. I'll ring Sergeant Smith and tell him you will *not* need a hire car.'

'Perhaps you're right,' Roland said. 'OK. I give in. You'd make a good nurse. You have the bossy touch.'

In fact, he thought, he'd be glad to lie down for a

while. But first he must have that word with Mike.

Inspector Murgatroyd rose to his feet. 'Well,' he said. 'Going for a nice trip up the Dales are we? Something I'm always promising myself. Have a nice time both of you.'

CHAPTER TWELVE

'I won't be a minute,' Marion said. 'I must sign these letters.'

Roland was waiting for her, in her office.

'How do you feel now?' she asked him. 'I'm not convinced that you're fit for this jaunt. You should have stayed in hospital.'

'We've been through all that,' Roland said. 'Let's leave it. How long will it take us to get there?' He was anxious to be off.

'As I said before, it's not much more than thirty miles, but it's a twisting, hilly road. We shan't be able to keep up much of a speed.'

Norma came into the room, carrying a letter folder. She looked at Roland uncertainly, not speaking to him. Marion took the folder and handed over the letters already signed.

'Thank you very much, Norma. I'm truly grateful.'

'Is there anything else?' Norma asked. Her voice was subdued. The life had gone out of her, Roland thought.

'No, thank you.'

'You're sure, Marion? Mr Washington's not busy.' She seemed reluctant to leave.

'Quite sure. I've switched the phone through to your office. I'll be in at the usual time tomorrow.'

152

Norma hesitated by Roland's chair; hovered, as if she wanted to speak to him, and then changed her mind and went out. He wondered what she'd been going to say.

'There! That's it! I'm finished,' Marion said.

She moved across to look at herself in the mirror set in the back of the coat cupboard door.

'You don't need any embellishment,' Roland told her. 'You're exactly right as you are.'

She was wearing a sleeveless dress of some fine cotton material in a soft, clear green, the bottom of the skirt bordered with a design in black.

'You should always wear green,' Roland said.

Looking in the mirror, Marion caught his look of appreciation. 'I do practically,' she said. 'Hadn't you noticed?'

She brought out a black crocheted shawl. 'In case it turns chilly,' she said. 'There! Sorry to have kept you waiting.'

She smiled at him and Roland thought how attractive she looked. He wished they were going for a perfectly ordinary day out; a fellow and a girl. Maybe when this was over they would.

Suddenly the smile left Marion's face.

'What's wrong?'

'How callous of me,' she said quietly. 'I've been so intent on getting away . . .'

'What's worrying you?'

'Something Inspector Murgatroyd said about Norma. Just before you came in this morning he told me Norma could be in danger. I think he was about to say more when you arrived. He wouldn't say that unless he meant it, would he? Unless he was using it as a trap.'

'A trap?'

153

'To get me to tell him something about Norma. But in fact I don't know anything.'

'You might,' Roland said thoughtfully. 'We don't always recognise just how much we do know about a person. Things we've seen or heard which seem unimportant, so that we push them out of sight.'

'Then you think it's true that Norma's in danger?' Marion sounded puzzled and Roland remembered that she knew nothing of Norma's visit to Maxton's room. Well, that was the Inspector's area, not his.

'It could be true. If she's as innocent as she proclaims, then I'd say she was in a sticky position. Most people seem to know that she had some link with Maxton. If she really had nothing to do with his killing, then whoever did it might well be after her. It depends what she knows. Or what the killer thinks she knows.'

Marion shivered. 'You sound so matter-of-fact about it,' she protested. 'I feel I want to pick her up and take her with me; keep her out of harm's way.'

'She'll be safe enough with Washington,' Roland pointed out. 'He wouldn't harm a hair of her head.'

'How do you know? If he'd had a hand in . . .'

'She'd still be safe. He wouldn't hurt Norma.'

'You really think so?'

'I really do,' Roland assured her.

'I'm not so certain,' Marion said slowly. 'Oh I'm sure he wouldn't normally want to harm her, but he's acting so strangely. He's like a man possessed. And you remember Norma said just now that he wasn't busy? It so happens that there's stacks of work waiting and he's just not doing anything. Every time I go into the office he's staring out of the window. And he can't bear Norma out of his sight.'

154

'There's not much we can do,' Roland said. 'For a start, I have to go after the Vice-Chancellor. If Norma is innocent she'd be safer if she told the truth to Inspector Murgatroyd. If he wasn't working in the dark about her he'd know where the danger lay and he could do something about it. He has resources that you and I don't possess. The last thing he wants is another tragedy on his hands.'

'I suppose you're right,' Marion said. She draped the shawl around her shoulders, feeling chilly. With the thought of Norma her whole mood had changed. The brightness had gone out of the day. Then she had an idea.

'We could telephone Mike Carshalton,' she said. 'Ask him to keep an eye on Norma when she leaves work.'

'What reason do we give?' Roland asked. But in fact Mike wouldn't need a reason given. He was in this, whatever it was, with Norma.

'Make up something. He'll take it from you.'

'All right then. If it'll make you feel better.'

'It will,' Marion assured him. She looked up the number, dialled, handed the receiver to Roland.

Mike himself answered the telephone. He sounded concerned, but not unduly surprised, by the request.

'Sure I'll stick with her,' he promised. 'Every minute she'll let me, that is. I've been trying to contact you,' he continued.

'And I you. Have you anything new for me?'

'Yes. That's why I wanted you.'

'Well come on man! Spit it out!'

'Professor Fletcher was here last night. I didn't see him, and I'm sure no one else did or they'd have said so. I worked after everyone had gone, on an

155

experiment for my thesis. I left everything tidy, and locked up. This morning I was first in and the things on the bench were different. No one else in the lab would have used my bench. And he'd certainly been in his office.'

'How come?'

'Because of his pipe. He never smokes in the lab, of course, but in his office he smokes a lot: some foul tobacco that a shop in Northwell blends especially for him. It's unmistakable, and this morning his office was thick with it.'

'I see. Now look here, Mike, I can't stay on campus today, but will you do everything you can to track down your boss? Try everywhere you can think of. And if you do find him, ask him to contact Inspector Murgatroyd if I'm not back. It's important. I'll be back this evening. I'm not sure what time.'

'OK,' Mike said.

'And Mike . . . take care,' Roland said.

'What was all that?' Marion asked. 'Will he keep an eye on Norma?'

'What? Oh yes, he'll do that.'

'And the rest?'

'Fletcher's been on campus. Last night, in his laboratory and office. Now *there's* a man who could be either dangerous or, equally well, in danger. Have you any idea where he'd go to ground?'

'None at all. If he's not in his lodgings.'

'I've got to have a word with Inspector Murgatroyd,' Roland said. 'I'll be as quick as I can, and then we must get going.' He put his finger under her chin, tilted her face until her eyes met his.

'Cheer up, love!'

'All right,' she said. 'I'm sorry I fussed about

156

Norma.'

Roland smiled. 'Don't apologise for a tender heart.' He kissed her gently on the mouth. 'That's to be going on with,' he said. 'More than that and we'll never make it to the Vice-Chancellor.'

She gave him a push in the direction of the door. 'Go and see your Inspector. I'll wait here.'

Ten minutes later Roland returned and they walked out together into the summer sunshine. Overhead the tall trees made changing patterns against the sky. In the treetops the rooks fussed about, balancing precariously on the edges of their nests, raucously admonishing their young; or so it seemed. Marion took off her shawl and felt the warmth of the sun on her bare arms. It was to be, from now on, one of those special days. She felt it. Nothing could go wrong. She smiled up at Roland as they walked across the campus to the car-park.

'Not exactly handy to your building, the car-park,' Roland said a little later.

'No. I think the idea was that it should be close to the entrance, which I suppose is reasonable. We're always being promised one nearer to the Administration building when funds allow. Goodness knows when that will be. There's never enough money.'

'One doesn't think of universities as being short of cash,' Roland said.

'This one is. We work on a shoestring. Always making cuts; going from crisis to crisis. Actually, Bruce Washington is quite good at balancing the books.'

'Don't you have any endowments?'

'Very few. Not like the older universities. People seem shy of giving money to the new ones. I think

157

hey don't trust them. They think the money will go
raight to the Communist Party funds, or worse.
e could do with a whacking big grant for the
nce side.'

' can imagine that's expensive,' Roland said.
'Where's your car?'

'Over there by the wall. I usually park it there,
well out of the way. Do you mind if I leave the top
down?'

They settled themselves in. Marion started the
car and drove slowly out of the park. As they passed
the entrance block she waved to Sergeant Smith
who was standing in the doorway, directing a visitor.

'You've forgiven him for telling me where to find
the Vice-Chancellor?' Roland asked.

'It's up to the Vice-Chancellor to do that,'
Marion said. 'I don't suppose the Sergeant had
much chance against your particular line of
inquisition. Anyway, I'm in a forgiving mood.'

They drove out of the entrance and down the hill.

'By the way,' Marion said. 'All I'm going to do is
deliver you to the nearest point to the cottage. I'm
not coming with you beyond that. The road ends
about a mile or so before the house and you have to
take a track. If you'd like to search in the glove
compartment you'll find a map. You can check the
journey.'

'Do you want me to navigate?'

Marion laughed. 'I've been travelling around the
Dales since I was a child. On foot; later on by
bicycle; and now the lazy way.'

Roland studied the map. 'Do we make for
Kettlewell?'

'That's right. Then along the river valley to
Buckden. After that we turn off into

Langstrothdale. My very favourite.'

'Is that where the cottage is?'

'Oh no! It's much more remote. We drive up to the head of the dale and then start looking.'

'From the map I'd say it's hilly country,' Roland said.

'It is. The river cuts into a valley between the fells, but quite often the road runs parallel, half-way up the fellside. It's a twisting road, too, but that's what makes it interesting. Why don't you relax and have a sleep? Remember you're an invalid.'

'I am relaxed,' Roland said. 'I'd rather not sleep. I don't want to miss any of this.'

For the moment he was utterly contented, enjoying the unfamiliar scenery and the warmth of the day. Then as the little car covered the miles the questions began to thrust themselves to the front of his mind again. What could Fletcher have been doing in his laboratory last night? Why was it necessary to pay a clandestine visit—always supposing Mike was right? Marion had not seemed unduly surprised at the news of Fletcher's reappearance. He turned to look at her. Her eyes were fixed on the road ahead, her capable hands relaxed on the wheel, but she sensed his gaze. She tightened her grip on the steering wheel to take a sharp bend on an incline.

They drove through Skipton and out into the open country again. Where a road went off to the right for Grassington, they kept forward. Close on their left, now, the hills climbed upward, and on the right dropped steeply down to the river. Dry limestone walls, badly broken in places and sometimes almost missing, bordered the road and snaked up and across the fells, making a random

159

pattern of enclosures on the emerald-green grass. In the meadows down by the river there were patches of yellow kingcups.

'By the way,' Marion said, 'Norma fetched me some sandwiches from the refectory. Shall we stop somewhere and eat them, or do you want to press on and eat as we go?'

'You *are* organised,' Roland said. 'Actually, I'm quite hungry. Why don't we have a break?'

'Right! When I find a bit of road that's wide enough I'll pull into the side.'

The place she finally chose was high above the river, on one of the few straight stretches. She backed the car into a gateway on the left and they got out and crossed the road. The wall here was broken down and they climbed through without difficulty to sit on the fellside.

They ate in near silence. The sun was strong now. There were no trees to give any shade but the slight breeze, blowing over the hills, tempered the heat. In the valley the river rushed and sparkled over the stones and children played in the shallows.

'It's a far cry from sudden death,' Marion said. 'Are you always thinking about crimes and suchlike? I don't think I could stand it.'

She turned towards him, holding a hand to her face to shield her eyes from the sun. The warmth of the day had brought the colour into her cheeks. She was one of those people who begin to live when the temperature rises.

'I do have other thoughts from time to time,' Roland said. 'Especially in a place like this. Listen!'

Larks sang overhead and in the distance curlews called. A bee, hard at work in a patch of clover, buzzed near at hand, and further down the meadow sheep bleated.

'This place is in my blood,' Marion said. 'Generations of my family have lived in these parts. You can't escape it, no matter where you go.'

'Come here,' Roland said. He took her hand in his and pulled her towards him. She put her arms around his neck and lay back on the short-cropped grass, drawing him down with her. He kissed her soundly and she responded with enthusiasm. 'All the same,' Roland said after a while, 'I can't help wondering why Fletcher had to return so secretly.'

Marion sat up and pushed him away from her. 'You're impossible!' she said.

'It's not a new complaint,' he admitted. 'Come back here.'

'I will not! We'll go right back to the car.'

'Pity!' Roland said. 'I was enjoying myself. I thought you were.'

Back in the car again Roland, fastening his seat belt, said, 'You're not really angry with me are you?'

'I'm furious,' Marion said. 'Naturally.'

He watched her while she let in the clutch, eased the car out of the gateway. There was the suggestion of a smile around her lips and he knew she was not as angry as she pretended to be.

Marion drove forward along the road, gathering speed.

'Stop looking at me,' she said. 'I have to concentrate on my driving here. No distractions allowed.' She braked the car before a steep bend.

'All right,' he said.

Going down the hill, Roland was at first unaware that anything was wrong, thinking only that Marion was taking it too fast. Then he glanced at her and saw that her hands gripped the wheel, her body was

161

tense, her face contorted with terror.

'The brakes!' she screamed. 'It's the brakes! I can't stop!'

The car shot down the steep gradient. Marion's foot was on the floor. Roland pulled on the handbrake, with no effect. As the road turned sharply to the left the car went forward and the gap in the limestone wall rushed towards them. There was a long scream from Marion as the car leaped over the remains of the wall and plunged down the fellside. As it turned over Roland, for a brief moment, saw the green grass and the blue sky merge into each other.

CHAPTER THIRTEEN

Before Roland and Marion had left the campus Inspector Murgatroyd was already on his way to Picketts, with Naylor this time in the passenger seat.

'I found out a bit about Maxton,' Naylor said. 'The Dean of Chemistry was fairly sure that Maxton had met Fletcher at a conference in Chicago. Something he called the "platinum" conference, organised by a private company, not by the university there. Apparently that's not unusual.'

The Inspector grunted. 'Well that bit fits. Did he say anything else?'

'He knew Fletcher had been there last year, though he'd not talked about it much when he got back. He hadn't mentioned issuing an invitation to Maxton, which the Dean thought he should have done. To him, he meant, as a matter of courtesy because Maxton would be working in the Chemistry Department. But Fletcher was a nonconformist, he

162

said. Didn't like doing things by the book.'

'Then how did he know Fletcher issued the invitation?'

'Maxton said so. And since Fletcher had left for the States, and the Dean wasn't sure just where he'd be, they took Maxton's word for it. They're a funny lot. All seem to be going their own sweet way, not bothering.'

'It's known as intellectual freedom,' the Inspector said gravely.

'We could do with it in the police force,' Detective-

Sergeant Naylor said. 'I haven't had a day off for a fortnight.'

'My heart bleeds,' the Inspector said. 'Have you ever been to Picketts' factory?'

'Only to their sports grounds,' Naylor said. 'The police once played them at rugger.'

'Rugby league. Nasty rough game,' the Inspector said. 'Now in the south they play something more refined. Who won?'

'They did.'

They drove into the factory down a wide, gravelled drive with flowerbeds on each side. The Inspector pulled into the parking bay in front of the main entrance. They got out of the car and walked across the gravel towards the plate glass doors, which opened automatically at their approach.

'All very posh,' the Inspector remarked. 'I suppose the place where the work's done is all hidden away at the back. I'd like to speak to the Managing Director,' he said to the woman at the reception desk.

'Have you an appointment sir?' she asked him.

'No.' He handed her his card. 'Please tell him it's

very important and that I won't keep him long.'

She spoke briefly on the telephone and then said, 'He has someone with him at the moment, but he'll see you in a few minutes. Would you take a seat please?'

While they waited, sitting on a black, plastic-covered settee flanked on each side by rubber plants, he picked up a house magazine from a table and scanned the pages.

'I see Joe Benson has been presented with a clock after forty years' service, and Mrs Heather Click, formerly of our Packing Department, has had twins,' the Inspector said. 'What about the Washingtons then? Find out anything more?'

'Give me time, sir!' Naylor said. 'Do you think perhaps I could go to London to investigate?'

'I do not, lad. Full of vice and corruption, London—or so they tell me. Not the place for a Yorkshire bobby, apart from the cost of the train fare. You asked for someone to get on to it down there?'

'Yes sir,' Naylor admitted.

'Good lad! Then we should hear fairly soon. Hello, hello!'

He had been turning the pages of the magazine while they were talking. 'Listen to this. Picketts Limited, one of the Carshalton Group of Companies. Did you know that, Detective-Sergeant Naylor?'

A young woman came into the entrance hall, spoke to the receptionist and then walked across to the two men.

'Mr Pearce will see you now,' she said.

'The Managing Director?'

'That's right.'

164

They followed her along a corridor and she showed them into the Managing Director's office.

'Thank you for sparing us the time,' the Inspector said. He usually said something like that. Made the other party feel well-disposed towards you, even though they knew they'd not had much choice.

'What's it all about?' Pearce said jovially. 'We haven't been breaking the law, I hope.'

'So do I, sir. No, it's quite simple really. I just want to ask a few questions about a young lady who used to work here.'

'Ah, then you want Mr Edwards, our Personnel Manager. I don't actually know all the staff myself. Like to, naturally, but you know how it is. Of course you were quite right to come to me in the first place, but I'll have my secretary take you to Mr Edwards.' He stretched his hand towards the telephone.

'Just a minute, sir, before you ring.'

'Well?'

'You make all kinds of car components here, I believe?'

'Well, not *every* kind, Inspector. But a good many.'

'Exhaust systems?'

'Yes. Is this relevant?'

'It could be,' the Inspector said. 'We'll have to see. I suppose you sometimes co-operate with the university, them being so near, and having a Mechanical Engineering Department?'

'Well perhaps occasionally,' Pearce said. 'Not necessarily that department. They come to us for bits of information, perhaps. Or to use a piece of machinery. Our Research and Development Department would know more about that.'

'Ah yes! You've got a very good R and D

165

Department here, I understand. Perhaps more than one would expect in a factory of this size? Well that's what I hear, but you can't believe everything you hear can you?'

'No you can't, Inspector. But there's no secret about our Research and Development Department. It was greatly expanded when we became part of the Carshalton Group a few months ago. We're rather proud of it. And of course it serves other members of the Group as well as ourselves.'

'I see, sir. And would you know what was going on in the department?'

'Well of course I would,' Pearce said testily. 'In broad outline, that is. What are you getting at, Inspector? Did the girl you're enquiring about work in R and D?'

'Miss Norma Wishbone? Did she, I wonder?' the Inspector said. Then he watched recognition come into Pearce's face.

'Miss Wishbone? Ah yes! Now I *do* remember her. She worked in finance, Inspector. Nothing to do with Research. I hope she's not in any trouble?'

'Then perhaps we should see your Personnel Manager,' the Inspector said. 'But while I'm here I would like a word with your Research and Development Manager.'

'Well that's rather different,' Pearce said. 'You'll appreciate that what goes on in that department is mostly confidential.'

'Of course, sir. Perhaps you'd rather we saw him in your office?' Inspector Murgatroyd said smoothly.

'I think that would be best,' Pearce said. He rang through to his secretary. 'Please ask Mr Robinson if he'd come up to my office for a few minutes. Right away, please.'

A few minutes later the Research and Development Manager bounced into the room. 'Look here,' he said, 'I was in the middle of something important! What's it all about?'

'Calm down, Robbie! This is Inspector Murgatroyd and Detective-Sergeant Naylor. They want to ask a few questions about your department.'

'My department?' The man made no attempt to hide his irritation. 'Whatever for?'

'It won't take long,' the Inspector said soothingly. Sometimes when he heard himself talk like this he thought he sounded like a dentist, preparing a patient for an extraction. Well perhaps it was a bit like that. 'You may have read in the papers that a Dr Maxton was killed up at the university a few days ago? We don't know much about him, except that he was a scientist. We think he might, just might, have been interested in a project which your department was working on in co-operation with the university.'

'Maxton? I don't know him,' Robinson said.

'You're quite sure?'

'Certain. I've never heard of him.'

'Are we co-operating on anything at the moment?' Pearce asked his manager. 'With the university, I mean.'

'No. Nothing at all.'

'I see,' Inspector Murgatroyd said. 'Do you by any chance know Professor Fletcher?' He hoped Challis would appreciate what he was doing on his behalf, while he was gadding up the Dales with Miss Richmond.

'Oh yes,' Robinson said. 'I know him quite well.

He's abroad at the moment.'

So he hadn't contacted Picketts since his return, the Inspector noted.

'I believe he sometimes co-operates with you?' he said.

Robinson looked at him keenly. 'Did,' he said. 'But quite some time ago now. Fletcher, as far as I know, hasn't co-operated with anyone for the last couple of years. Rumour says he's not doing any science.'

'And do you believe rumour?' Inspector Murgatroyd asked.

'No,' Robinson said. 'Not in this case.'

'Well, thank you very much,' the Inspector said. 'I mustn't keep you two gentlemen any longer. You've been most helpful. Now if I could see your Personnel Manager? Tie up a few more loose ends.'

The Research Manager left in a hurry. Pearce's secretary came in. 'Please take these gentlemen to Mr Edwards,' her boss said. 'I'll phone and tell him you're on the way.'

*   *   *

Mr Edwards, a short fat man, looked at them over the top of his National Health half-moon spectacles.

'Wishbone?' he said. 'And it is Miss Wishbone, not her father, you're enquiring about?'

'Her father? Does he work here?' Inspector Murgatroyd hoped he concealed his surprise.

'Well, in a manner of speaking,' Edwards said.

How in God's name did you work somewhere in a manner of speaking, the Inspector asked himself. Out loud he merely said, 'How?'

'He's not exactly on our payroll. He has a small

168

contract cleaning firm, just himself and three or four helpers.'

'And he cleans all the offices?'

'Not just the offices. The whole building,' Edwards said.

'Every department?'

'Of course. In the evenings. They start at five-thirty and work through until they've finished.'

'So you don't see him much?' the Inspector asked.

'Sometimes I see him around when I'm leaving. And of course if I want to see him about anything special, or if he wants to see me, he'll come in a bit earlier. But that doesn't often happen. He had a bad patch when his wife died a few months ago; he used to come in and talk a bit then; nothing special. He knows the routine and there aren't many snags.'

'You've known him long?' the Inspector said. 'You're quite satisfied with him, then?'

'Oh absolutely! He's been with us for years. We're very happy with him. I hope you're not telling me there's anything wrong there?'

'I'm not,' the Inspector said. 'I'd in no way considered him as the villain of the piece.' That was true enough. He hadn't considered him at all; hadn't cast his net wide enough. How many times had he grumbled at Naylor for the very same omission?

'I'm glad to hear it. And his daughter, Norma? I thought it was Norma you wanted to ask about.'

'It was,' the Inspector said. 'Just routine stuff. When did she join, who did she work for? That sort of thing.'

'She came to us straight from secretarial college. Her father saw me and asked if we had a vacancy,

169

and as it happened there was one. That would be . . . well it's on her card.'

He swivelled around in his chair and consulted a card index file. 'Yes. Exactly two years ago this week. She started as one of the secretaries in the Finance Department and after three months she got the job of secretary to the Accountant. He spoke very highly of her.'

'Spoke?'

'He's no longer here. Been transferred to another company in the Group.'

'Oh yes of course. You're part of the Carshalton Group. Why did Miss Wishbone leave?'

'She said it was because she wanted to work in the university. Actually, it's recognised in my job that one seldom knows why a person leaves a job, only the reason they give. The only time you know for certain is when they're pregnant or retired.'

'And you think the reason she gave wasn't the true one?'

'I don't know. It sounds a good enough reason. The university's attractive to young people—all those students. But she wasn't bubbling over about it, as you'd have expected. I got the feeling that she was reluctant.'

'But a step up?' the Inspector suggested.

The Personnel Manager shrugged his shoulders. 'We pay much better wages than the university. And we're on flexitime, so that there's a lot of freedom to come and go.'

'Strange creatures, women,' Inspector Murgatroyd said with feeling.

'I deal with them all the time,' Edwards said. 'I never understand them. But of course I love 'em,' he added.

170

'Sure!' The Inspector rose to his feet. 'Come along Detective-Sergeant Naylor. We've taken up enough of Mr Edwards's time. Thank you very much for your help, sir. Runswick Avenue, the Wishbones live. Thirty-seven, isn't it?'

Mr Edwards looked at the card. 'Thirty-nine,' he corrected.

They shook hands and left.

'What next?' Naylor asked when they were outside again.

'What next?' Inspector Murgatroyd sounded surprised by the question. 'Thirty-nine Runswick Avenue, of course.'

*   *   *

The Inspector's first emotion when Henry Wishbone opened the door to them was astonishment that the man standing in the hall could have fathered the beautiful Norma. At first glance there was no point of similarity. He was small—not more than five-feet-four-inches—thin, round-shouldered, balding. His features were a job lot, assembled in a haphazard fashion in a sallow skin, blue around the lips and chin where he badly needed a shave.

'Mr Henry Wishbone?' the Inspector asked.

'Yes.' He admitted it reluctantly, as if he would rather not have been.

The Inspector identified himself and his assistant. 'May we come in for a minute?' he said.

It was then that he noticed the man's one resemblance to his daughter. They had the same beautiful, heavy-lashed eyes; Henry Wishbone's curiously out of place in his homely face. And with the same look of fear in them, the Inspector noted with interest.

They followed Wishbone down the passage into what in better days would have been a breakfast room or living kitchen, and was now an untidy overflow of the scullery beyond. The remains of a meal was still on the table, egg yolk drying on the plate.

'May we sit down?' the Inspector asked.

'Oh yes. Yes.' Wishbone cleared two chairs, but remained standing himself. He was quite still, as if waiting for something to happen.

'It's a bit of a mess in here,' he said softly. 'My wife—my late wife—used to keep it spick-and-span. Norma does her best in the evenings, but the wife didn't bring her up to do housework, her being the only one. And she doesn't have much time.'

And you haven't the heart, the Inspector thought. Wishbone hadn't asked why they'd come. It was almost as if he'd been expecting them.

'Norma's my daughter,' he explained.

'We know. Please sit down, Mr Wishbone. Do you know what I've come about?'

Wishbone hesitated, then said, 'No.'

'You've no idea?'

'No.' He looked terrified. Why didn't he ask if it was about his daughter, the Inspector wondered. It was as if he daren't commit himself to anything.

'You knew Dr Maxton?' the Inspector said suddenly.

'I ...' Wishbone seemed to have difficulty in finding his voice.

'Of course you knew Dr Maxton. He lived a few doors away. He was friendly with your daughter. Used to give her a lift in his car. Got her a job in the university.'

172

'Did Norma tell you that?' Wishbone said.

'Your daughter's been quite frank with us,' the Inspector said, feeling Naylor's eyes on him as he told the lie. 'I hope you're going to be the same.'

'I don't know anything beyond what she's told you,' Henry Wishbone said.

'Well you don't know what she *has* told us, do you?' the Inspector said. 'You know Maxton was killed. We all know that. You know Norma was friendly with him and that she was actually seen with him just before he died. We all know that, too.'

For a second, but only for a second, the Inspector hated what he was doing. Henry Wishbone was as miserable a piece of humanity as he'd seen in a long time. His face was chalk-white; his whole body sagged, as if he wore a heavy garment of fear. Fear, or guilt, the Inspector wondered, brushing away his momentary compassion. Wishbone could have been the one.

'Where were *you* when your daughter was at the Vice-Chancellor's party with Dr Maxton?' he asked.

'I was working,' Wishbone said. His reply was without hesitation. 'There was extra work that night at Picketts. We clean off the floors with the machine every so often, and then polish them. It means staying late.'

'Anyone to prove that you were there?'

'My mates. I worked alongside them. They'll tell you that.'

Whether or not, the Inspector thought.

'But Norma couldn't have done it! Not what you're thinking!' For the first time there was life, though anguished, in Wishbone's voice.

'Oh?' The Inspector sounded interested. 'Why not?'

'She just couldn't. It ... well, it isn't in her. Norma's like her mother ... like her mother was. A gentle person. Wouldn't hurt nobody.'

'She hated Maxton,' the Inspector said. 'She told me that herself. Did you hate him, Mr Wishbone? Did you hate Maxton?'

There was silence.

'If you and Norma are both as innocent as you say,' the Inspector continued, 'Norma could be in danger. Work it out for yourself.'

He kept quiet for a few seconds, watching Henry Wishbone, observing the fear and doubt succeed each other in his face.

'Did *you* hate Dr Maxton?' the Inspector repeated eventually.

'Yes,' Wishbone said. 'Yes I hated him all right.' He buried his face in his hands.

'Why?' The Inspector pulled his chair nearer to the other man's; bent towards him, speaking softly. 'What did he ask you to do?'

Wishbone raised his head. 'If I tell you, it's because you say my Norma could be in danger,' he said. 'If you're not being straight with me then I hope you'll be punished. The way I've been punished.'

'It's straight. I really believe she is. That is, if you and she, or either one of you, didn't kill Maxton.'

'Right then,' Wishbone said. 'Maxton wanted me to get papers from Picketts. Not really steal them. I wouldn't have done that. Couldn't have. One of our perks—the cleaners' perks, that is—is that we can take the waste paper. We bag it up, and when we've got enough we sell it.'

'From the waste paper baskets you mean?'

'That's it. Only things what have been thrown

174

out. We're allowed to do it. You can ask anybody.'

'It's usual I believe.'

'Well Maxton wanted me to give him the waste paper from some of the bins.' Wishbone stopped, looked at Inspector Murgatroyd. The Inspector leaned forward.

'Come on man! Give me the rest. Which bins? Which departments? What did he pay you? I want the lot.'

'The Research and Development Department and the Managing Director's area. His secretary's office.'

'What did you do?'

'All I had to do was put the contents of those waste paper baskets in a separate sack.'

'You didn't look for anything special?'

'No. I never looked at anything. Just put it in the sack.'

'And how did you get the stuff to Maxton?'

'We kept the sacks in a yard until the firm we sold 'em to came to collect them. I'd put a mark on the ones for Dr Maxton and keep them separate. He collected them. I never knew how. Didn't want to.'

Why in God's name, the Inspector thought, don't people like Picketts invest in a few document shredders? You'd think a company like that would be more efficient.

'He paid you well?'

'Yes. But I didn't do it just for the money. Oh, there were a few bills to settle after my wife died. I was a bit short. But it wasn't that. It was . . . well, a bit of something out of the rut. I was very down after Vesta died. Nothing seemed to mean anything any more.'

'How long did this go on?' the Inspector asked.

'A few months. Then he got mad because, he said, he wasn't getting anything. Said there was nothing in the waste that was any good to him. I told him he couldn't blame me for that. Then he said . . .' Wishbone hesitated.

'Go on.'

'He wanted me to break into the files. I refused. I'd only ever agreed to the paper because we were allowed to take it. I wouldn't do the files. He said if I didn't he'd go to Picketts, and to the police. I'd lose my job and go to prison he said.'

'I see. So he got Norma to do it?'

'No. She'd left Picketts. He'd got her a job at the university. Talked as if he did it as a favour. I don't think she wanted to go, but she said it was all right. She wouldn't really talk about it.'

'Did Norma know what you were up to?'

'I never told her anything,' Wishbone said.

But Maxton did, I'll bet my cotton socks, the Inspector thought. And used the same bit of blackmail he'd used on her father. Do as I say or it's prison for your dad. Why had he never listened when people said, 'Norma's very fond of her dad'? It stuck out a mile. Well now he had to get the next instalment from Norma, which shouldn't be difficult when she heard her dad had come clean.

'I'm leaving now, Mr Wishbone,' he said. 'Don't think of going away anywhere, will you? And by the way, you'd better take care of yourself as well as of Norma.'

*   *   *

'I'd like to call in the station to see whether anything's come through about the Washingtons,' Detective-Sergeant Naylor said as they left

Wishbone's house. 'I presume we're on our way to the university and Miss Norma Wishbone?'

'That's right, lad. And this should be a *fruitful* interview. But we'll call in the station first,' he added kindly.

CHAPTER FOURTEEN

As Marion opened her eyes Roland was looking at her, his face drawn with anxiety. He touched her cheek.

'Are you all right?' he asked.

'Yes, I think so. My foot hurts.' Her voice, in her own ears, sounded a long way off, and as if it belonged to someone else. 'Are you OK?'

'Yes.'

The car was on its side. It had not, as Roland had feared in that final second when he had seen the ground and sky rushing towards him, turned completely over, but had tipped on its side as it came to a stop on a small plateau part-way down the slope. They were both still strapped in their seats, with Marion's side of the car nearest to the ground. Lucky, in the circumstances, that they'd had the top down. They'd get out easily. But he shuddered to think what might have happened to them if the car had actually somersaulted.

'I'm going to climb out,' he said. 'Keep still. I'll have you out in a jiffy.' He unfastened his seat belt and climbed over the back seat, on to the grass at Marion's side of the car.

'Can you undo your belt?' he asked. 'Then I'll pull you free. Don't struggle. Let me take the weight. How bad is your foot?'

177

'Not terrible.' Marion twisted in her seat and Roland took hold of her under the arms and eased her out on to the grassy bank. She lay there shivering, her eyes closed, while he examined her foot carefully. The skin was broken and discoloured, bleeding a little, but so far there was no swelling.

'I think it's just a nasty graze. You've probably banged it against a pedal,' he said. 'Look here, I'm going to climb up to the road, go and find a phone box, and get an ambulance. I might be gone some time. Will you be all right?'

She opened her eyes again. 'Ambulance? Don't be daft. I don't need an ambulance. Give me a minute or two and I'll climb up to the road with you.'

'Oh no you won't,' Roland said. 'But if you're absolutely sure you don't want to go to hospital . . .' He had a dread of doing so himself. They'd possibly both be kept in.

'I certainly don't. I really feel better already. If we could just get to the nearest village, then we could sort ourselves out.'

'Right! I'll climb up to the road and thumb a lift. You stay here and rest, and when I've got a car to stop I'll come back and collect you.' He found her shawl in the back of the car and wrapped it around her shoulders. 'All right?'

'Fine!'

'I hope I shan't be long,' he said. 'It all depends how often cars come along this road.'

But she was no longer listening to his words. She was looking at the little red car, lying on its side on the grass.

'Look,' she said. 'We must have been deflected

by that rock, and then slowed down by this bit of a plateau. Otherwise nothing would have stopped us hurtling down to the bottom.' Beads of sweat broke out on her face as she stared at the downward slope of the hill.

'Well we did stop,' Roland said gently. 'And we're all right. Try not to think about the rest just now.'

She turned and looked at him, a question in her eyes. 'The brakes, Roland? There was nothing wrong with them yesterday. I had my car back from servicing. The brakes were just fine. And all the way from the university ... there was no sign that I remember. But as I came along the last bit ... nothing! What happened, Roland?'

'I don't know. But we'll find out.'

'Do you think someone could have tampered with them?'

'Could have is possible. Did, we don't know. Let's not think about it right now.'

'I can't just stop thinking about it,' Marion protested. 'It's a horrible thought. Why *my* car?'

'Because you were taking me,' Roland said. 'It's as simple as that. Whoever's at the bottom of this— and just about the whole world and his wife knew we were making the trip—isn't too particular about who else gets hurt. I seem not to be a safe person to be with. You'd be better off avoiding my company.'

'Rubbish!' Marion said. 'I must say, though, that if someone is after you they're not very skilled at it. I mean, there was no certainty that anything terrible would happen this way. It just might have. It was a gamble.'

In spite of the turn the conversation had taken, Marion seemed to be recovering her spirits. She was not so ashen now, and she propped herself up

179

on her elbows.

'I know,' Roland said thoughtfully. 'I get the feeling that these occurrences are just delaying tactics. I'm wanted out of the way to allow something else to happen. I wonder what?'

'I don't much like it,' Marion said.

'Well, I'm going up to the road now, to stop a car. Lie still and rest. Don't try to climb up the bank on your own.'

'It would have to be a crawl. I'm not sure that I could put any weight on my foot. It seems to be swelling up now.'

Roland left her and clambered up to the road. He felt surprisingly fit, considering all things. It must be his adrenalin, rising to the occasion. He stood at the side of the road and signalled an approaching car, but it went straight past him, as did also the second one. The third car to come around the bend was a silver-blue Daimler and this time he stood in the middle of the road, waving both his arms. The car slowed to a halt a few yards short of him. He walked forward.

It couldn't be! Fate couldn't do this to them! But it was. In the passenger seat of the car sat the Vice-Chancellor's wife. The driver, a tall, burly man in late middle-age, was unknown to Roland.

'Good-afternoon Mrs Spencer,' Roland said. It was obvious that she didn't remember him. 'I'm Roland Challis. I met you the other evening.' We met at the murder, he felt like saying. He spoke to the car driver. 'There's been an accident. Our brakes failed. The car's half-way down the hill. And the driver. It's Marion Richmond,' he said, turning to Mrs Spencer.

'Miss Richmond? Good heavens! She's my

husband's secretary, Lord Carshalton,' Mrs Spencer said. 'What in the world is she doing here?'

'Waiting for help,' Roland said briskly. So this was Lord Carshalton. Where was he taking Mrs Spencer? It couldn't possibly be on a pleasure jaunt.

Lord Carshalton was already out of the car; then he turned back and took something from the glove compartment.

'Brandy,' he explained. 'Always carry a flask, just in case. Now where is this young woman?'

He followed Roland over the broken wall and scrambled down the hill after him. Marion was sitting up now and looked considerably better.

'This is Lord Carshalton,' Roland said. 'By strange coincidence his was the first car to stop. We know your son,' he explained.

'A small world! A very small world!' Lord Carshalton said. 'Here, young lady, have a drink of this. Put a bit of life into you.' Marion took the flask and sipped the brandy.

'Lord Carshalton has Mrs Spencer in his car with him,' Roland warned, conversationally.

Marion choked over the drink. 'Did you say Mrs Spencer?'

'Yes.'

'I thought you did.' She took a long drink of the brandy before handing the flask back to its owner.

'Is it just possible that you were on your way to see the Vice-Chancellor?' Roland asked.

'Indeed I was.'

'That's great,' Roland said. 'So were we. And I've got to get there. It's a matter of some urgency.'

'So is my visit,' Lord Carshalton said. 'Most important business or I can assure you I wouldn't be driving up here. Is he expecting you?'

'No,' Roland said. 'And you?'

'No. Nor, I gather, his lady wife.'

'Well, well! What an interesting party he's going to have! I'm hoping, Lord Carshalton, that you'll be kind enough to give Miss Richmond and myself a lift there?'

'But of course my dear fellow. As long as it's understood that I must have my tête-à-tête with the Vice-Chancellor. I'm sure you understand.'

'Perfectly. The same thing goes for me. And if I may, I'd like to stop off at the police station and the garage when we get to the next village.'

'No trouble,' Lord Carshalton said affably. 'Now, Miss Richmond, if you'll just lean all your weight on Mr Challis and myself, we'll have you in my car in no time at all.'

Really, Mrs Spencer thought, watching her husband's secretary approach, carefully supported by the two men, really it's too bad. So inconsiderate! So far she had not made much progress with Lord Carshalton. He was polite enough, seeing to her every comfort, making trivial conversation, but she had the feeling that his mind was on other things. She was aware that she had not yet really got through to him, but with the eternal optimism which was one of her better qualities she felt—or had felt—that in the last few miles, alone in the wild Dales country (as she put it to herself) she would come into her own. Now they were to be burdened by this wretched girl and some young man who claimed to know her. She was sure Lord Carshalton was as disappointed as she was; but of course he was too much of a gentleman to show it.

'Here we are then,' Lord Carshalton said kindly. 'Into the back seat with you. There's lots of room.

182

You can put your feet up on Mr Challis's lap. I'm sure he won't mind.'

'You're very kind,' Marion said.

Mrs Spencer forced a chilly smile to her lips. 'Are you all right?' she asked.

'Yes, thank you Mrs Spencer,' Marion replied.

'So unfortunate!'

What she means, Marion thought, is so careless. She didn't answer.

'Now are you sure you wouldn't rather let the hospital take a look at that foot of yours?' Lord Carshalton said. 'We could drive back to Skipton. No trouble, I assure you.'

'Really, no,' Marion said. 'I feel fine. And there's nothing seriously wrong with my foot. I'm sure of that. I really don't want to go to hospital.'

'Very well then, if you're sure. We'll call at the garage and get them to do something about your car, and then I think Mr Challis wants to call in at the police station. After that we'll take you as quickly as possible up to the Vice-Chancellor's cottage and Mrs Spencer can make you comfortable there.'

Mrs Spencer stared at him, trying not to look as horrified as she felt. 'You mean . . . we're all going to my husband's cottage? All of us?'

'Why yes, dear lady,' Lord Carshalton said. 'And I think if you were to give Miss Richmond a cold compress . . .'

'Cold poison more like,' Marion whispered to Roland. 'I don't want to be any trouble,' she said out loud. 'If there's an hotel in the village I'd be quite happy to stay there while Roland goes up to see the Vice-Chancellor.'

'But why should Mr Challis wish to see my

husband?' Mrs Spencer said. 'He hardly knows him.'

'Business, my dear,' Lord Carshalton said. 'Don't you worry your head about it.'

'William won't be pleased,' Mrs Spencer said. 'I can promise you that. Why, he doesn't even like *me* arriving unexpectedly!' To which, it seemed, no one could find an answer.

When they reached the village, which turned out to be no more than a couple of miles along the road, Lord Carshalton stopped his car outside the police station. Roland went in, and emerged a few minutes later accompanied by a policeman. They walked to the car.

'Constable Blunt recommends the local garage,' Roland said.

'They're very reliable,' the constable nodded. 'And they have a breakdown truck. You're not the first people to go over the wall, not by a long chalk. If there's anything more I can do for you, just pop in and let me know, sir.' He turned, and went back into the station.

'I want to go to the garage with you,' Marion said. 'I'm the best person to tell them about my car.'

'I don't think you should attempt to walk,' Roland told her.

'Then I'll hop,' she said tersely. Couldn't he see that anything was preferable to staying in the car with Mrs Spencer.

'And while you're seeing to that,' Lord Carshalton said, 'I shall look around the village and see if there's anyone who'll give us a cup of tea. I'm sure we could all do with one.'

'I'll come with you,' Mrs Spencer said.

'Are you sure you wouldn't rather rest in the car?

It would do you good,' Lord Carshalton said persuasively.

'So thoughtful of you,' Mrs Spencer said. 'But I'm quite sure. And I'll be company for you. I wouldn't dream of letting you do it on your own.'

As the constable had hinted, the owner of the garage showed little surprise when he heard about the accident. Marion got the feeling that he went out regularly to rescue cars from the fellside.

'Will you be able to give us a fairly quick report on what went wrong?' Roland asked. 'It's important.'

'I'm sure it was the brakes,' Marion said. 'But the car's been serviced only this week, so I'm puzzled to know why.'

'I'll get it up on the ramp right away,' the man promised. 'We're not busy. Should know in an hour or two, if that suits you. Be able to give you an estimate for repairs as well.'

'Great,' Roland said. He turned to Marion. 'We shall have to beg a lift back to Northwell with Lord Carshalton. He's got to take Mrs Spencer back anyway.'

'Lord save us,' Marion said. 'You're right, though.' She spoke to the garage owner. 'We'll call back later today for the verdict.'

'Right you are, miss. If the garage is closed, knock on the house door.'

From the other end of the village Lord Carshalton and Mrs Spencer walked towards them.

'Why does no one put Mrs Spencer in a runaway car?' Marion asked.

'Don't worry. She's got it coming to her,' Roland said.

'The hotel will give us tea,' Lord Carshalton

called out happily as they met up. 'Now you take my arm, Miss Richmond. Lean all your weight on me.'

The sitting room of the hotel, into which they were directed by a white-aproned woman who smiled as if she was actually pleased to see four customers, was dark, the windows being too small and too heavily-curtained to let in much light. The chintz-covered armchairs, however, looked comfortable and Marion was glad to sink into one of them. By the time the waitress had found a small stool on which to prop up her foot, and Lord Carshalton had placed a cushion behind her back she was almost comfortable again. If only some magic would cause Mrs Spencer to disappear, Marion thought, she would be happy to sit here for a long, long time. Even to fall asleep.

Half a dozen low tables were set for tea, but it was early yet and the only other occupant of the room was a fair-haired man who sat with his back to them in a chair close to the window. It was not until Marion had closed her eyes in relaxation that recognition leaped into her mind. She opened her eyes, let out a shout of surprise and tried to rise to her feet, thereby knocking her handbag to the floor and spilling its contents on the carpet.

'Leon! Leon, what are you doing here?' she called out sharply. 'It's Professor Fletcher!' she said to Roland.

The man stood up, turned around and walked across the room to them. Reluctantly, Roland thought, watching him with great interest.

'Hello Marion,' Fletcher said. 'You look as though you've been in the wars. Good-afternoon, Mrs Spencer.'

His words were ordinary civilities, but Roland

186

noticed that the hand he held out was trembling. When he was introduced, and shook it, it was cold.

'I thought you were in the States,' Marion said. She gave no sign of having heard that he had been in the university on the previous night.

'I came back,' Fletcher replied. 'As you see.'

'Well I'm very pleased to meet you,' Lord Carshalton said, beaming. 'I've heard a lot about you from my son. You must come and join us for tea. My word, we're becoming quite a party! And what brings you to this remote part of the world? Trout fishing perhaps?'

'No,' Fletcher said. He looked around the circle of faces, each one looking to him for an answer. 'I'm on my way to see the Vice-Chancellor.'

Marion broke into a peal of laughter. Mrs Spencer gave her a hostile look.

'I can't help it,' Marion apologised. 'I'm picturing the Vice-Chancellor's face when he sees us roll up like a coach party!'

'It's not a matter for facetiousness, Miss Richmond,' Mrs Spencer said. 'You should know that if anyone does. My husband values his privacy above all things. I simply can't think why you and Mr Challis are here, and I should have thought that you, Professor Fletcher, might have waited until my husband returned to the university. I do know, of course, that Lord Carshalton has a matter of the utmost importance to discuss with my husband.' And now, she realised, she would have precious little opportunity of finding out what it was.

'Have you a car, Professor Fletcher?' Roland asked suddenly.

'Yes. The yellow Mini outside.'

'Ah!' Mrs Spencer said quickly. 'Then that's

splendid. Mr Challis and Miss Richmond can travel with *you*.'

'Certainly not,' Lord Carshalton protested. 'We can't possibly allow Miss Richmond to travel in the back of the Mini when there's plenty of room in my Daimler. No offence meant, Professor.'

'But she could have the whole of the back seat of Professor Fletcher's car to herself,' Mrs Spencer pointed out.

'In fact,' Roland said, 'it would make better sense if Marion had the whole of the back seat of Lord Carshalton's car to herself and I travelled with Professor Fletcher. That was what I was about to suggest. If you'll have me,' he said to Fletcher.

'Of course.' It was a reluctant agreement. Marion glared at Roland and he smiled back at her sweetly.

'Please excuse me for a moment!' he said, and went out of the room.

*   *   *

The police station was fortunately near to the hotel and Constable Blunt was still on duty.

'I need to speak to Inspector Murgatroyd of the Northwell CID,' Roland told him. 'It's urgent. Can you get me through to him at once? And if he's not in, will you ask if they'll put out a call asking him to ring me here at once?'

*   *   *

'You're lucky,' Inspector Murgatroyd said a few minutes later, down the line. 'I only walked in a few minutes ago. I've got news for you.'

'Splendid!' Roland said. 'And I for you. Now listen.'

188

'Fine,' the Inspector said when Roland ⸺
finished. 'Now you listen to me . . .'

*   *   *

'I'm sorry to have been away so long,' ⸺
apologised, returning to the tea-table. 'A⸺
upset. Must be reaction from the accident.

Marion stared at him in complete disbelief.

CHAPTER FIFTEEN

'Anything for me?' Detective-Sergeant Naylor asked the duty sergeant as he and Inspector Murgatroyd entered the police station.

'On your desk.'

They went through to the inner office. Detective-Sergeant Naylor picked up a foolscap folder from his desk. Inspector Murgatroyd stood behind him and read over his shoulder.

'I thought you told me Washington wasn't a political animal?' the Inspector said.

'That's what I gathered, sir. Not now at any rate. This does go back a bit. Ten years. They've had to dig for it.'

'Hm! A member of the Communist Party, and active at that—secretary of the local group. Resigned from that office and from the Party five years ago. Before leaving LSE that would be. No reason given. I wonder?'

'What, sir?'

'Lots of things. *Did* he resign? Why? Does it matter anyway? And where did his wife come into it?'

'If at all,' the Detective-Sergeant said. 'According

189

to this she was never a party member. Leftish, but never as far as her husband.'

'He was still a member after they married,' the Inspector said. 'And she's an American. Prominent New England family. Moneybags. Not the kind of family to spawn a left-wing lecturer in Political Economy at the London School of Economics. And not comfortable for an American lady to be married to a real live Communist.'

'Well he isn't now,' Detective-Sergeant Naylor pointed out. 'I mean, he's given it up. Perhaps that was why.'

'Could be. We shall have to find out, shan't we?'

'I don't see where it would tie in with Maxton's death,' Naylor said.

'And that's another thing we'll have to find out,' Inspector Murgatroyd said.

'Do you want me to see him?'

'Not this time. I think I'd like a word with him myself. I have a feeling I've been neglecting the Bursar a little. And his wife. Perhaps I'll see them together. Works quite well sometimes.'

'Shall I see Miss Wishbone then?' Detective-Sergeant Naylor asked hopefully.

'Nay lad, she's mine. I'll tell thee what though,' the Inspector added kindly, 'tha can come wi' me!'

He's excited, Detective-Sergeant Naylor thought. He only breaks into Yorkshire dialect when things are hotting up.

'Thank you very much I'm sure,' Naylor replied.

The telephone rang. He leaned across the desk and picked up the receiver.

'It's a Mr Challis for Inspector Murgatroyd,' the operator said. 'Says it's urgent. Shall I put him through?'

'Will you speak to Mr Challis, sir?' Detective-Sergeant Naylor asked the Inspector.

The Inspector took the receiver from him, nudged him out of the chair and sat down himself.

'You're lucky,' he said down the line. 'I only walked in a few minutes ago. I've got news for you.'

Detective-Sergeant Naylor watched the Inspector while he listened to his caller. There was nothing to be gained from his expression, which remained deadpan. It was a while before he spoke.

'Fine. Now you listen to me.'

He gave Challis the outline of his visit to Picketts and his interview with Henry Wishbone.

'No collaboration,' he said. 'In fact, like your people, Picketts seemed a bit puzzled by Fletcher's silence. The tie-up with Carshalton could be interesting. I wonder what his nibs wants with the V-C? No. I don't think Wishbone knows anything. Norma might be another matter.'

He broke off to listen to the caller.

'It's a possibility,' he said. 'Anyway, I'm on my way to see the lady. And the Bursar and his missus. I'd like to see you when you get back this evening. The station will know where I am. So long.' He put the receiver down and turned to Naylor.

'They're having a bit of a house party up there,' he said. 'Or about to. Lord Carshalton, Mrs Vice-Chancellor, our young hero and Maid Marion, and would you believe it Professor Fletcher, are all about to make an unexpected call on the Vice-Chancellor.'

Detective-Sergeant Naylor stared at him.

'Fletcher? Did you say Professor Fletcher?'

'That's right. Picked him up in the hotel, as easy as you please.'

191

'Why? I mean why was he there?'

'How do I know? That's what Mr Challis is about to find out. Oh! Did I tell you that Challis and Miss Richmond had had an accident? Brake failure. Car shot over a bit of broken wall and fetched up halfway down the hillside.'

'Brake failure?'

'So they say. Could have been very nasty.'

'It sure could. I still don't get it though. Why are they with Lord Carshalton, and what has Mrs Spencer got to do with it.'

Inspector Murgatroyd stood up and started for the door. 'There lad,' he said. 'Don't you bother your head about that little lot. We've got matters of our own to see to. Who shall it be first, do you think? Miss Norma Wishbone or the Washingtons. And the last two together or singly?'

'Play it by ear, sir. See who's available.'

'A good idea.'

Passing the desk on his way out of the building, Inspector Murgatroyd said, 'If Mr Challis phones again, get in touch with me. Wherever I am.'

Probably just settling down to my supper, he thought, and a good programme on the telly.

*   *   *

Entering the Administration building the Inspector nodded to the porter on duty and walked down the corridor to the stairway.

'Perhaps we'll see the Bursar first,' he said to Detective-Sergeant Naylor. 'See what gives.'

He knocked on the Bursar's door and there was no reply. The two men entered. The room was empty and the large desk clear of work. Inspector Murgatroyd looked around. It was difficult to say how much the room expressed its owner's personality and how much was simply university furnishing for the man's particular grading. The larger than usual desk maybe, and all the gadgetry. The time-plotting map on the wall with all the coloured pins in it. Perhaps these indicated a man who liked to appear more important than at heart he knew himself to be. Underneath the man's extrovert facade he suspected a basic insecurity in Washington. While he was thus thinking, Norma came into the room.

'The Bursar's not in,' she said.

'So I see. Unless he's hiding!'

She looked at him uncertainly. 'He's not well. Mrs Washington rang up to say he had a stomach upset. He won't be in today.'

'I see. Well, never mind. Perhaps we'll have a little talk with you, Miss Wishbone.'

'I don't know anything about Mr Washington,' she said. 'He's considerate. He's a good boss. But I don't know anything about him.'

'I wasn't thinking of asking you about Mr Washington,' the Inspector said. 'I thought we might have another little talk about *you*.'

Norma backed towards the door. 'You've talked to me before,' she said. Her voice was strained. 'I can't tell you anything else.'

Detective-Sergeant Naylor, watching the Inspector's face, knew that he was about to pounce, and disliked him for it.

'But that was before we'd seen your father,' Inspector Murgatroyd said, his voice like thick cream.

He stood without moving, watching the effect of his words on the girl, seeing her face change colour,

193

noting the terror in her eyes. It was Detective-Sergeant Naylor who stepped forward and took her arm and led her to a chair. He had been afraid that she would collapse on the spot.

'My news seems to upset you, Miss Wishbone,' the Inspector said. 'Now let's all sit down comfortably and sort it out, shall we?'

He drew up an armchair so that he sat close to her, and motioned the Detective-Sergeant to do likewise.

'So!' he said. 'What's it all about, then?'

Norma made an effort to speak. 'My father never did anything wrong,' she said. 'He's a good man, my father!'

For a moment Inspector Murgatroyd wondered what that weak bundle of humanity, Henry Wishbone, had done to deserve the loyalty of his lovely daughter. Would either of *his* daughters stick up for *him* like this? He pushed the sobering thought to the back of his mind.

'You know what your father did, don't you Norma?' he said.

'It wasn't wrong. He was allowed to do it,' she protested.

'Of course it was wrong, my dear. He sold the stuff to Dr Maxton. That wasn't in the contract, was it?'

She was silent.

'And when Dr Maxton found the waste paper wasn't enough he wanted your father to break into the files—'

'He never did that,' she interrupted. 'I know he wouldn't do that!'

She's not sure, the Inspector thought. There was a question in her face which belied her positive

194

words. She only knows what Maxton told her.

'Did your father tell you that?'

'He would never do it!' she repeated.

'Did you talk to your father about it?' the Inspector asked. 'Or did you just take Dr Maxton's word for what had happened.'

She raised her face and looked at the Inspector, her face suddenly alive with hope.

'You mean . . . you mean my father didn't do anything? You mean Dr Maxton made it all up?'

For one moment the Inspector wished he could answer 'yes' to her question. And then where would that lead them? Would she have done whatever she had done if she hadn't believed Maxton?

'You believed him,' he said. 'You must have had a reason to believe him.'

She said nothing. He watched the hope fade from her face.

'Norma,' the Inspector said, 'we already know what your father did. He's told us. And you know as well as I do that Maxton was threatening him. He told us that too. So why not just tell me the rest? What did Maxton want from you?'

'Will it help my father if I do?' she asked.

'I don't know,' the Inspector admitted. 'I can't say. I don't see that it can make things worse.'

She seemed smaller, more fragile, overpowered by the size of the ostentatious armchair. She bit her lower lip until Inspector Murgatroyd saw the blood come.

'All right,' she said. 'I'll tell you.'

'Start at the beginning,' the Inspector said. 'How you came to know Dr Maxton. It doesn't matter if you've told me before. I'd like to know it all again.'

'Like I told you before,' Norma said, 'I got to

195

know Dr Maxton because he lodged with Mrs Thompson and he used to give me a lift sometimes, if he saw me standing at the bus stop. I was working at Picketts.'

'And you told him that your father worked there, and what he did?'

'Yes. I didn't think anything about it. And at first I didn't know he'd made any arrangement with my dad. He must have done that when I was out of the house, during the day.'

'Your father never discussed it with you?'

'No never. I could see he was worried about something, and I asked him what it was, but he wouldn't say anything. Said it was just missing Mum, but I knew it was more than that. Then one day in the car Dr Maxton said my dad was in serious trouble, but he could get him out of it if I would do him a favour.'

'Did he tell you what the trouble was?'

'He said he'd been stealing information from Picketts and selling it. He said it was a matter for the police. I said I didn't believe him, my dad would never do that, but he said it was true and he showed me a sheet of typing to prove it. I recognised it was Picketts. So I had to believe him.'

'And what was the favour?'

She hesitated.

'Come on,' the Inspector encouraged.

When she started to speak again the words came out with a rush, as if all she wanted was to rid herself of them as fast as possible. 'He wanted me to take a job at the university, which he said he could get for me.'

'Well? That wasn't all?'

'Yes it was. At first I didn't want to go. I was

happy at Picketts. But I had to. He made me.' For a second a happier expression flitted across her face—and was gone again.

And you met Mike Carshalton, the Inspector thought.

'So you came to work for the Bursar? And then what?'

'Dr Maxton wanted me to get information about Professor Fletcher. I didn't know the Professor, but we held his file. I knew he did some very important work.'

'Because Mike Carshalton told you?'

She jumped; raised her hand to her mouth in fright. 'Mike had nothing to do with it!' she cried.

'Have I said he did?' the Inspector said patiently. 'Calm down! So Maxton told you to get Professor Fletcher's file?'

'Yes. I kept putting him off, saying I couldn't get the key from Marion, and so on.'

'But you could have?'

'Yes.'

'So?'

'On the day the Vice-Chancellor had his sherry party Dr Maxton came in—to the party I mean. He was very, very angry. I had to go with him because I thought he was going to say something out loud about my dad. He took me on to the balcony and he told me that if I didn't get the file the very next day, then he would go to the police. But he also said . . .' She broke off.

'Go on.'

'He said that Mike Carshalton would have some information he wanted, because Professor Fletcher was his boss. I reckoned I was going to have to get that as well. I couldn't bear it.' Tears welled in her es. She buried her face in her trembling hands.

The Inspector pulled her hands away and tilted er face so that she looked directly into his eyes.

'So you picked up a handy object and hit him on ne head?'

'I did not! I did not!' Norma screamed. 'I've told ou, I didn't do it!'

The Inspector grabbed her wrists. 'What did you do then? Look at me! Answer me!'

'I told him I felt sick and I'd have to go to the toilet. I had to get away for a minute to think what to do. He said if I didn't come back straight away he'd find Mike Carshalton and tell him everything, and then go to the police.'

'Didn't you see that he couldn't talk to Carshalton without incriminating himself?'

'Not then. I couldn't think straight. You don't know what it's like.'

'So you returned?'

'When I was in the toilet I realised I'd have to get the file. I couldn't see any way out. When I came back to tell him, he was lying on the floor, his head all bloody. He was unconscious. I don't know whether he was dead.'

'What did you do?'

'I thought, all my troubles are over. Then I remembered something else. It was strange how I stopped panicking and thought. I realised he might have some of the papers he'd got from my dad in his lodgings, and the police would find them. So . . .' She looked nauseated at the memory.

'So you felt in his pocket for his bunch of keys, and next morning you let yourself into his room. Is that what you were going to tell me?'

'Yes,' Norma whispered. 'I put the keys into my

handbag and went back into the party. Mike was looking for me.'

'Did you find what you wanted in Maxton's room?' the Inspector asked.

'No. There was nothing. Someone had been there before me.'

And we won't go into who found you there, the Inspector thought.

'Do you expect me to believe this?' he asked.

'It's the truth,' Norma said wearily. 'And in case you want to know, Mike knows all about it now. I told him myself. He believes me.'

The Inspector smiled. 'That's important isn't it?'

'Very,' Norma replied.

'And does your father know of all this? Have you talked to him? About any of it.'

'Nothing at all. I didn't want to worry him. He doesn't have to know, does he?'

'Not for the moment,' the Inspector conceded. 'What about your Uncle George? I'm sure Sergeant Smith would be quite upset if he knew what his favourite niece was going through. Perhaps you should have gone to him for help.'

'His only niece,' Norma corrected. 'I thought about it. He's very fond of my dad as well. We're really his family. But I didn't see how he could help, and the fewer people who knew, the better. I had to tell Mike because it wouldn't have been honest otherwise. What will happen to my dad, Inspector?'

The Inspector shrugged. 'I don't really know,' he admitted. 'As it stands, it's a case for Picketts really. They'll decide what to do. For the moment it would be better to leave it as it is. It was a serious thing your dad did, no doubt about that. But as far as I can see no harm has come of it.' Except perhaps

Maxton's death, he added to himself.

'Can I go now?' Norma asked.

'I should think so. For the time being. A stomach upset you say your boss has?'

Norma looked surprised at the change of subject. 'Yes. That's what Mrs Washington said on the telephone.'

'Ah yes! A nice lady, Mrs Washington. You get on with her all right?'

'I don't really know her,' Norma said. 'She seems very nice. She's ever so fond of Mr Washington.'

'And that's nice,' the Inspector said. 'Don't you think that's nice, Detective-Sergeant Naylor?'

'Yes sir,' Naylor said. 'Very gratifying.'

'Then I think perhaps we'll nip along and see Mr and Mrs Washington,' the Inspector said. 'There's just about time before we go off duty.' He turned to Norma. 'Thank you for your co-operation, Miss Wishbone. Remember what I said about looking after yourself.'

CHAPTER SIXTEEN

Detective-Sergeant Naylor looked at his watch. 'Do you reckon we'll be through by finishing time, sir?' he asked.

'*Finishing* time, Detective-Sergeant?' Inspector Murgatroyd said. 'What's finishing time?'

'We are supposed to have one,' Naylor protested.

The Inspector shook his head. 'That's theory, lad. Nothing to do with real life. We finish when we've done.'

'I only wondered.'

'You've got a date, I suppose. That young

woman.' The Inspector's voice was morose. 'Well, she might as well get used to waiting around.'

'She is. We both are. She's a policewoman.'

The Inspector took his eyes off the road for a second to stare at his assistant. 'You must be stark staring mad! I doubt if policemen should marry at all, but to marry a WPC ... ! That's asking for trouble. When will you ever see her?'

'Absence makes the heart grow fonder,' Detective-Sergeant Naylor quoted.

'Fonder of being absent,' the Inspector reminded him. 'Here we are then. Bentwood Lane.' He turned the car into the narrow road which led off to the right at the end of the village of Otwood. 'Candlemass Cottage we want. Where do they get these fancy names from?'

'We're just coming to it, sir,' Naylor observed. 'On the left here.'

The Inspector braked gently, then stopped the car in front of an elaborate iron gate.

'Very nice too,' he said. 'Now when I was a lad, "cottage" meant two up and two down with a lavatory out at the back. Nothing like this.'

A short circular drive led to a double-fronted house of fine proportions. Ivy climbed around the deep sash windows, covering the grey stone walls almost as far as the roof.

'Some people like it,' the Inspector said, ringing the bell. 'Me, I pull it down wherever it appears.'

'What?'

'Ivy. Spoils the stonework. That's what me and the late Queen Mary have in common. Implacable enemies of ivy.' He rapped with the iron door knocker for good measure and before he had finished his tattoo Mrs Washington opened the door to them. Why does practically everyone look frightened the minute they set eyes on me, the Inspector asked himself. It was depressing.

'Mrs Washington! Good-afternoon. May we come in?'

'I'm sorry,' she said. 'My husband's not well.' She made no attempt to invite them into the house, holding the door no more than half open while they waited on the step.

'I know,' the Inspector sympathised. 'Stomach upset isn't it? Miss Wishbone told me. I hope he's feeling a bit better; but if not, perhaps you could help.'

'I don't see how,' she said. 'What is it you want?'

'Perhaps if we could come in for a minute,' Inspector Murgatroyd suggested.

She hesitated. 'Very well,' she said in the end. She held open the door reluctantly and the two men walked into the large square hall. Rooms led off on either side and on the left was a wide, crimson-carpeted staircase with an intricate iron rail. The Bursar, clad in a blue silk dressing-gown, was descending the stairs. His red hair stood out in tufts, as if he had tossed and turned in bed, and he was unhealthily pale. Inspector Murgatroyd had no difficulty in believing that a gastric upset was the true reason for his absence from the university.

'What's all this, Sylvia?' Washington asked irritably. 'What do you want, Inspector? I'm really not well you know.'

'So I see,' the Inspector said. 'You don't look at all well. I'm sorry about that, sir. Something you've eaten, is it? Or perhaps you've picked up a bug? A lot of them about.'

'What do you want?' Washington repeated.

'I'd just like a word or two with you, sir. Both you and your wife. Or if you're not fit enough, then I could just talk to Mrs Washington.'

It was interesting, Inspector Murgatroyd thought, to see the other man's reaction to that; the wariness in his eyes. No way did he want his wife to be questioned in his absence. Was it for the lady's protection, or would she say something her husband would rather she didn't?

'Very well then,' Washington said, not troubling to hide his distaste. 'I don't want my wife bothered. Come into the sitting room.'

'We'd like Mrs Washington to be present as well,' the Inspector pressed gently. 'She could be very helpful.'

The Washingtons looked at each other. There was hostility in Mrs Washington's face when she turned back to the Inspector.

'I don't think I can add anything to what I've already told you,' she said. 'But if you insist . . .'

'*Not* a word I care for,' the Inspector said lightly. 'I'm glad you're willing to co-operate.'

The Bursar led the way into a room which opened off the back of the hall. It was a long room, with a French window opening on to a well-kept lawn. The carpets and furniture were expensive; there were original paintings on the wall. He didn't manage this on a Bursar's salary, the Inspector reckoned. This was Mrs Bursar's contribution, without a doubt. All this and a lovely wife. Why did he want to go after young girls, however pretty?

'Please sit down,' the Bursar said. 'I suppose this is what you call helping the police with their enquiries?'

'A bit like that, sir. Not quite the same, though.

That's a phrase we tend to use when we've got someone at the station. Before we charge him.'

'Well at least it hasn't come to that!'

Washington's attempt at a joke fell flat on its face. Mrs Washington continued to look apprehensive, sitting forward on the edge of her chair, her back held as stiff as a board.

'Let's hope it won't,' Inspector Murgatroyd said gravely. Really, they could hardly look more guilty if they'd been caught red-handed, clutching the blunt instrument.

'Can one ask how the case is going?' Washington asked.

'Very well,' the Inspector said. 'Most satisfactory. One or two loose ends to tie up, of course.' He met Detective-Sergeant Naylor's sharp glance with a bland stare.

'Why did you leave the London School of Economics, sir?' the Inspector asked swiftly.

Washington looked up in surprise.

'Oh we know you were there,' the Inspector said. 'Part of our job, you might say. Getting the facts. Not a secret is it? I'm sure you don't mind.'

'Not at all,' Washington said. The words were polite but there was anger in his eyes. 'Though I wouldn't have your job for a fortune. Prying into people's lives.'

'Nasty,' the Inspector agreed. 'But there you are, sir. Someone has to do it!'

'I don't see why,' the Bursar snapped.

'Don't you sir?' The Inspector's tone was reproachful. 'Then perhaps I should remind you that this is a case of murder. Someone hated, or feared, Dr Maxton enough to want him out of the way, and in the end didn't hesitate to despatch him.

204

You wouldn't want the murderer to get away with it, would you now?'

'I would! I hope you never find out who did it!' Mrs Washington said the words quietly, and with the utmost venom, her eyes bright with hatred.

'Sylvia!' Washington cried. 'Don't be so bloody foolish! You don't know what you're saying.'

'Oh yes I do,' she said passionately. 'And I won't pretend, Bruce. I'm glad he's dead. I wish all the luck in the world to whoever did it!'

The Bursar shook his head, shifted in his chair, gnawed the knuckles of his left hand with strong white teeth.

'He was blackmailing you, of course,' the Inspector said with sympathy. It was not so much a question as a statement of fact.

Washington jerked his head up. 'Nonsense! Why should Maxton blackmail us?'

'You tell me,' the Inspector invited.

'That's utter rubbish,' Washington said loudly. 'Look here, if this is all you have to say—'

'Oh it isn't,' Inspector Murgatroyd said. 'Not by a long chalk. I just thought it would save a lot of time if you told me your version of the story.'

'What story?' Washington demanded. 'What are you talking about?'

Mrs Washington rose abruptly, walked across to the mantelpiece and stared at the arrangement of flowers in the grate. Then she turned around and faced the three men. 'It's not rubbish,' she said.

Her husband put out a hand to restrain her and she caught it in her own and moved closer to him, standing by his side.

'No Bruce,' she said. 'Stop pretending.'

She turned to the Inspector.

'Maxton *was* blackmailing my husband. That is quite true. I dare say he was blackmailing other people. He was . . . filth!' She spat out the words as if the thought of him had poisoned her.

'Why? Why was he blackmailing you?' Inspector Murgatroyd asked Washington.

Mrs Washington gripped her husband's hand tightly. 'I'll tell you why,' she said. 'He was blackmailing Bruce because he'd been a member of the Communist Party. An active member.'

Tell me something I don't know, the Inspector thought; but said nothing. Washington, he noticed, remained taut. He was still wary of something. The Inspector allowed the silence to continue.

Mrs Washington was the first to break it. 'Well? Is there anything else you want to know, Inspector?'

He stared at her. She couldn't be as naïve as all that.

'Quite a lot, madam,' he said. 'How did Dr Maxton know you'd been a Communist? I take it it was all a long time ago, or am I wrong?'

'You're right,' Washington said. 'I was a member for five years. I was secretary of the local group. Believed in what I was doing and worked hard. Then I gave it up. I've had nothing to do with the Party since before I came to Northwell.'

'You haven't told me how Dr Maxton knew?'

'The kind of coincidence that happens in real life,' Washington said bitterly. 'He attended a rally I helped to organise in London. I was on the platform, and then afterwards there was a social get-together. He noticed me, and when we met in the university here he remembered me.'

'Do you remember him?'

'No.'

'Did you meet Dr Maxton in the past, Mrs Washington?' the Inspector asked.

'I don't remember him,' she said. 'He wasn't a memorable character, not until you got into his clutches. Anyway, I was never a Communist.'

'Un-American,' the Inspector said.

She gave him a cold look.

'Now what I don't quite understand was why Dr Maxton could blackmail you because you were a member of the Party. I mean, lots of people are. It's not downright wicked is it? Did it matter all that much?'

Mrs Washington rushed to answer. 'Doesn't it matter in the police force, Inspector? Would it increase *your* chance of promotion, for instance? Or help you to get another job?'

The Inspector nodded. 'I *see!*' he said. 'So you wanted to take another job and your prospective employer wouldn't have a Commie? Not even an ex-one. Is that it?'

'No!' Washington said. 'I never said that.'

'I'm sorry. I'm a bit confused. Let me ask you something else then. What form did this blackmail take? Money? Information? What was it Maxton wanted of you?'

'Money,' Washington said. 'I had nothing else he wanted.'

'Information?'

'I don't know what you're talking about.'

'So he demanded money. And you had that. How much?'

'I didn't have it,' Washington said. 'I only have my salary. I've never managed to save. My wife paid him.'

'My husband finds it hard to accept that what's

207

mine is his,' Mrs Washington broke in. 'It wasn't the five hundred pounds which mattered to me. It was paying it to a skunk like Maxton.'

'But you paid?'

'Yes. Of course it was no time at all before he came back for more. We should have known. He'd have bled us forever.'

'Had he not died,' the Inspector said softly.

'As you say.'

'When was the last time he demanded money?'

Mrs Washington looked at her husband. Now I think she really is scared, the Inspector thought.

'On the day he died. In the afternoon,' Washington said. Then he raised his voice surprisingly and shouted at the Inspector, 'I told him to go to hell! Said I'd never pay him another penny.'

'And?'

'He said he thought my wife would.'

'I see,' the Inspector said. He was beginning to. 'And did you, Mrs Washington?'

'He came here the same afternoon,' she admitted. 'I told him I'd get hold of the money in a day or two.'

So Maxton's silence was worth more to Mrs Washington than to her husband. Why was that? He looked at the two of them in turn. Mrs Washington, her hand on her husband's shoulder, protective. The Bursar, in spite of his size, seeming now the smaller and weaker of the two. Then he saw Washington's face drain of colour, almost turn green. The man put a hand to his mouth and without excusing himself ran out of the room. Mrs Washington followed him.

'*Must* be something he ate,' Inspector

208

Murgatroyd said to Detective-Sergeant Naylor. 'Now why don't you go and wait for me in the car. I shan't be long. Just got one or two more questions I want to ask Mrs Washington.'

Naylor left and minutes later Mrs Washington came back into the room.

'I thought you would have gone, Inspector,' she said.

'Not much longer,' he assured her. 'I'm sorry your husband was taken bad.'

'I've put him to bed. He's not getting up again today for anyone. What more do you want from me, Inspector?' She sounded weary, dispirited.

'First of all I'd like to look at your passports,' the Inspector said. 'Yours and your husband's.'

He had, without a doubt, frightened her. He heard the catch of her breath and watched her cheeks flush.

'Passports?'

'If you please, Mrs Washington. I'm afraid I must insist.' He held out his hand.

She went to a mahogany bureau, unlocked it and took them from a small inner drawer. She held them close to her, not wanting to give them up.

'Please, Mrs Washington.'

Not taking her eyes from his face she handed the passports to the Inspector. He opened them, flicked through the pages.

'Sit down Mrs Washington,' he said.

She obeyed him as if hypnotised. He held Washington's passport in his left hand and waved it in her direction.

'This is what it's all about, Mrs Washington, isn't it?'

'How did you know?' she whispered.

'It wasn't difficult. You didn't really expect me to believe that you'd pay a blackmailer—a woman of your spirit—just because your husband had been a Party member? It's a free country, Mrs Washington. He could be a Marxist-Maoist Conservative if he wanted to. But *your* country doesn't like Communists. He wouldn't get very far there. In fact he wouldn't get more than a limited period visa, would he? And have to make a fresh application every time he wanted to go. But see what this one says.' He held the passport out to her. She turned away, not looking at it.

He opened it and read it out to her. '"Indefinitely"', it says here. "For multiple applications". Now I wonder why they allowed Mr Washington an indefinite visa? To come and go as he pleased. Could it be that they didn't know he'd been a Party member? They're funny about that, you know. Never seems to matter how long ago it happened. "Inadmissible" they call it on the form.'

'That's right,' she said. 'Together with drug addicts, lunatics and criminals.'

'All the same, he'd probably have got a visa for a short stay. Tell me why that wouldn't do? Or shall I guess?'

'I'll tell you,' she said. 'It's not difficult to guess. I wanted us to settle down in the States. Bruce could get a good job in the family business; something worthy of him. He's not appreciated here. We could be happy in the States; make something of our lives. I could work too. There's nothing for me in a place like Northwell. Everything's gone wrong since we came here.'

'Why did you leave London?' he asked.

She hesitated before answering.

'That's not difficult to guess either. I expect you know. Another woman. Or rather, more than one.'

'And in Northwell?' he asked gently. He hated this but it was necessary.

'Ask anyone. They'd be only too ready to tell,' she said. 'Norma isn't the first. But Bruce was serious about her. That's why he was able to tell Maxton to go to hell, in the end. He didn't want to leave her.'

'And you were willing to pay up because you still hoped he'd go?'

'For his own sake. He could never have Norma, you know. But he couldn't see that.'

'How did Maxton know about the visa?'

She flushed. 'Because I was stupid. All I can say is, at that time I didn't know Maxton well enough. I let it out in conversation when he was there. Just that we hoped to settle in the States before too long. He jumped to the right conclusion. He didn't need to see the visas. All he had to do—and that was what he threatened—was to raise a query with the United States Embassy.'

'Who would have found out that your husband had ticked the wrong box on the form, and put his signature to it? Quite a serious offence in their eyes; and of course the end of his hopes for a job there.'

'Yes. What are you going to do?'

'Me? What about?'

'The visa.'

'Oh that! That's a matter for your Embassy,' Inspector Murgatroyd said. 'I'm busy with a case of murder. Now if your husband no longer wanted to go to the States it really disposes of his motive against Maxton, wouldn't you say?'

She looked him in the eye. 'But strengthens

211

mine, you mean?'

'I didn't say that.' But it could. 'And now I think I'd better be off.'

The Inspector rose to his feet. Mrs Washington conducted him to the door. He started off down the path, and then turned back. Mrs Washington was standing in the doorway.

'By the way,' he called. 'A bit of campus gossip. It's my belief that we're going to have wedding bells before long. Miss Norma Wishbone and Mr Mike Carshalton. I meant to tell your husband but it went right out of my mind. Perhaps you'll do it for me.'

She tried to smile, and then closed the door.

'I heard what you said,' Detective-Sergeant Naylor said. 'I didn't know about that.'

'Second sight,' the Inspector told him, getting into the car. 'The gift of prophecy. Very useful sometimes.'

CHAPTER SEVENTEEN

'If you're ready then,' Professor Fletcher said. 'I'd like to get away.'

Roland was pleased to move. It was obvious that Fletcher was not happy about the way they'd all met up. The tea party was beginning to be a strain; Marion was plainly furious and the whole thing was only made bearable by Lord Carshalton's unfailing good manners.

'I should like to finish my tea,' Mrs Spencer said.

'You come along when you're ready. Don't hurry,' Professor Fletcher said shortly. 'I know where I'm going.'

Mrs Spencer looked at him with surprise. 'How

212

do you know?' she asked.

He didn't answer; simply walked out of the room, Roland following him.

The yellow Mini was parked in front of the hotel. Fletcher scarcely waited for Roland to seat himself before driving off. He drove in silence, following the sign for Buckden. The tight set of his mouth, the manner in which he looked rigidly ahead, did not encourage conversation. All the same, Roland decided, talk there had to be. He broke the silence.

'I've been looking forward to meeting you. You're really quite an elusive chap.'

'Am I supposed to know you?' Fletcher said rudely.

Roland explained himself. 'The Vice-Chancellor knows all about it,' he ended.

'Then we'll wait until we see the Vice-Chancellor, shall we?' Fletcher said. His manner was disagreeable and he made it quite plain that he considered Roland an unwelcome intrusion. Which I suppose I am, Roland admitted to himself.

'It's not entirely one-sided though,' Roland pointed out. 'You stand to gain. It could be that you need money in fairly large quantities—an open-ended grant—for your research. If my people think it's worthwhile that's the kind of thing they're able to provide; and without putting it on record as the Research Councils would have to do.'

'A bit late in the day,' Fletcher said.

'Whose fault is that?'

They drove in silence for a while, turning left in Buckden, crossing the old packhorse bridge and covering the narrow road towards Hubberholme at a speed well above the limit. There was no sign of the Daimler behind them.

213

'I'm sorry,' Fletcher said eventually. He sounded less aggressive. 'It's just that I don't like people looking over my shoulder.'

'Is that why you haven't been publishing?'

'Look, I'm not prepared to talk about it until we've seen the Vice-Chancellor,' Fletcher said.

'By which time the others will have caught us up.'

Past Hubberholme the dale grew wilder, the fells on either side of the valley closing in on them; the river, still swollen from the Spring rains, rushing in miniature waterfalls over the rocks. Then they crossed a narrow wooden bridge and left the river behind them, climbing now to the top of the fell. Almost at the summit, Fletcher pulled in to the side of the road.

'The rest is on foot,' he said. He pointed to a track which went off to the left. There was no sign of a house. 'It's about three-quarters of a mile,' he said.

*   *   *

The Vice-Chancellor, coming out of his cottage to fetch water from the well, lifted his head to look— as he never failed to do—at the scene before him. The steep green fells with their rocky outcrops; the fields which climbed up to meet them. No other building in sight and not a human being to mar the solitude. All's well with the world, he thought—and then he saw them. Leon Fletcher, and someone with him, walking at a steady pace towards the house. It was that Challis fellow, whom in a way he was not surprised to see since he'd deliberately run away without talking to him. He had judged the time not to be ripe for talking. Now if Leon Fletcher had finished his stuff it would be all right

214

to let Challis in on it. How very strange that they should be together. The two men saw him, and waved. He sat on the edge of the well and waited for them to reach him.

'You did it?' was his first question to Fletcher.

'Yes. Everything's OK,' Fletcher answered.

'Come into the house,' the Vice-Chancellor said. 'I expect you've made yourselves acquainted?'

'Professor Fletcher thought it better not to talk to me,' Roland said. 'I hope you're going to tell him that it's all fair and square.'

'Of course. I think now, that we can tell you whatever your people want to know,' the Vice-Chancellor said. 'I'm sorry to have kept you hanging around like this.'

'I think I should warn you that you've got other visitors on the way,' Roland said, smiling. 'Your wife, Lord Carshalton, and your secretary. They'll be here any minute.'

The Vice-Chancellor stood as if glued to the ground. His mouth sagged open; his thin face seemed to grow thinner. *'My wife?'* he said hoarsely. 'Lavinia? On her way here?'

'With Lord Carshalton and Marion,' Roland confirmed.

'But *why*?' It was a cry of anguish. His instinct was to escape; to run away, hide; to stay hidden until they'd all given up and gone home again. Force of habit and a lurking sense of duty made him push the temptation behind him.

'I don't know why Lord Carshalton and Mrs Spencer are coming—though he says he has business with you. Marion started out to bring me.' Roland explained about the accident. 'So we haven't much time before they arrive. What shall

215

we do?'

The Vice-Chancellor thought for a moment and then said, 'We'll go for a walk. I think that's the answer.' He spoke in a serious, businesslike way, quite unlike the manner in which Roland had so far seen him. 'Come along,' he urged. 'From what you say we've no time to lose.' He looked anxiously in the direction of the track which led to the road, but so far the horizon was empty. 'Follow me.'

At the back of the cottage there was a wide, flat meadow, and then the fellside rose steep and craggy. They walked and climbed without speaking until they reached a small plateau half-way up the hill.

'We'll sit here,' the Vice-Chancellor said. 'Fletcher, you can do the talking.'

'When I get my breath back,' Professor Fletcher said. 'You're used to this place; I'm not.'

'A laboratory type,' the Vice-Chancellor said. 'Well that much I envy you. Perhaps if I could have done more of that I wouldn't have needed to escape.'

His tone was wistful. Roland looked at him with interest. It hadn't occurred to him before now that the Vice-Chancellor was a frustrated scientist.

'Right then,' Fletcher said. 'I'll be with you in a minute.' He took a pipe, and a roll of tobacco, out of his jacket pocket and started all the preliminaries of smoking, measuring the amount of tobacco, pressing it down into the bowl, first with his fingers and then with a small silver instrument which he took from his waistcoat pocket. Then he carefully held the lighted match horizontally over the bowl and after a second or two was rewarded with clouds of blue smoke ascending into the clear air. Mike

216

'Don't get the idea that I don't care side,' the Vice-Chancellor broke in. 'I encouraged Leon in every way possi

was right, Roland thought. It wasn't an aroma you'd forget in a hurry.

'There!' Fletcher said with satisfaction. He turned to Roland. 'Do you understand chemistry?'

'Try me,' Roland said. 'But keep it simple.'

Fletcher had a pleasant voice. Low-pitched, gentle; a hint of a West Country accent. 'The problem is this,' he said. 'Car exhaust fumes, as you know, contain harmful pollutants. Carbon monoxide and oxides of nitrogen. Nasty, poisonous stuff. In Japan and the United States catalytic converters are fitted to car exhaust systems and these convert the pollutant gases to much less harmful ones: carbon monoxide to the dioxide and nitric oxide to nitrous oxide or nitrogen—though you don't need to know the details.'

'I'm with you,' Roland said. 'But if the solution's already in use in Japan and the United States, what's the problem?'

'Cost. The catalyst for the present converter is based on platinum. I don't need to tell you that that's prohibitively expensive. Out of the question for most countries.'

'So we breathe the poison?'

'Depending on the density of the traffic. Take a city as crowded as Tokyo—'

'What's the answer?' Roland asked. 'You reckon you've got it?'

'I believe so,' Fletcher said modestly. 'The answer is ruthenium. I believe I've found a new catalyst, based on ruthenium instead of platinum. What happens is that it catalyses the interaction of carbon monoxide and oxides of nitrogen to give carbon dioxide, excess of carbon monoxide and nitrogen gas. After the catalyst treatment the

217

remaining carbon oxides are absorbed. Are you still with me?'

'Yes I think so.'

'To simplify it, only nitrogen, oxygen and water—all perfectly harmless—escape.'

'And the cost?' Roland asked. 'Ruthenium is a precious metal, surely?'

'That's true,' Fletcher agreed. 'But not nearly as expensive as platinum. And it's inevitably isolated during the work-up of ores for other precious metals—platinum for instance.'

'A sort of by-product?'

'If you like. There are huge stockpiles. It's not cheap at the moment, but that's purely artificial. It could cost a good deal less. And an outlet would be a godsend to the precious metal people. And there'd be a continuing supply.'

There was silence. Then Roland said, 'And that's it?'

'That's it.'

'The implications are enormous,' Roland said thoughtfully. 'Financially, I mean. You realise that?'

'I didn't,' Fletcher said. 'It took the Vice-Chancellor to see that.' He waved his hand in acknowledgement.

'Just something I have to be aware of,' the Vice-Chancellor said deprecatingly. 'I don't enjoy thinking in terms of money.'

'You were thinking about pollution?' Roland asked Fletcher.

'That's so.'

'Don't get the idea that I don't care about that side,' the Vice-Chancellor broke in. 'I do. I'd have encouraged Leon in every way possible, even with to let Challis in on it. How very strange that they should be together. The two men saw him, and waved. He sat on the edge of the well and waited for them to reach him.

'You did it?' was his first question to Fletcher.

'Yes. Everything's OK,' Fletcher answered.

'Come into the house,' the Vice-Chancellor said. 'I expect you've made yourselves acquainted?'

'Professor Fletcher thought it better not to talk to me,' Roland said. 'I hope you're going to tell him that it's all fair and square.'

'Of course. I think now, that we can tell you whatever your people want to know,' the Vice-Chancellor said. 'I'm sorry to have kept you hanging around like this.'

'I think I should warn you that you've got other visitors on the way,' Roland said, smiling. 'Your wife, Lord Carshalton, and your secretary. They'll be here any minute.'

The Vice-Chancellor stood as if glued to the ground. His mouth sagged open; his thin face seemed to grow thinner. *My wife?* he said hoarsely. 'Lavinia? On her way here?'

'With Lord Carshalton and Marion,' Roland confirmed.

'But *why*?' It was a cry of anguish. His instinct was to escape; to run away, hide; to stay hidden until they'd all given up and gone home again. Force of habit and a lurking sense of duty made him push the temptation behind him.

'I don't know why Lord Carshalton and Mrs Spencer are coming—though he says he has business with you. Marion started out to bring me.' Roland explained about the accident. 'So we haven't much time before they arrive. What shall

215

we do?'

The Vice-Chancellor thought for a moment and then said, 'We'll go for a walk. I think that's the answer.' He spoke in a serious, businesslike way, quite unlike the manner in which Roland had so far seen him. 'Come along,' he urged. 'From what you say we've no time to lose.' He looked anxiously in the direction of the track which led to the road, but so far the horizon was empty. 'Follow me.'

At the back of the cottage there was a wide, flat meadow, and then the fellside rose steep and craggy. They walked and climbed without speaking until they reached a small plateau half-way up the hill.

'We'll sit here,' the Vice-Chancellor said. 'Fletcher, you can do the talking.'

'When I get my breath back,' Professor Fletcher said. 'You're used to this place; I'm not.'

'A laboratory type,' the Vice-Chancellor said. 'Well that much I envy you. Perhaps if I could have done more of that I wouldn't have needed to escape.'

His tone was wistful. Roland looked at him with interest. It hadn't occurred to him before now that the Vice-Chancellor was a frustrated scientist.

'Right then,' Fletcher said. 'I'll be with you in a minute.' He took a pipe, and a roll of tobacco, out of his jacket pocket and started all the preliminaries of smoking, measuring the amount of tobacco, pressing it down into the bowl, first with his fingers and then with a small silver instrument which he took from his waistcoat pocket. Then he carefully held the lighted match horizontally over the bowl and after a second or two was rewarded with clouds of blue smoke ascending into the clear air. Mike

216

'no money involved.'

'I can vouch for that,' Fletcher said.

'I believe you,' Roland said. 'I'd like to discuss the implications, of course, but if I'm not mistaken here comes the rest of the party!' He pointed down the hillside, towards the track. Marion, supported by Lord Carshalton and an unwilling Mrs Spencer, were advancing inexorably towards the cottage.

The Vice-Chancellor sighed, shook his head. 'I suppose I'll have to go,' he said. 'If it were only my wife . . . but Lord Carshalton, and Marion. Have you no idea what Lord Carshalton wants?' he asked Roland.

'None whatever.'

'Do you suppose he might be about to offer us a large sum of money? In gratitude for looking after his son, I mean. I suppose the stuff's practically coming out of his ears.'

Roland laughed. 'I hope you're right. But why the urgency?'

'I know,' the Vice-Chancellor said. 'People only rush to give one bad news. Well if you'll excuse me I think I'd better go and see to them. Is there anything else you want to ask me?'

'Nothing that can't wait, or that perhaps Professor Fletcher can't answer.'

'I would like to have stayed,' the Vice-Chancellor said, getting to his feet. 'But the two of you continue, by all means. I'm taking it that whatever Leon tells you will remain between you and your people?'

'As far as I'm concerned, yes,' Roland said. 'I don't know what information you might have to give to the police. There's still a murder investigation going on, and what Professor Fletcher has told me could be relevant to that.'

'It won't matter that I talk to the police,' Fletcher said. 'I'm about to write it all up for publication anyway.'

'Well I'll be off,' the Vice-Chancellor said.

The two men watched him go with reluctant steps to meet his visitors.

'Interesting,' Roland said.

'You mean the Vice-Chancellor?'

Roland nodded.

'He would have been a first class biologist—great perhaps, who can tell—if the ambition of that bitch of a wife of his hadn't prevented it,' Fletcher said. 'I've read his early papers. He really had something. Now, although he's important as a Vice-Chancellor, he sees people who were at university with him advancing in science. Fellows of the Royal Society, Nobel prizewinners, all that.'

'Was that what he wanted?'

'Not exactly. Not the prizes. He just wanted to do the research. There's a book on the life of the robin—'

'I know it,' Roland said.

'Well he told me once that if he could have written something like that, it would have been the crowning point of his life. "Now *there's* achievement," he said. I think that's why he's been so sympathetic to me. To a certain extent he's been able to identify with me.'

'Why did you go to the States?' Roland asked. 'Did you really go on sabbatical? Why did you return without telling anyone? Why did you say, just a few minutes ago, that it no longer mattered who knew?'

Fletcher smiled. 'To answer in order. I didn't go

220

on sabbatical, of course. I went to use an instrument at MIT—Massachusetts Institute of Technology—to make some measurements and verify some results. In fact, there's a similar instrument in Oxford, but I didn't want it known that I was using it. Then I went to the University of New York at Ithaca to consult another scientist there.'

'And you flew back because ... ?'

'Because I'd got my results. I had a bit more to do in the lab and then the whole thing could be sewn up. We'd agreed, the Vice-Chancellor and I, that I should lie low until I'd completed, and for that reason I've been staying hereabouts since I came back. In Kettlewell, in fact. I've been back to the university and done what I had to do there—'

'Puffing on your pipe meanwhile,' Roland said, smiling.

Professor Fletcher looked at him in astonishment. 'Good Lord! I never thought about it!'

'What's made you decide to publish? Why didn't you publish earlier?'

'There's no written rule which says a scientist has got to publish. Most of us do so as early as possible, partly in order to—well—stake a claim, I suppose you could say. I took the gamble of not doing so because I wanted to get to the conclusion and file the patent.'

'And you've done so?'

'I've done that. Since I returned from the States.'

'You stand to be a rich man,' Roland said.

Fletcher looked at him in surprise. 'Oh no! You misunderstand me. The patent's been filed on behalf of the university. That's where the money will go.'

'Not to the scientist?'

'Of course not,' Fletcher said.

'And what about Maxton?' Roland asked. 'Where does he fit into all this, if at all?'

Professor Fletcher's expression changed. A flush reddened his fair skin. 'It's not an edifying story,' he said quietly. 'I was at a conference in Chicago. I got drunk—for the very last time let me say—and talked about my work in too much detail. Anybody could have picked it up and some people doubtless did—which was another reason why I had to work quickly. Maxton was one of them. He isn't a real scientist. He's a nasty little industrial spy who knows just enough science to work on the fringes. He picks up what he can and profits from it. Sells it to the highest bidder. I didn't invite him here, of course, and when I heard he was in Northwell I was already in the middle of my work at MIT. Couldn't leave it.'

'Well Maxton got his comeuppance,' Roland said. 'I wonder from whom?'

Professor Fletcher didn't answer the question. 'I think that about wraps it up,' he said. 'If you don't mind I'd like to get back.'

They walked down to the cottage and entered together. In the small sitting room Lord Carshalton and the Vice-Chancellor sat in facing armchairs, but there was no sign of Marion or Mrs Spencer.

'My wife has gone out for a walk,' the Vice-Chancellor said. 'Marion is resting in the bedroom.' He turned to Roland. 'I'm glad you're back, Challis. Lord Carshalton has something very interesting. I think it's really a matter for the police, and in my opinion we shall have to get in touch with Inspector Murgatroyd, but Carshalton has agreed that we might discuss it with you. Your experience might help.'

So no large sums of money being handed out, Roland thought.

'Look here,' Professor Fletcher interrupted. 'It's not my concern is it? I really want to get back to my laboratory. I've got writing to do. Will you mind if I leave you?'

The Vice-Chancellor smiled. 'Spoken like a single-minded scientist,' he said.

'I'll be in the lab if I'm wanted,' Fletcher said. He was clearly anxious to be off.

When he had gone Lord Carshalton said, 'I'll come straight to the point, Challis. I received this communication in the post yesterday. It seemed to me that it concerned the University of Northwell as well as myself, and that's why I came to see the Vice-Chancellor. I'm not convinced, however, that I should involve the police.'

He handed a single sheet of paper to Roland. It was plain white typing paper with the words it contained spread out unevenly over the whole page. Roland held the sheet by the edges and read the message.

'VALUABLE INFO SUMMER BALL R252300 POLICE INFO OR NO PLAY LOVED ONES DANGER.'

'Done in Letraset,' Roland said. 'Badly done too. Someone who's not used to it.'

'The envelope likewise,' Lord Carshalton said. 'And as it happens, the postmark smudged so that we don't know which day it was posted. The way things are it could have been several days ago.'

'When did you get it?'

'Yesterday. I couldn't decide what to do; thought I'd sleep on it.'

'Have you had anything like this before?' Roland asked him.

'Well I get crank letters, of course. Threats too, sometimes. People in my position expect that. But I reckon this threatens my son. I've no other close relations. That's why I'm not sure about going to the police.'

'But it's blackmail,' Roland pointed out.

'It's not an easy decision,' Lord Carshalton said sharply. 'That's why I slept on it even before seeing the Vice-Chancellor. Mike means everything to me and kidnapping is the name of the game nowadays.'

'I sympathise,' Roland said. 'But I imagine you're not a man to give in to threats.'

'No. But I intend to keep the appointment. Find out what it's about and make my judgement.'

'Do you understand what the figures mean?' Roland asked the Vice-Chancellor. 'R252300?'

'Oh yes. Anyone in the university would know that. It's the way the rooms are numbered. R25 is Room 5 on the second floor of the Senior Common Room building. Not just the Senior Common Room building, of course. The Students' Union rooms are there and the Junior Common Room.'

'And 2300 is the time. Eleven p.m.,' Roland said. 'Not very subtle.'

'It's Boys Own Paper stuff,' Lord Carshalton said. 'That doesn't make it any less of a threat to my son.'

'I still think you should have a word with Inspector Murgatroyd,' the Vice-Chancellor said.

224

'Me too,' Roland said. 'You want the writer of this thing caught, don't you? You can't do it single-handed.'

'Very well then,' Lord Carshalton said grudgingly. He took back the letter, folded it and returned it to the envelope which he put into his pocket.

'I'm calling on the Inspector as soon as I get back to Northwell,' Roland said. 'Perhaps you'd like to come with me. And I hate to say it, Vice-Chancellor, but I think you should come back. You ought to be on the spot.'

The Vice-Chancellor sighed. 'I suppose you're right,' he said. 'I was coming the day after tomorrow for the Summer Ball. But I'll make it tomorrow. Not tonight,' he added firmly. 'If you'll be so kind, Carshalton, my wife can go back with you. I'll follow in the morning.' Thus he salvaged another evening's peace.

*   *   *

On the return journey to Northwell, Roland and Marion sitting in the back of the Daimler and a frustrated Mrs Spencer beside Lord Carshalton, they called in at the garage. The owner saw them coming and came out to meet them.

'Well?' Roland said.

'Brake fluid. Run right out of it. Lucky nothing worse happened to you.'

'But how?' Marion asked. 'The car's just been serviced; I know the brake fluid was checked.'

The mechanic shook his head. 'It's very puzzling, miss. There's a loose nut—the bleeding nipple it's called. As you've driven along it's got looser, and

225

the brake fluid has dribbled out, a little at a time, until the point where there wasn't enough left. Come with me and I'll show you what I mean.'

They followed him into the garage, where the car was still up on the ramp.

'There,' he said. 'You see how loose it is? The others are quite tight. What's more, sir, they're caked with grease and dirt. The grease is rubbed off this one where it's been shifted with a spanner. It's quite plain to see.'

'Simple isn't it?' Roland said. 'The kind of thing anyone might know about?'

'That's right!'

*   *   *

When the telephone rang, Inspector Murgatroyd swallowed a mouthful of his wife's delicious steak and kidney pie and rose from the table to answer it.

'I see,' he said. 'Lord Carshalton as well? You're sure it's urgent? I'll be down at the station in about fifteen minutes then.'

He went back to the table and attacked the pie with speed.

'And I suppose you're going to tell me you've got no time for pudding?' his wife said.

''Fraid not love.'

'Treacle sponge and custard,' she said bitterly. 'Why do I bother?'

He left the house, the saliva running at the thought of the treat he was leaving behind.

*   *   *

In the station he heard Lord Carshalton's story, looked at the letter.

226

'Do you mind if I keep this, sir?' he asked. 'Might be some fingerprints, though I doubt it. They learn about that in the infants nowadays.'

'It's all yours,' Lord Carshalton said. 'And since I've come to you, Inspector, I expect you to look after my son.' His tone was grim.

'We shall do our best,' Inspector Murgatroyd said. 'And perhaps I should warn you that you might be in some danger yourself. It is possible that the letter writer and Maxton's killer are one and the same. Of course we'll protect you every bit of the way—as far as we can, that is.'

'Thank you,' Lord Carshalton said. 'Do you know who this person is likely to be? Can you tell me who to expect?'

'I think I know,' the Inspector said mildly. 'I'm not sure that it would help if anyone else knew. Well, if there's nothing else at the moment, I'll see you at the ball. By the way, were you intending being at the ball?'

'Oh yes. I'd asked my son to get tickets. He's bringing a girl he wants me to meet. A corker, he says.'

A worried Lord Carshalton left the police station and Roland Challis stayed behind. Over the next half-hour he told Inspector Murgatroyd about his conversation with Professor Fletcher and the Vice-Chancellor. The Inspector gave Challis the details of his interview with Norma, but omitted to mention the Washingtons.

'So you really think you know who it was?' Roland said.

'I can see the motive, the means and the opportunity,' the Inspector said. 'Let's see what the Summer Ball brings, shall we?'

227

CHAPTER EIGHTEEN

The Summer Ball of the University of Northwell at Otwood, if not in full swing, had made a good start. The five-piece band, Pip Cosmo and his Northwellians, who played for most functions within a ten-mile radius and had, as a matter of local patriotism, to be engaged, were hard at work on selections from musical comedies arranged for steady, middle-of-the-road dancing. Later on, when things had hotted up, their place would be taken, for part of the time, by the Sycamores, a local group of exceptional loudness and incomprehensibility, much favoured by students and the *avant garde* academics. Since Pip Cosmo himself, together with two of his Northwellians, were also Sycamores, they were in for a strenuous evening. For now, he beat time languidly, saving himself for the frenzy to come.

Inspector Murgatroyd stood in the entrance hall waiting for his wife. Since she had been bandbox perfect when she had left him ten minutes ago to take off her coat, he couldn't imagine what she could be doing to herself.

The ball was taking place in the building which normally housed—by an unfortunate architectural error—both Junior and Senior Common Rooms and the Students' Union. It was a mix which on ordinary days did not work too well, but this evening all promised to be harmony. With the exception of one room in the Union area, the whole floor had been dedicated to the ball. Mrs Spencer and her ladies, together with the entire resources of the Northwell Council Parks Department, had transformed the several connecting areas into a sort of Yorkshire jungle.

'Quite splendid!' Mrs Spencer said, surveying the scene. She had worked hard all day, ordering people about, and had allowed herself a bare hour in which to go home and change into her royal blue gown and improve on her hairdresser's arrangement with a little more backcombing and a drenching with lacquer. She had taken up a strategic position not too far from the door so that she might welcome Lord Carshalton before anyone else got at him. From where she stood she could see through to the entrance, watch Sergeant George Robey Smith welcoming visitors in, directing them to the cloakrooms. He acted as if it were *his* ball, she thought, taking place in his private palace.

She noticed Inspector Murgatroyd standing in the foyer, and then saw a woman, presumably his wife, emerge from the cloakroom to join him. She wondered who had issued the invitation and braced herself to receive them. Across the room she could see her husband, talking to his secretary. It was really too bad of William, whose place was by her side. She was tempted to cross the floor and retrieve him, but the thought that in so doing she might miss out on Lord Carshalton's entrance kept her glued to the spot. The Inspector! She could send him.

'Ah, Inspector Murgatroyd,' she said. 'And your wife. So nice . . . I wonder if you'd be kind enough to go and tell my husband that he's rather urgently wanted here? I'm afraid his secretary may be detaining him. Thank you so much!' She waved them on.

'I'll introduce you to Mr Challis and Miss Richmond,' the Inspector said to his wife. 'You'll

229

like them. And the Vice-Chancellor—though whether I'll give him the message is another matter. Let him enjoy his freedom while he can, I say.'

Mrs Spencer continued to watch the entrance, while at the same time casting anxious looks in her husband's direction.

He seemed to be making not the slightest attempt to join her. But at last her vigilance, in one direction at least, and that the most important, was rewarded. Through the front entrance, into the foyer, stepped Lord Carshalton. How splendid he looked in his white frilly shirt and black velvet jacket! Unfortunately he was closely accompanied by his son and Miss Norma Wishbone, whose arm he held as they stopped to speak to Sergeant Smith. I wonder if he knows that our Head Porter is her uncle, Mrs Spencer thought. Perhaps he should. She also realised that she would have no option but to invite Norma to sit at the table which had been reserved for the Vice-Chancellor's party. She turned and waved frantically at her husband as Lord Carshalton and his party entered.

Marion saw the wave. 'There's Norma,' she said. 'Doesn't she look gorgeous?'

'My word yes!' the Vice-Chancellor said. 'And I see my wife is signalling to me. Excuse me please.' He sped away in time to greet his guests just as Mike was about to take Norma on to the dance floor.

'May I have the pleasure, Miss Wishbone?' the Vice-Chancellor said, cutting in and whisking her away. Lord Carshalton watched them go, envying the Vice-Chancellor his quick thinking.

'Perhaps, Lord Carshalton, *we* should dance,' Mrs Spencer said. 'Others don't always like to do so before they've seen the Vice-Chancellor's lady take the floor.'

And so it went on. The floor became more crowded, the bar did a roaring trade. The Sycamores took over from the Northwellians and the tempo increased. The parks and gardens foliage stood up well to the heat. Lord Carshalton danced with Norma until his son protested and took her away. Detective-Sergeant Naylor gyrated with his policewoman, whose off-duty had for once coincided with his. Marion, resting her foot, sat beside a potted palm with Roland.

'I wonder why Bruce and Sylvia Washington aren't here,' she said. 'He was well again yesterday.'

At about half-past ten everyone collected supper from the buffet which was laid out on the balcony. It was a lavish feast since the catering committee had taken advantage of Mrs Spencer's trip to the Dales to order more of everything. It was towards the end of the supper interval (though it was not really an interval in the musical sense since the Northwellians took over from the Sycamores and played the Sound of Music, thus leaving Pip Cosmo and two of his musicians without an opportunity to eat) that Mrs Spencer noticed that her husband had disappeared yet again, and was this time nowhere to be seen. Roland excused himself to Marion and went off, and Mrs Murgatroyd wondered what her husband was doing all this time in the cloakroom.

In Room 5, which was a room normally set aside for rehearsals of the Music Society, Lord Carshalton sat alone. Guitars, music stands, cellos and violins in cases, were scattered around the room. Two grand pianos were littered with sheet music. He looked at his watch and compared the time with the clock on the wall. Exactly eleven o'clock. When he had walked up the stairs, this whole floor had seemed deserted: another world from the rowdy goings-on downstairs. Strains of music, the thud of drums, sounded through the floor. The Sycamores had taken over again. He took out a cigar, trimmed the end, lit it and blew the fragrant smoke in a cloud above his head. He wondered what lay ahead and was apprehensive, though since this morning when Inspector Murgatroyd had called a meeting of himself, the Vice-Chancellor and Challis, he was fairly certain who to expect.

At two minutes past eleven the door opened and Sergeant Smith entered and walked across the room, moving quietly for so large a man. He stood at attention, resplendent in his uniform, perfect to the last detail, in front of Lord Carshalton. The two men looked at each other. Lord Carshalton was the first to speak. 'You have something for me, I believe?'

Sergeant Smith walked forward and stood two paces closer to Lord Carshalton, who remained seated.

'For a price,' Sergeant Smith said. His voice was firm and confident.

'You don't beat about the bush,' Lord Carshalton said. 'How much?'

'It's worth a lot of money. I'm not letting it go for peanuts,' Sergeant Smith said.

'I said how much.'

The Sergeant hesitated for a moment and then said, 'Twenty thousand pounds.'

Lord Carshalton smiled. 'And what can you give me that's worth twenty thousand pounds?'

'Plenty. You could make a killing. I've got the details for an exhaust system that every manufacturer in the world will be crying out for.'

'Have you really?'

The Sergeant flushed.

'Then why let *me* have it?' Lord Carshalton said. 'Why not keep it for yourself?'

'Don't give me that,' Sergeant Smith said roughly. 'You know the answer to that. It's people who have money who can make money. People like me, without two ha'pennies to rub together, can't make money honestly.'

'As a matter of interest,' Lord Carshalton said. 'Why do you want money? Do you think that it brings happiness?'

'What's it got to do with you why I want it?' Sergeant Smith said gruffly. 'You, sitting there smoking your fat cigar! It's never done you no harm!'

'On the contrary, it's got me right where I'm sitting now!'

'And will get you out of it again,' the Sergeant reminded him. 'Power! That's what money buys. Not food, or clothes, or fine houses—though I have every intention of a nice little villa in Spain—but *power*. People jump when you've got money. Defer to you. It puts you in the officer class. You can rule the world with money.'

'Not with twenty thousand pounds you can't,' Lord Carshalton said.

'That's only the beginning. Money makes money,' the Sergeant said.

'Then have you brought the information with you?'

'Of course I haven't, any more than you've

brought the money with you. We make another arrangement for that. I've brought a bit of it.' The Sergeant handed over a sheet of paper. 'And I've got the rest. I went to a lot of trouble to get it. You arrange the money and I'll come up with the goods.'

Lord Carshalton studied the paper. 'Twenty thousand pounds is a lot of money. It would take me a day or two.'

'I know that. I want used tenners. And let's say that meanwhile, I'm very interested in your son. Can't take my eyes off him.'

'You're threatening me?'

'That's right. You've got the idea.'

'I still think it's a lot of money.' Carshalton moved his hand so that he could see his watch.

'That's my price,' Sergeant Smith said. 'And you know very well it's nothing to the money you'll get out of it. So make up your mind quick. I'm supposed to be on duty.'

'Very well,' Lord Carshalton said. 'We'll work something out.'

'In the meantime I'll have my bit of paper back,' Sergeant Smith said, holding out his hand.

Lord Carshalton stood up, put his cigar down on the ashtray, handed the sheet of paper to the Sergeant.

'I thought you'd see sense,' Sergeant Smith said. 'A clever man like you.'

He had folded the paper carefully and was putting it back into his pocket when the door opened and Inspector Murgatroyd, accompanied by Detective-Sergeant Naylor, came into the room. The Vice-Chancellor and Roland Challis were close behind, but before they could enter Sergeant Smith rushed forward, passing the policemen like a bullet

234

from a gun. The Vice-Chancellor, blocking the doorway, hit the ground with a thud. Through the gap where the Vice-Chancellor had stood, leaping over his body, Sergeant Smith ran out of the room, pursued by Roland, the Inspector and Detective-Sergeant Naylor, and Lord Carshalton. The Vice-Chancellor rose shakily to his feet, rubbing his chin.

Sergeant Smith was well ahead along the corridor, making for the stairs. He was incredibly fast, Roland thought, for someone of his size. It was his speed of movement which had taken them all unawares. For a second he was lost to sight as he rounded the corner towards the stairs. The music from the Sycamores came up strongly now, and mingled with it was a curious, dirge-like chanting sound.

Then as Roland, slightly ahead of the Inspector and his assistant, who were now well in front of an out-of-condition Lord Carshalton, came in sight of the staircase, the chanting became louder.

'My God it can't be!' Roland said. But it was.

At the foot of the stairs, completely blocking them, was a group of students with banners. At least twenty of them. They stood solidly shoulder to shoulder, chanting their slogans, on their way from the Union room, hopefully to create havoc in the ballroom. 'Homes not Hovels!' they shouted. 'Give us homes!' And the girl Fiona, whom Roland had not seen since the demo on the night of Maxton's murder, was well to the front of the group, waving her banner. What a wonderful way she had of turning up at the crucial moment!

'Stop him!' Roland yelled. 'FIONA! STOP SERGEANT SMITH!'

The Sergeant was already decimating the group,

cutting through them like a knife through butter. It took Fiona rather less than a second to hear Roland's yell, sum up the situation, and take action. With a skill born of long practice on the playing fields of her expensive school, she wielded her banner into a strategic position where the Sergeant, in his headlong flight, could only fall over it. He sprawled on the ground as Roland and the Inspector reached him.

*   *   *

'And he's been charged with murder?' Roland said to Inspector Murgatroyd next day. They were seated in the Inspector's office, drinking coffee from cardboard cups.

'Yes. When I recognised the motive, the rest slotted in. It usually does. Sergeant Smith was a man of strange contradictions. And he had this inordinate sense of power.'

'That's true,' Roland said. 'He was known for it.'

'And a great love for his family. When his beloved sister died I think he concentrated the love he'd had for her on Norma and that pathetic father of hers.'

'How did he know that Norma was in trouble with Maxton?'

'She didn't tell him. But Henry Wishbone, who had to confide in someone and didn't want it to be his daughter, had told him what he'd been doing at Picketts. The Sergeant saw Maxton's effect on Norma and put two and two together. Remember his reputation for knowing everything. It was well founded.'

'I think,' the Inspector went on, 'that at first he saw Maxton simply as someone who was making Norma unhappy, and therefore had to be dealt with. He'd had a bloody war and lives weren't that sacred to him, especially the life of a mongrel foreigner, as he would have put it. And of course the opportunity was there at the party. He was all over the place. He only had to pick his moment. If one hadn't presented itself he'd probably have arranged something.'

'You think that the money was an afterthought?'

'Yes I do. A fairly quick afterthought. If Maxton had been after it, why not he. And the thought grew on him because it meant power. But he hadn't enough intelligence to go about it very well.'

'He got the information from Fletcher's file?'

'He's already confessed that. Though what he couldn't recognise was that it was incomplete. It was simply enough for him to get it. He holds master keys for safety and security reasons—a point we should have got on to ourselves and didn't. And it was Smith, of course, who searched Maxton's room before Norma got there, and for much the same reason.'

'That figures. And Smith who coshed me,' Roland said. 'I've found out since yesterday that the telemessage had been transmitted over the phone and the switchboard had put the call through to Sergeant Smith because he always knew where people were to be found. What Marion had was the confirming copy. And of course Marion's car. It was more or less on his doorstep, wasn't it? What about the weapon?'

The Inspector shrugged. 'I still think it was an ashtray. Sergeant Smith was busy cleaning and polishing them, you remember. But we shall see.'

'I wonder what will happen to Norma's father,' Roland mused. 'That's tricky.'

'Nothing, I shouldn't think. After all, Lord Carshalton *is* Picketts. And Norma's still on her way to being his daughter-in-law. Nothing seems to have changed that. Perhaps I am psychic after all!'

'What?'

'Nothing. Now you tell me something for a change. What's in the air *vis-à-vis* Fletcher's invention and Lord Carshalton?'

'That's fairly simple,' Roland said. 'Lord Carshalton will develop and manufacture the system and the university will get the royalties. My lot are quite happy now that it's not going out of the country. There's a great deal of money in it as well as prestige.'

'I can imagine,' the Inspector said. 'Well, anything else not clear to you or shall we go and get the taste of this coffee out of our mouths with a beer?'

Roland hesitated. 'There is something,' he said. 'Did *you* know that the Washingtons were on the point of clearing out? Couldn't you have prevented them?'

The Inspector looked hurt. 'Me? Now how do you think *I* could have had every plane out of Heathrow watched? Besides, I never thought they'd done anything; not anything I'd have considered criminal. If it had turned out otherwise I could have got them back.'

'But why did they go to the States so suddenly?' Roland persisted.

The Inspector spread his hands. 'Search me. The time was ripe, I suppose. I really know very little about them.' And no smart alec from London is getting it out of me, he thought.

'Well aside from that everything seems to fit,'

238

Roland said. 'Oh there's just one other thing I haven't been able to discover. I don't suppose you could help me?'

'What's that?'

'Mrs Thompson's pursuits. What are they?'

'Bingo, I suspect,' Inspector Murgatroyd said. 'Like me to put someone on to it?'

The LARGE PRINT HOME LIBRARY

If you have enjoyed this Large Print book and would like to build up your own collection of Large Print books and have them delivered direct to your door, please contact The Large Print Home Library.

The Large Print Home Library offers you a full service:

☆ **Created to support your local library**

☆ **Delivery direct to your door**

☆ **Easy-to-read type & attractively bound**

☆ **The very best authors**

☆ **Special low prices**

For further details either call Customer Services on 01225 443400 or write to us at:

The Large Print Home Library
FREEPOST (BA 1686/1)
Bath BA2 3SZ